Rise of the Ripper

Amanda M Tams

Copyright© 2024 Amanda M Tams
Cover Luke Tams
All rights reserved. No part of this book may be reproduced or used in any form without permission from the author or publisher except for using quotations in a book review.

ISBN-9798301750489:

Acknowledgements

References taken from Casebook: Jack The Ripper.
Produced by Stephen P Ryder and Johnno
WWW

CONTENTS

Acknowledgements

1	Victorian London	1
2	Hanover Road	27
3	Albury Street	58
4	William 1887	73
5	Emily 1889	96
6	1893	109
7	Rise of the Ripper	117
8	Emily's Downfall	130
9	The Trial	160
10	Asylum	170
11	Jasper	190
12	Suicide and Murder	220
13	Arthur Jacob	230
14	Tony	247
15	The Body in the Tree	288
16	Revelations	302
17	Jack	323

Introduction

INTRODUCTION

Although this is a work of fiction, facts have been used to give the story depth. All the deceased mentioned were true unfortunates of the time, all unnamed and unclaimed victims throughout the years.
We all know of Jack the Ripper, but how many of us know him?
Please let me introduce you...

Chapter 1

VICTORIAN LONDON

Poor Alice missed out on the gift from the prettiness fairy. A woman aged forty, dumpy and a heavy drinker who smokes roll-up cigarettes and keeps a clay pipe charged with the cheapest of shag tobaccos, which she hides in the pouch of her worn skirt. Thus, folk nicknamed Alice Mackenzie, Clay Pipe Alice.

For all of her shortcomings, around the doors on Gun Street, where Alice shacks up with her common-law husband John, they all acknowledge Alice as a pleasant, helpful soul. However, neighbours, including the local constabulary, believe she is a woman of easy virtue.

The July evening is as balmy as one can expect in the gloom of the dank, suspicion-laden streets, like the arteries of Whitechapel. The threat of summer rain and murky mists persists when Alice and George, a blind youth, go out for the night. Their attire is the same as any Victorian slum dweller, patched and not too clean. She guides the boy by the elbow through the busy thoroughfares.

Outside the taproom next to the Cambridge Music Hall on Commercial Street, the couple stagger arm in arm. Both are enjoying their evening on the town and are well in their cups, oblivious to their surroundings.

Laughing loudly, they aren't concentrating when,

without warning, George trips, misses his footing and stumbles, almost taking them both to the ground. Alice's voice booms out with a resonant, hoarse, throaty cry.

'Hold yer 'orses, Georgie, lad, be careful. You'll be having us over.'

She totters but manages to keep them upright. People gawp and walk on, the couple are no threat to them, only a pair of harmless drunks out for the night.

At the same time, a nearby bystander asks himself why he decided to go to the theatre because he doesn't enjoy it. Why he bothers still puzzles him. Sylvia, his wife, enjoyed the ugly men prancing about as women on the stage, but he always thought it offensive, so he asked himself again; now she is not here. Why does he go?

Frustrated and agitated, he waits for something or someone. Screwing his heels into the cobbles, his body trembles. He balls his right fist and slams the knuckles into the palm of his left hand. On contact the pain on contact causes him to wince. Enough is too much; he's off but as he turns a coarse, raucous, bedroom chuckle rumbles across the cobbles and like a bullet whizzing past, stops his stride and he staggers into the shadows.

The inflexion is familiar, but it can't be. It's impossible and he should know. There is nothing more he would like to do than dismiss the cackle of laughter, which makes his head spin and has him double-check. Is he wrong? He questions his memory of the repellant laugh winging across the cobbles and the familiarity causes his insides to squirm, but he knows it can't be who he thinks it is. Turning, he spots a couple stumbling on the path

Seeing them stumble, he swoops in to help and his dark, lengthy coat billows behind him like giant bat wings in his haste. He helps them and discovers that the man she calls George is blind.

This knowledge empowers something in him and triggers memories of previous adrenaline rushes. It helps birth an understanding of his recent frustrations.

Theatricals are not what he's after. It's the strange, nighttime call of the crowds he's answering, which grows daily and he's finding it harder and harder to resist. A flash of insight hits him as the woman's voice resounds. A laugh that sparks another memory of a long-forgotten desire. How did he manage to wait so long?

Alice can just see the outline of a fair and neat moustache in the dim glow of the streetlight as the Samaritan steps forward. 'Thanks, mister. t'is good of yer.' She steadies herself and George.

'Glad to be of assistance.' His voice is soft and cultured. She brushes George down and then squints at the helpful stranger. At first glance, she fancies the cut of his jib and supposes he may be a potential customer. He doesn't strike her as typical of the area, like sailors on liberty or between tours of duty. This man dresses like a toff.

'May I be of further help?' He asks, studying them both.

'Thanks, but we're alright now. It's about time I

took him back. Clumsy tonight aren't you matey.' She glowers at the boy, thinking she's missing out on a customer.

'Didn't I tell you to put more water in it, lad? Better remember for next time, hey.'

Holding his head to one side and turning an ear to her voice, George nods, a lopsided, inebriated grin stretches his face, displaying his ragged black stumps and gummy gaps.

'Of course, you could indulge me with a drink, Mister, but after I deliver my pal to his abode. I can always come back.'

Alice pats her hair; it's a ludicrous move like she's about to go to a soiree. She also keeps her lips tight to hide the gap from a missing tooth in her upper jaw, but she flashes him a well-practised and, as she imagines, seductive, sexy smile. Shrugging George's hand away from her arm she said, 'Hold on, Georgie. Dunna fret, lad, I won't desert you.'

Trying to improve her image, she straightens the nape and neckline of the once-fashionable bodice, now patched under the armpits and stained. Nothing alters, no matter how many prods, or primps and preens. God ran out of gifts on the day she came to be. No amount of tweaking can alter anything.

The blind boy panics and flaps his arms like a fledgling on its first flight, clawing at the air locked in his murky world of darkness eager for human touch. Alice stays his hands and casts the helpful stranger a coy smile.

He nods and drawls. 'I will look forward to a

pleasant diversion. Should we arrange to meet here once you've delivered your charge?' He turns to go.

'It'll be a while, sir. Gun Street is a fair stride from here,' says Alice.

'Don't be concerned, I will return.' He bows from the waist as if acknowledging someone of value and grace. Alice stares after him, thinking he's a toff and turns on George, annoyed.

'Strewth, Georgie. What a night for me to take you for a drink when I might be with the posh gent. I have a thirst for a toff to buy the gin tonight. An' if I play me cards right, I may even earn a coin or two.' Her laughter rings out.

People stare their way, tutting as they shuffle on past. To all who pass, it's obvious it's the man's idea of a cruel joke. Titters rise on the lips of the pedestrians, and they say, 'Another pitiable soul soon to go home penniless. What well-to-do fellow would come back for this baggage?'

Alice will drag George back if need be. 'Come on, shift. Let's whip down this old frog and toad,' she says as she grabs him by the hand.

Myopically, she peers back to examine the man marching further down the Aldgate Railway Station road. 'Shame he didn't wait. What do you think, Georgie?'

'What about, Ducks?'

'Him buying me a drink, nitwit, don't you reckon he's rather dapper?' Mortified at what she said. 'Oh gosh, I'm all of a dither. Sorry, mate, you're blind, ain't ya. I dunna fink, do I? Blimey, me and my mouth.'

'Dunna fuss, gal, he did sound sharp. Thing is, gal, you can't tell who's about, not these days, and after what that beast the ripper did, you've gotta be careful. T'is not so long ago. It ain't safe on yer own at night, and you've never seen this geezer afore 'av yer. Is he a Jack Tar?'

'No. I don't fink so, ducks, he's kitted out like a toff, I fink he's up to snuff.'

Sighing, she stretches her neck round to get what may be a final glimpse. 'Who can truly say? From what I can tell of him as he strides down the road, he don't walk with no sailor's gait. Remember, he did come to our aid, so can't be that bad.'

'Please, gal, be careful. Don't you go. Think about them women killed last year, them that nutter did in. Okay, they say he's gone, but can we really be sure, lass? Let's go back to the Bells.'

'No chance, Georgie boy. It's home for you, mate. You can't keep upright as is.'

After musing on it, she believes her pal may be correct, but she is still loath to let a handsome and moneyed fella, from what she can see of him, go untapped.

Alice leads the sightless boy amidst the hectic folk of Whitechapel and reaches Gun Street minutes after the church clock strikes eight. She says ta rah to him at his door and enters her own squalid abode.

'Where you bin, bitch?' John, her partner, slams his fist against the door. 'Go on, what excuse are you gonna give this time?'

'What's that supposed to mean? What's up with you? Don't you go bawlin' at me the second I come in, John because I won't take any lip.'

'That bloody Ryder woman barged in, shouting the odds and threatening to kick us out.' His bawl almost flapped the roof tiles. 'So come on, where's the rent I gave you earlier? I'm warning you, woman, this must stop. he dosh isn't for you to piss up the wall, and where's me grub?'

Alice's high spirits disappear within seconds of arriving home and she's angry at John for spoiling her good humour. In a voice to match his, another argument ensues to the amusement of the rest of the lodgers, but they don't care. That pair always argue.

'Shove it, I'm off; get yer own vittles,' hangs on the air as she retreats in double quick time. As purposeful as her gin-sodden brain can be while descending the rickety staircase, she remembers to clear the first broken tread but stumbles on the third loose stair riser.

'Stinking death trap.' She curses each step and more so when she bumps into the landlady.

Ryder had hung around waiting for Alice and when she saw her, greeted her with, 'Where's the poxy rent, Alice? Come on, stump up.' Her eyes roll heavenward.

'John says he gave the money to you, and I want what's due now.'

'Hark at yersen.' Alice shrugs tightening her shawl around her shoulders. 'I give ya me word, I wud of paid, if he gave me the dosh.'

'Well, he said he 'as, so gimme it now or else.'

'Cross me 'art.' Clay pipe Alice crosses the right side of her chest with a finger. 'Frisk me, cos I ain't got a single coin, I'm tellin' ya. Ask him.'

'You are one lyin' tart with a tongue so twisted it could pull corks. You poured the lot down yer neck, ain't ya, ya drunken tart. You better not light yon pipe.' Ryder looks at Alice's skirt, where she keeps her clay pipe. 'Cos you'll go up in one massive bang with the amount of alcohol you supped tonight. You reek of gin, ya rat-arsed bitch.'

'Tart, I'll give you tart, you old hag. Who do you fink you are calling ratted, I'm respected, round here, I am,' bawls Alice.

'Who you kiddin', Alice? You ain't nothin' but a whore.'

'Ah, get over yersen, Ryder. You need more than rent to have me on me back, not like you and your hoity-toity cat's lap. That's what you want them to fink. I know them cups of char of yours is full of mother's ruin, so don't kid a kidder. Yer breath cud strip paint. You can't fool me who the dipso is an' if ya suggestin' more, you better guard ya back. Now I'm away from this doss hole, so I'm warning you, leave off.'

Eager for another drink, Alice sidles away, but the landlady persists grabbing the paisley shawl from her shoulders. 'Gimme me money else you'll be out on your arses.' Ryder won't crumble and she won't let her go out unless she stumps up.

Alice grinds her choppers and warms her jaw for a

battle of choice words. The women go hammer and tongue for half an hour and Alice's diatribe grows more incoherent with each flurry until she's drained, not only out of breath but also suitable obscenities.

Using her shoulder, she shoves the landlady aside and leaves her with, 'If I'm skint, I can't give it ya, can I blast you? Talk to him fer yer stinking dosh an' let me tell you, while yer in me face, you should be renumer... renuma—bloody hell, paying us to live here and not demand rent off honest folk. Aye, cos you're not the only one with lodgers. Let me tell ye, yer missin' a trick. The bloodsucking beasts are forever crawling up our walls; ya oughta make them cough up because ya do nothin' to rid us of 'em. We can't even tek a piss without treading on the buggers.'

At a pace to make a drill sergeant proud, she marches off to the Ten Bells pub, her clay pipe gripped between her teeth, scanning the path behind to make sure Ryder isn't treading on her heels for more harsh words.

Taking a breath, Alice retrieves a bottle of cheap gin from a pouch sewn in her skirt and swigs a mouthful swishing it around her mouth, savouring the flavour like a long-lost lover before swallowing. A gentleman passing by gawps and presses a handkerchief to his face. It's obvious to her that he is either off course or up to nefarious deeds. No real gentlemen wander these paths, they do their best to bypass them.

'Wot's up wiv ya? It's an emergency, mate. I need to wet me whistle,' she says. 'An' the rag to yer neb don't hide yer ugly mug. Pretendin' to avoid the stink don't wash with anyone, I'm tellin' ya,' says Alice as the man ups his pace and scuttles on.

She licks gin-spotted lips to ensure every last drop is gone and blots her mouth on her sleeve before she pockets the bottle. Salvaging the money, she denied having to Ryder she squeezes the coins and anticipates the forthcoming drinks.

Her foul temper disappears like the morning mist and the image of the dapper chap slips away, off into the background of her booze-soaked brain.

In the Bells, as the locals call the pub, Alice downs the throat-burning jigger gin, coughs, and dabs her mouth with the back of her hand, ready to flirt with the male customers. Pestering them for pennies or a tot, but none want to play because all are well acquainted with old clay pipe and her man.

By 11:30, bored with the lackadaisical customers, she recalls the man who helped her and George earlier. 'Aw, I bet he'll buy me a tot or two,' she says to no one in particular.

In her rush to leave, she gulps her last swig of gin, which catches in her throat and goes down the wrong way. The regulars in the bar erupt into laughter making lewd remarks about Clay pipe not capable of carrying her drink as she coughs and splutters. 'Stuff you lot, I'm off, I 'ave a chap waiting for me.' Alice flounces out but lurches into a table, causing more giggles and curses from the regulars.

'Don't tell your John, gal. He'll bash your face in,

an' what he'll do to the gent ain't worth finkin' about.' The cry follows her as she attempts to leave.

She rights herself, getting ready to go. 'Oh, lordy. I bet he's scarpered by now. You buggers can shift out of me way.'

Fuelled by liquor and staggering to the door, she blunders out so fast that she ends up hugging the grimy stone pillar at the entrance as a lover does. With a shake of her head and a mutter, Alice straightens up and totters off, creating an amusing spectacle for any onlookers as she heads for Flower and Dean Street connecting to the now-infamous Brick Lane, the junction from where came the last sighting of Mary Nichols after leaving the Frying Pan bar the night before her gruesome slaying by the so-called Jack the Ripper.

Resolute, Alice makes headway as she staggers on mumbling, 'Blimey, I hope he's come back, he did say he would, and I need sum dosh. Better still a jigger or two, but remember gal, beggars can't be choosers.'

She pauses and gawps trying to steady herself as the path weaves before her, or is she tight?

Talking aloud, she says, 'Take fings steady, gal, now tread carefully. You don't want to end up arse over tit.'

Erect but more confident in her head than her legs, Alice embarks on her trek, pleased with herself until she trips over a drunk and screams smacking into a doorframe. His feet were sticking out of a doorway. 'Ya smashed, git, you'll do a body an injury,' she says.

'Shift ya backside.' She aims a kick at his patched boots, misses, and almost topples again.

'Hey, how come you got three pins?' She squints shaking her head as both his legs come into focus and slip out again.

'Oh, my, I am pissed.' She shakes her head and steadying herself, gets ready to hurry on her way. As she hurries, a voice from behind reaches her, 'How you doing, Alice?'

Margaret, her friend, and two other women are sitting on the stone steps of the barber's shop, smoking their clay pipes, and chatting about their day.

'All right, I can't stop now.' Says Alice, dashing on. Her target is Castle Alley, a dark, dank passage, which cuts through to Whitechapel High Street. In drunken undertones, she chatters to herself. 'Not the type of place a well-bred young woman heads for.' A picture of herself dressed as a lady comes to mind and she grunts. 'Ha, well at least I can thank the Lord for summat by not being well-bred or young, and honest, gal, times money.'

A belly chuckle rumbles under her skirt, and she squints through the gloom for eavesdroppers in the dim night.

With a shrug, tinged with regret, she glances down at her best brown skirt topped by an almost white chemise and apron. Lifting the hem to look at her button boots, which haven't seen polish in many a day, she sees she's wearing one brown and one black stocking. 'Strewth, I can't even dress mesen proper these days,' she grumbles and staggers on.

'Oh Lordy, me poor duds.' Sighing deeply, she is tickled at the sound of her voice, which, in the dark, gives a modicum of comfort. It's not safe on the street at night. 'Like having a friend at me side, safety in numbers, like.' She says before being attacked by a fit of hiccoughs and releasing an unladylike fart.

The local church bells ring out at midnight. Alice walks towards the Music Hall, still clinging to the possibility of meeting the stranger. If he's not there, someone else may want her offerings. Three pence will buy her a double gin.

Rushing on, sweat seeps beneath her oxters, soaking into her already stained bodice. 'Gawd, I'm gonna burst,' she groans as her heart pumps the alcohol through her kidneys into her bladder, and she concentrates on not peeing herself.

Aided by the fuddling of her spirit-addled mind, she fails to detect a man trailing her through the hazy gloom, wearing a long coat, tall hat and clutching a carpet bag.

'Oh, lordy, I don't 'alf need a piss.' She crosses her legs and scans the road. 'Oh, my, why didn't I go back there before.' Alice checks behind her, which looks clear, but in the dark, who can tell who or what hides in the curtain of black murk?

Hurrying, she dashes into the passage, and pulls her skirt and petticoats up, hoping she won't get disturbed. She doesn't waste time in examining the alleyway for vagrants, stray drunks, or footpads who bed down for the night in such places because she's about to wet herself as she hunkers down.

Enjoying the relief as she squats, the last bong from the church clock hangs in the surrounding gloom, and it dawns on her that today is her sister's birthday.

'July 17th, blimey, me little sister, Kath, is thirty-two, daft cow. Aw, don't be unkind. You're pissed an' jealous cos she's younger than you. Aye,' she answers herself, 'but I'm not drunk enough.'

She tries to straighten up but struggles, not only to reorganise her clothing but remaining vertical. 'Cor, I'm glad I'm no gentlewoman with a pair of draws to fiddle with.' Her chunters echo along the alley.

A noise nearby startles her, but steady is the way to go, which is as fast as the huge amount of gin she swallowed allows. Alice glances up at the windows overlooking the alley but only one glows from candlelight, no one is watching.

Panicking in case a rat is fancying a bite of her backside, she twists around when, with no time to scream, a gloved hand smothers her mouth. A moustached man thrusts his face close and indicates with a wag of his forefinger that he demands complete silence. 'Shh, I won't harm you.' He says.

It's a distinguished voice. He relaxes his grip to ease the pressure, brandishing Alice's cheeks with finger marks.

'I didn't mean to be rough; please, let me apologise. It's not my intention to scare you.' His tender intonations put her more at ease.

'Well, you did, and half to death, mister. What do you want? Wait a minute.' She screws her eyes and studies what little she can of him in the subdued light. Something about his cultured voice struck her from before, and not so long ago, but where? Her eyes dart to the entrance and back as he backs them into the dark alley. 'Here, aren't you the gent who offered to buy me a drink?'

'Yes, I am, and I did.'

'Well, what are you doing...? Here you.' She nudges him. 'Did you follow me?'

Flattered, the well-dressed gentleman sought her out but thinking back to what George said unsettles her. Blind George said the nights aren't safe for anyone, much less for ladies out unaccompanied. She considers the murders of the previous year. The memories wipe a smile from her face, and her eyes seek out the alley entrance.

'Do you mind?' He slips his fingers into his waistcoat placket, removes a few coins and pushes them under her nose. Mingled with the blend of the city and his sweaty palm, the aroma tempts her twitching nostrils, unstoppable like waves rippling to the shore. The man jingles them in her face. Alice can almost feel them in her grimy hand, and her face creases into a grin.

'Well, aye, I suppose if you want a bit of a lark before we take a sup, ducks.'

'Oh, yes, I want.' In his haste to stash them, one tumbles to the floor and bounces along the cobbles. Avaricious enough to mark where the coin rests, Alice hopes he will forget, and if she's lucky, she can claim an extra penny or sixpence. She doesn't know they will find only a farthing and her old clay pipe underneath her extinct corpse.

'Turn around,' he says, trembling with husky passion. Giggling, she twirls her back to him, wiggles her hips, and hitches up her skirt, ready to fulfil his request. 'Is this what you be after, me ducks?' A moan fills the alley, and she smacks her lips as she relishes the gin she is sure will follow.

Time doesn't permit Alice to picture further as a blow strikes her in the ribs. 'Oh God, no, Georgie, help.' A vision of the boys' warning and second sight flashes before her. Why didn't she take heed? Why did she always think she would be the one to avoid these things and nothing would happen to her?

Incapable of screaming, she slumps forward, powerless to breathe. The pretend gentleman jerks his hand under her chin and snaps her head to the right and backwards. She flops, and he catches her, lowers her to the floor, and sighs, not relishing placing his hands beneath her sweat-stained oxters to drag her dead weight. He struggles, panting with the effort.

He separates the costermonger's barrows and props her against the slime-ridden, urine-stained brickwork shaking his right hand, which throbs painfully.

The stranger tugs her skirt above her waist and bares her legs and stomach. His heart leaps as excitement courses through his veins while running the razor-sharp steel up her abdomen. The keen edge enables him to complete one cut straight up to her throat, where he stops under her left breast.

Exhilarated, he never thought to enjoy this type of thrill again. How wrong can a person be, and the proof lies beneath him? With one knee on her chest, he strives to concentrate. His eyes glaze over in the sheer eagerness of the task. 'Damn the bitch,' he mutters. This is harder than he remembers. 'Oh yes, it's been too long.'

At least Alice didn't suffer from either of the stabs to her neck or glimpse the wink of the blade, and she didn't flinch as the steel pierced her skin and glided across her neckline from left to right, slicing her gullet.

The only sound to prove she ever lived occurs as blood gurgles up between her lips and bubbles from the slashed carotid artery. Unworried about rats, money, or jigger gin, she leaves this world abused and humiliated, yet now in peace.

A noise at the alley entrance interrupts his enjoyment, and with a swift swipe of his lengthy cloak, he manages to cover them, blending them into the shadows. Pressed against her warm, smoke-damaged form, he holds his breath and prays not to inhale the stink of salty blood and unwashed flesh, which now assaults his sensitivities. His urge dwindles as her lifeblood oozes from her body and leaches through his shirt.

A hungry PC, Joseph Allen, is ready for a rest, it's about a quarter past midnight, and he's on for the night shift. The aroma from the pie he bought an hour before tempts him, and he decides to take a bite, so he pops into Castle Alley seeking refuge next to a streetlight. It's safer to eat near the dim glow of the lamp than in the open threat of the street, but it's not an ideal location for a meal.

The killer psyches himself and holds his breath. After he's waited for such a long time, for a Bobby swinging his billy club to stroll into the same place and ruin his night is too much to bear. He thinks why the hell couldn't he skive elsewhere; the killer's bloodlust is not yet spent, but he keeps deathly still.

The officers would on occasion, though not as much since the rise of the ripper, peek at the shenanigans in the passage as voyeurs before they stopped their fun to drag off a few doxies. More adept clients manage to run quicker than the well-oiled whores they took for a fumble.

Joseph takes the pie from a knapsack slung over his shoulder, checks all is clear, and bites into the thick crust as he leans against the wall, secure from attack. After the previous year's horrendous murders in the locality, he's not taking the chance of anyone overwhelming him from behind.

Bending one knee, he presses his foot on the brickwork and savours the cold, gelatinous liquor between the chunks of meat. In minutes, though, another Bobby with the same idea enters the alley. They nod to each other; no words are necessary.

Joseph, ready to leave, still chewing on the last bite of the pie, takes a minute to relieve himself against the wall. Without seeing anything else of note, both of the Bobbies depart, with not a word spoken. The sound of hobnail boots scraping on the cobbles signals to the murderer they are heading in opposite directions.

To examine the alley, he raises his head and takes a long breath through his mouth. Irritated at the height of his excitement, he mutters, 'Why, why, why do they stop me?' With a grunt, he rises from the lifeless body of Alice and screws his face in disgust. His pleasure over, his lust abates, washed away in the mire of his surroundings.

She was nothing more than a bitch earning gin and a crust from between her thighs, he thinks, while his body and mind scream for an undefined release.

Fearful of discovery and disappointed, he sneaks out of the alley leading to the High Street to confirm the whereabouts of the law where there's a plentiful supply of doorways to pop in hide as he heads for Aldgate Station.

The heavens open releasing a short, ferocious torrent of rain that bounces off the filth-ridden cobbles leaving a haze to rise from the tepid surface on the hottest days of the year. It lingers aiding the killer in making his way to Aldgate.

At the station he weaves between the rolling stock to reach the work sheds where he ducks. His eyes hunt out the building, surrounded by unkempt undergrowth, the shed furthest from the road.

Voices call out in the distance. 'He's back. The Ripper's, back an' he's dun another woman in. Come on everybody get a move on. Let's find the bastard. He can't be far because they say she's still warm, an' the pavement's dry underneath her, so it's just happened.'

The killer crouches, his heart pounds in rhythm with the horses' hooves thudding along the thoroughfare. A hackney thunders past, and from the sound of growling wheels, he knows the vehicle is a Clarence, and at this late hour and the speed it's travelling, an anxious cabby is keen to put the hostile thoroughfares behind him.

Unseen, the killer lifts his head and rakes the bleak night praising his providence—no Black Maria yet. He shivers but makes his way to the last brick-built shed on the plot, using steady, progressive strides and trying not to leave any discernible path. He reaches the wall and slumps against the weather-beaten brickwork to think. Shrouded in darkness, he listens until he's sure he's not been seen.

Always alert, he kneels on the soggy grass before a crumbling wall and removes a few loose bricks from the base before hiding his case and hat inside the wall's cavity. He checks to ensure the way is clear. Nothing unnerves him, so he replaces the bricks, rests, and relives what happened. The rain slows to a drizzle.

Earlier that day, when he visited this same place to retrieve the tools of his trade, he was surprised to find them in fine fettle. It's been eight months since his previous call. The equipment needed a wet stone and oiling, and he's glad he took heed when his uncle taught him how to make the most of them.

After a quick breath, he checks his handiwork and

plumps the foliage. It's not ideal, but he does what he can. He was always careful to take different paths to and from this shed. The last time he came here is never far from his mind.

Memories tinged with heartache, and an equal amount of pleasure fill him, yet he still clings to regrets until he attempts to stretch the fingers on his right hand. It doesn't matter how much he massages or stretches them, the middle and forefinger curl. His grip is impeded to a vast degree due to what he calls 'an incident' back in November when he damaged his tendons.

Searching around his feet for a specific spot, he grins when he spots a patch of flourishing daisies. A sardonic smile breaches his face, he whispers, 'By, and didn't I pay in so many ways for one night's work.'

Ever since that fateful night, he's struggled to teach himself to use his left hand. Tonight was a bit of a failure in many ways, not only with the bobby turning up, but his hand isn't as supple or durable as he had hoped. He doubts he killed her outright. When he opened her torso, blood still pumped through the slash on the left side of her neck and only stopped when he ripped her open.

He needs more practice. He hates a sloppy job, but here in these slums, enough opportunities will arise. Mindful of the blast of whistles and the clatter of hobnailed boots coming from the pathways, he remains hidden and unhurried and works out his options.

His clothing is covered in gore, and he recalls

shielding Alice's body with his. The memory of her vital fluids leaching through his shirt, on his hands, and face, makes him shudder, he must cleanse himself. He tilts his face to the drizzle, hoping to wash most of the blood away while he rubs his fingers in the long, wet grass.

A blast from a police whistle forces him to lie flat. The thuds of heavy footwear on the cobbles seem much closer. The cries of 'Help' join the affray of the locals as officers from near and far converge on the district. His head spins, he must escape. They must not find him, not yet, not until he finishes his mission. Angry at himself for skulking away in the dark with his task unfinished and his lust unsatisfied, he laments in a sotto voice. 'Why don't they let me do my work? What is wrong with them?'

The wheels of a goods train squeal and spin to gain purchase and gather enough momentum to pull away from the siding. The killer gives chase and leaps on the last waggon, hanging on for grim life he discovers it's the guards' van he's hanging onto. With a heaving torso, he pants and presses against the ladder. His left hand grips the rungs, his right hooked on for balance.

His knuckles shine white, and only one hand stops him from falling off to land on the rail tracks. He grumbles and mourns the limited use of his hand and fingers, aware of his tentative grasp and the occupied van.

The throbbing engine begins to slow. He can't make anything out in the gloom ahead or along the side of the train. What if this is the wrong train? By now, if he's on the Greenwich Line, he should be able to glimpse the glow of the firebox from the locomotive as it sways on the bend of the viaduct.

The thought he's mistaken is hard to take, his heart races, where the hell is he? A sudden glimmer of flames on the curve shines out and he sighs with relief.

Any time after the whistle blew meant the train was crossing the bridge and would be an excellent time to wave goodbye to the chugging beast, which urged him to jump off, jump off, jump off, in rhythm with the wheels singing out on the track, committing him to plan his escape.

Taking his life in his hands, he gambles and leaps into the unknown. His cloak flares, suggesting an enormous bird in flight, before hitting the ground, where, with an inelegant thud, he bounces down the bank. He doesn't realise he's holding his breath until each stone and branch of brushwood makes him gasp as he rolls and bumps over them.

Unhurt but breathless, he's pleased to discover he's nigh on top of Deptford Market Yard. Once the heat dies down, he can find his way back, but he needs a place to wash first. He takes no delight in the lingering odour of blood about his person.

After dispatching his victims, he examined his feelings about the way he left them to the shame of bearing their most intimate regions for all the world to gawp upon. His self-analysis establishes he is more disgusted by the noisome rank of the body than by dispatching them to the afterlife, wherever or whatever that may be.

Unsteady, he gets to his feet and tests the terrain and his joints. Thank goodness his bones are sound, he thinks as he gingerly puts a foot forward, every joint, lump, and bump aches. He gazes past the railway embankment to the dim glow of the street gaslights through their glass shields and ponders on his next move and then like a moth drawn to light, he heads towards them.

He reaches into his waistcoat pocket but, his fob is gone, and he curses wondering on the time. Scanning the dark sky for a moment he suddenly chuckles. Why is he trying to tell the time through the cloudy murk hiding the stars when, at a distance, a church clock strikes half past the hour, but which hour? He decides to seek refuge in St. Paul's Churchyard, where he can rest among the dead for a while. Worn out and sore, yet exhilarated, he grins again at escaping unnoticed.

In the gloom and resting with his back against a headstone, voices reach him from down the road as people stumble from the pubs, which will serve for hours. He was familiar with the area and the various public houses nearby, where typically he would appreciate groups of men to mingle with, but not in his current state. He longs to wash his person before sunrise and before anyone spots him.

The King's Head pub is on the crossroads of Creek and Church Street. He'll head there. He rejoiced again at his luck in finding the train he jumped was heading in the right direction.

The pub owns stables on the land behind them and he can clean himself with little possibility of being disturbed by any horse-drawn vehicles arriving at this hour, but he needs to rest, liberating the city of its filth is exhausting, and this last attempt is no exception making him wonder, is he getting too old? No, never, his motivation is strong; he must finish. Drowsiness hits him, both in the head and the body, prompting him to take a nap. The dead aren't fussy about with whom they keep company, he will wash later.

At 1:30 in the morning, a brougham races up the street. Jameson, the driver, is uncomfortable with the lateness and curses the time wasted by witnessing a bad incident where they shot the animal blocking the roadway, forcing them to wait for the knackerman to retrieve the corpse. To avoid more delays, he climbed down and asked some gathered bystanders. 'Come on, give a hand here. Let's shift this so we can all enjoy our beds before dawn.'

'How much?' One shabby-looking chap with a pipe dangling from his mouth held his hand out and rubbed his fingers with his thumb. Growing ever more jittery about his employer out after dark, he said, 'Here, buy yourselves a tot on the mistress,' and threw a few coins at the group of men.

He won't relax until he delivers his employer and prays she won't suffer any adverse effects from this night. The men had manhandled the vehicle to the side, making enough room to pass.

At the Creek Street crossroads, he crosses over to

Union Street without stopping, a scream pierces the air and the stallion rears in the shafts. After anxious seconds, he brings the skittish stallion to a standstill and ties him on a short rein. He gave a cursory brush to the horse's muzzle and returned to discover a man lying prostrate and bleeding.

Chapter 2

HANOVER ROAD
(Present Day)

Larry glares through his study window on an overcast and gloomy morning. A cloudy sky creates a murky outlook. Raking his fingers through his overlong, ruffled hair, the weather suits his temper. He is quite dishevelled for a researcher of his distinguished calibre. The large window allows him to make out his reflection and his table, with his files and papers strewn everywhere.

He prays the weather holds true to the forecast, which says the day will pick up and be warm with sunshine. At the moment, it's like his humour and can't deteriorate, and it's still early.

He's a methodical person who hates untidiness, and his partner Glenda has got right up his nose. She has knocked his files onto the floor in a vindictive swipe and it's unforgivable.

'How dare you accuse me of snooping, Larry, you bastard?' She screams. 'This is my home, too. When I took the quilt out of the cupboard, that cardboard box fell out, and I only opened it to check if the stuff was important.'

His partner of five years is a petite and spirited

woman, still smarting from a previous argument when he yelled at her. She would claim he issued threats if anyone asked and ordered her out of his sight as he may not be responsible for his actions.

Never knowing when or wanting to back down, and bent on having her say, she slaps an A4-size buff envelope down. About to begin her tirade, but he bawls, 'Give me strength, woman, and lay off me. My time does not permit for this crap. It's this type of thing that makes me wonder why I relented.'

'Did what? Hey, Larry, mister freaking big shot?'

Her voice cuts through his meanderings. His image in the window sneers. His mind is not on arguing with her but on his work and the pending results of his trials. The end is in sight. He's so close to a resolution. He can do without her ranting about something private and nothing to do with her.

Twitching, he turns to his right. Is it a simple noise or a voice? Are they back? Doing his best to remain unaffected and wishing Glenda would shut her stupid mouth for once. She must let him think and stop them from taking over.

How can she so brazenly push his private property in his face? Of course, he read it, and the panic inside turned his world upside down. She has only skimmed through them with no idea of the truth they contained.

He's perplexed. Why did he take possession all those years ago? When the envelope contents struck a chord and answered hitherto unasked questions that helped to make him more determined to find a solution through his work. Would he be different if he hadn't accepted them?

'Ssh, keep your cool, you must prioritise.'

Larry believes these words are in his head, but he says them out loud.

No matter how hard he tries, he can't blank Glenda out, arguments are not on his agenda.

'Please put a bloody sock in it.' He says, but her voice thunders on, like a battering ram splintering his resolve to block her out. His twitching grows worse as her rants persist.

'Go on,' she says 'Did what, hey? What are you chuntering at now?'

More so nowadays than before, he's been ignoring her, so she is happy for him to pay her some mind. So much so, she will do anything for him to do so, but his anger explodes.

'Let another nosey woman in my life. You're all the same. Nosey, nagging bitches.' He stuns her into silence.

A flashback to the day he sat enjoying a quiet coffee in the sunshine, sitting on a rattan chair outside Starbucks, leaps to mind. A woman on her mobile walked into him, her ice-blue eyes and auburn hair glistened in the sunlight piquing his scientific mind

Larry is a genetic researcher, and he identified the colour combination of hair and eyes as being in the minority, which made her interesting in many ways. Flustered, she apologised. 'I'm so sorry. Can I buy you another?'

He appraised her from head to toe. 'No, I'm fine, a bit wet, yes, as you can see, but if you join me you can buy me another.' And she is still with him.

Glenda smothers her resentment. She hates to argue and understands he is at an essential stage in his work, but he shouldn't accuse her of snooping. She was only swapping the quilt with the warmer weather on the way. Why is the mess her fault? She pulled the quilt out, and it dragged a box with it, which burst open revealing opened envelopes and diaries.

At least this is the gist of what she told him when she presented him with one of the larger brown envelopes and asked him the meaning, but he bawled,

'What's it to you?'

So, she went through them all, excusing herself by saying anybody else would too.

Not comfortable reading diaries, she ignored them. Old memories of what a person did on a particular day don't interest her. She tried to keep one once, but the task she found was more than dull.

Rifling through it and dismissing certain papers, others she packed on one side, to go through them when he went out. At the bottom, a woman with love in her eyes stared out of a black and white photograph. This intrigued her, as he never spoke about previous girlfriends, and this one is beautiful.

She went to him and pushed the photo in his face, her top lip curled, and her nostril flared as she snarled, 'Is this one of the nagging bitches then?'

Larry can hardly believe it. 'You mean... after I

asked you to leave my things alone, and keep out of my way, you go through my private belongings until you find something to sink your malicious, bitter teeth into and this is it—one photograph? Umpteen times, I tell you to stop going through my stuff, you nosey bitch, and here you slap a photo and a document about a building I inherited years ago in front of me.'

A thought flicks through his head. This is not the time to go into these unimportant frivolities. His work is vital, not this crap. A voice over his right shoulder reminds him. 'Think about what she did to your files. Now you have to waste your valuable time sorting them out.'

'Please don't go on. Please shut up.'

Unsure whether he is talking to the voice close to his ear or Glenda. He doesn't want the voices back. He managed to shut them out for so long. He thought by now with some medication help, they had left him, but here she is, bringing it all back to him and he can't bear it. Why can't everybody leave him in peace? Clenching his fists, he's seething inside. This is a deliberate act of defiance, and yet…

'What happened to her, Larry? Are you still pining for her? Is this why you keep her hidden up there?' Glenda's lip curls in disdain as she sneers, 'So you can take her out for a gawp now and again. A pleasant palm friend, was she?'

With his voice, albeit under control, the floor resonates with his words, 'From your lips, "hidden". Does my or anyone's privacy mean nothing to you?

You are always nosing around; you can't stay out of any wretched thing, can you?'

'Privacy,' she rears, 'I can't take a damn shower without you wandering in to take a pee.'

With her hackles high and about to say more, he turns away and takes in a lung full of air. His hands rest on his hips, and as he sighs out, his middle-aged spread bulges over his waistband. With closed eyes and his mind whirling, he warns himself. 'Restrain yourself.' He mumbles, 'I can manage this.'

'What did you say?'

'What makes you think I'm speaking to you?'

'Well, who the hell else is here? Say something if you want, but don't chunter. The first step to madness is talking to yourself, Larry.' She sighs 'Why won't you just tell me, tell me something, anything; please, Larr?'

Interlocking his fingers behind his head, he glowers at his paperwork in disarray. 'You realise this is none of your damned business, so I would shift your bony arse if I were you before I lose my temper.'

She swallows. 'I'm sorry, Larr. Let's not row, we seem to spend all our days bitching at each other.' Sighing, he pauses and spreads out his words, 'Keep out of my belongings then.'

'How often should I apologise, and why didn't you just tell me about her?'

'Why, what is she to you? Let me tell you, nothing at all...' It's more of a growl pressed out between his teeth.

He snatches the pages and the photo, and his face softens as he gazes at the elfin features peering out. Standing as tall as her small frame allows, Glenda bristles, about to wade aggressively, but changes her mind and shifts tack. 'Okay, you are stressed about the tests, and I get it, but let's take a day off to clear your head a little. A day out would be fun.'

Lost for words. he absentmindedly runs his fingers over the broad leaves of the cheese plant on a jardinière adjacent to the window, he faces her and says, 'This monstera deliciosa needs water and a spray; I'll do it now. Did you buy the leaf milk I asked for?'

'Yes, I put the bottle in the cupboard, but don't bother about them. Larry, let's talk, please.'

'Will you let me finish? The trial results and data need to be analysed this weekend, so as I already said, I can't click my fingers and magic up more time.

'Yes, another weekend gone.

He explodes, exhausted, and at the end of his tether. 'I explained what I did when we bumped into each other, and yes, literally, and I made it clear. Now I'm this close,' He holds his forefinger and thumb apart, indicating a minute gap, 'I'm asking you to be patient. These latest tests will prove I'm right, I'm positive, so leave off before you regret it.'

Startled, she witnessed his anger at odd times. The stereotypical temperamental scientist, but not with the threats. This is scary and doesn't resemble him. He's acting like a different person.

Troubled, he glares at her, has he overstepped the mark; can he keep it together? A voice nearby says, 'Stop worrying; restraint is what you must have. We will take control of it all.'

He twitches, edgy, and answers. 'Not again, no, I can't go through this not again. Don't make me; you agreed.'

The spectacle sets Glenda wondering when he got that annoying tick. She's never detected a twitch before, and what's all this talking to thin air about?

Ashamed and embarrassed by hearing voices, he shies away from catching her eye. Once, long ago, he nurtured beliefs about them as an extra, like a sixth sense, sitting on his shoulder and taunting him. In his head, he believes they are his inner self, guiding him since he daren't think of interpreting them in any other way. He listens because, at times, they help to keep him steady and to concentrate on his work. They are a part of him even though he tries to get rid of them with tablets.

Memories of childhood, for the majority, offer no fondness for him. Unhappy and alone inside the circle of his adopted family, he craved love. Sad to say, he found the commodity in short supply and believes the lack of it may have birthed his voices.

They visited and talked to him in the night when sleep eluded him. When they questioned him, they gave him a modicum of comfort and helped him to find answers in times of crisis. He never admitted to anyone that he was conscious of them. He defined them as his mind searching out solutions.

At bottom, science is his life, and ghosts don't exist. He wouldn't converse with them as a boy, but as much as he hates to now, and deep down resents their presence, he does listen.

Glenda studies him as he composes himself and speaks more calmly. 'Plants are alive and become our responsibility if we take them in. They need us to feed and water them.'

Incapable of keeping her mouth closed as he pontificates, which is always annoying— but she can't resist screaming. 'Who do you think you're talking to and don't treat me like a blasted child? You take the biscuit, you. All your experiments are on animals.'

Physical pain strikes him as he bites the bullet and splutters, cutting her off. 'Don't start, woman. How many times do I have to warn you? Enough.'

'Well, they are living things. How you can do tests on them is beyond me, and here you are slavering and lavishing attention on flaming greenery. They're plants. They do not have feelings. You are a scientist.'

She throws her hands in the air, exasperated at the vast collection of glossy green foliage arranged around the room.

'Well, nothing is more obvious to me. Everything seems to be beyond you, Glenda, apart from jealousy.

'Oh, grow up, me, jealous, give over. It's your bloody double standards that get me.'

'We must love something.'

Aghast, but never silent, she cries, 'Something, am

I something? Is this your way of saying you don't love me?'

'At least I can say you are methodical in your perversity. Why try not to follow? You are working hard because nobody is that stupid. The trials are essential to helping people. I would do them on plants if possible. My priority is humankind, those who can benefit from my research and experiments. For myself, I love animals and would do investigations your way, but it's impossible—oh, you won't grasp it. You're like the rest of the doubters, so what's the point?'

'Try me. Straight up, I'll do my best. Think about it. You can't check data until the figures come in, can you? Let's do something together. Give ourselves some time away, anywhere away from here.'

In a rare moment of indecision, he says, 'But what if I'm on the wrong track? All my work will mean nothing.'

'What if you are on the right one? Think of the benefits you will bring to those needing your help. I have no idea what you do, and yes, I know you tried to explain, but I must confess you are fervent, and you will succeed. Anyhow, you said the data is ready at the weekend and not before.'

Glenda aims to take charge of this row, which she wishes she had never started. Though he is a terrifying spectacle when angry, he has never threatened her before, and this is the second time in a row he's dared to issue a threat of physical harm.

She lowered her voice attempting to calm the situation. 'A couple of hours, that's all I ask, please, or now. Can we talk now?'

She sits at the table, trying her best to sound light-hearted. 'Tell me about her and the property, Larry—wow, a real house not twenty miles away in the East End. Who left it to you? To be candid, since you told me about your adoption, I assumed you were alone in the world, well save for me.'

Larry is a man who is not so easy to win over, and he guesses what she's trying to do, and the annoying voices in his head are also trying to persuade him. 'She won't drop this, Larry. She wants to understand. What will you do now?'

'The house I inherited, as you say, is south of the river, not the east. I wish you'd keep up.' He's agitated, and mutters again, 'Women are all the same; they won't let things be.'

One wish of his is to banish these annoying, internal cynical mutterers in his head. All they do is goad him with the problem of the females in his life. A hitch, he is adamant about managing his way. The question is, will they give him the time to do so? He sounds brusque as he tries to dampen his anger. 'Wow, look at you, Glen, pound signs flash in your eyes. Well, you can digest this. You can kiss off contemplating any money.'

'You're not being fair; you're not.' Oblivious, she pushes on, missing the warning signals as inquisitiveness takes over. 'This one is about an inheritance with the deeds of an old property attached.' She didn't read the whole thing, only scanned a portion, but it looked like it was a family home, and yet, although he told her of his adoption, he said he had no real family, so why all the mystery?

Determined to press on while facing his wrath, the phrase "curiosity killed the cat" flashes across the recesses of her mind, but she can't resist asking,

'What's the plan?'

'Oh Lord, give me strength.' Spinning away, he slaps his hand against his forehead. Glenda carries on, unaware of any consequences.

'Don't call me a snoop, Larry. Why don't we go to the place? What's the name, oh, Albury Street?'

'No, why should I call you a snoop when you studied the confounded thing enough to remember the address.'

'Of course I did. What do you expect me to do?'

'Keep your composure, Larry; despite her, you are an educated man.' His head and shoulders twitch as he tells himself to remain cool. He breathes in and holds his breath, his inner voice cautions. 'Take control.'

Unheeding, or plain disregarding, his outburst, she's sure she can wheedle him around and she starts again. 'And may I reiterate, and no, don't gawp at me with a face like a smacked arse. I can use long words too. You need a break, and if you don't want to go away for a day or so, let's take a couple of hours off together. Come on, please?'

Her pleading is more like flirting as she uses

childlike tones and throws him a dazzling grin to lighten the mood. He is in no frame of mind to capitulate. 'Sounds like a real treat' he says, 'more time for us to argue.'

'Tell me, and I promise not to pick through your rubbish again.' The weak attempt to make a joke falls flat ad does nothing to help lift the tense atmosphere.

'To be frank,' he says, 'I tried to shrug it off.'

'You're joking.'

The tension lifts a touch when he pulls out a chair and sits opposite her. Taking his mobile, he tosses it across the table and strokes the leaves of a pot plant in the centre of the mayhem of paperwork while he gathers his thoughts.

Pausing, he raises his glance to an eager Glenda and swallows. 'I, err, well, as I told you, I am adopted, and I'm amazed they thought about me at all. One day, I'll check it all out, but, well, you know, with things as they are, I don't have the time.'

'No, how are things? What are they like, and how long has this been bugging you?'

'Oh, ages, I can't remember now.'

Powerless to grasp the idea of anyone inheriting a house, never mind relinquishing the responsibility of one and letting it rot in London. She studies him, puzzled. 'Why don't you sell or rent it to someone? Blimey, with the prices nowadays, you'd make a killing.'

His phone annoyingly interrupts them, and she cringes. She hates the aggressive Vivaldi's Summer

Storm ringtone he chose, but the tune matches their moods.

Instead of pinning the mobile to his ear, he slides the off slider, gulps, and stretches his neck. Prominent, his Adam's apple leaps as he grins. A hapless Glenda enjoys no notion of what she's saying, and he finds the situation almost funny.

'I've never been.'

'What, not ever?' She gapes, not believing him, but still can't or won't leave off with the questions.

'Bugger me, what the hell's wrong with you? I would at least have to look at it if I inherited a house. It's exciting, well, I think so.'

'Listen, Glenda, I can't permit the time for this trivia. With my investigations and the paperwork involved,' his eyes are on the ceiling, and tension rises with his temper, but throwing prudence out, Glenda carries on pushing.

'Is it derelict?'

Slapping his hand on the table, 'Leave me be, will you? For the last time, treat the subject like you do my money and let it go.'

A voice beside him whispers in his ear.

'Relax; you don't want them to come back again. They're watching. Now keep control.' Rubbing his nose, he twitches.

With a smirk like a Cheshire cat and her tone ridiculing, 'Oh, pack it in. We've done that once. Be more imaginative. You might like to play the crazy scientist, but as they say, we need a break, WE both do.'

'No, I'm almost there. DAMN AND BLAST YOU WOMAN. Let me be. I can't go, and I won't.' His words flow over her as if he never opened his mouth, and he might as well have handed her the spade as she dug in deeper.

'Let's go, Larr... please? You shouldn't tell me these things if you didn't want me to find out; come on, pretty please.'

'Tell you, I never said a word about it, DARLING, remember, you... to be polite, snooped. Or if I am less than polite, you stuck your ruddy snout in again, and my name is Larry.'

Rising from his chair, he pushes past her, leaving the room. She looks at the mess on the table without remorse but tries to make amends by tidying the files, but she also has no idea of their importance or the order in which to place them.

How can she make it up to him, she wonders as she fills the miniature watering can with distilled water, which he insists they use. She dribbles the water on his precious plants, not out of kindness, she scowls tutting, 'Rotten things, just die why don't you,' before going to find him, guessing he will be in the conservatory, his haven.

Unsurprised, she finds him chatting to his prize orchid collection, misting each plant. Listening to him talk for a minute, she stumped, because he's an intelligent man. Why he thinks the plants know he's talking to them, she can't fathom. She touches his shoulder. Larry neither flinches nor turns.

'Sorry,' she says.

He keeps spraying, but peers at her, guarding his mien.

'Oh, fiddle you. Can we move on now, Larry?'

Not bothering to respond, he picks tiny pieces of debris from the base of his phalaenopsis orchid.

'Please?'

'Already done, Glenda.'

'What is?'

'The moving on.'

'What does that mean?'

'You found the photo; I moved on.'

'Would you like to talk about her?'

'No.'

'Where is she?'

'She left long ago, and we didn't keep in touch.'

'Like your wife.'

'Don't you bring her into this.'

'Did you love her?' She focuses back on the photograph.

'Yes, at least I thought so. No, I did love her.'

'What happened?'

'Is this important?'

'I think so, if you are still...'

'I've already said, and will keep saying, things are different now, and it's a long time ago.'

'Are you saying they have changed between us, Larry?'

'What makes you ask?'

'Well, I'm no snoop, and you are so upset about me seeing the photo, and well, yes, all right, I did, but you are so uppity about every single thing. I'm more intrigued about the building now, though.'

Gripping the water gun, his fingers clench and unclench. He grins and pointing the nozzle at Glenda, sprays her full in the face. His grin bursts into full-blown laughter.

Annoyed, but seeing a chance to move in on his playful humour, she slaps at him. 'You better be careful, or I'll fetch the hose.'

A pause follows and they wonder which way to go, floundering for what to say next. Prompted to admit defeat, he says, 'It's unlucky, and some say it's haunted.'

'WHAT!'

'Haunted.'

'Says who?'

'The last agent said strange things happened, and invisible hands touched them. He said some potential renters said the place is eerie as though it's haunted. The word spooky passed his lips more than once.'

'I bct it's the agent. I bet he's a perv and a sly bum pincher who nips the backsides of potential customers as they walk past him. Bound to.' She chuckles at the idea.

'Perhaps.'

'Doesn't this pique your interest a little? I mean, as a scientist, you don't believe the nonsense about ghosts, do you?'

In a rare moment of goodwill, he tugs her down to sit next to him on the wicker sofa. 'All right, let me clarify. Yes, I am a man of science, and you remind me in the nicest of ways. I grant you, I am intrigued, and in the normal way of things, I'd enjoy nothing more than to prove the supernatural world is all hairy fairy.' He twitches.

'Says who, just because you say so, doesn't mean they don't exist.' She nudges him in the ribs with her elbow.

'Leave off, Glen. I am now inundated with more work since you left me a right mess to tidy up on the table.'

'I did it already.'

'Uh, no, the files are or were, all systemised and perspicuous, and crucial to helping humanity where the signposts of right and wrong will not be an issue. Now, no more, it doesn't concern you.'

'Hang on, I thought you said you would tell me.'

'Stop interrupting then.'

'Sorry, I'll zip it.' She makes a zipping motion across her lips with her fingers. 'Go on, what's her name?'

'What happened to you being only curious about the building?'

'Well, yes...and her.'

'Jenny—young, vivacious, nosey, and she walked out o me.' He strives to laugh. Inside, he is fighting the voices, compelling him to conceal them and not say anything more, because if he does, he can't go back. But he carries on.

'Like you, she craved more than I would give.'

'Like what?'

'I said. I never satisfied her with anything. She always wanted more.'

'Like what?'

'The house.'

'You're kidding?'

'No. Yes, I'm kidding, but she wasn't interested in my work and wanted me to spend more time with her. I tried, and I made it plain to you too, before you moved in. My work comes first.'

'You made that all very clear when you asked me, in your own enigmatic and wonderful way, "Right, if you want to move in, you can, but think on, you will always come second to my studies."'

'I never said I was a romantic.'

'True, but why keep this particular photo?' She wafts the picture in his face.

'Why not? At one time, Jenny used to play a major role in my life.'

'Where did she go?'

'No idea, she scarpered, took all her belongings, and I never set eyes on her again. I got home to find a note stuffed under the corner of a photograph of us both in a silver frame she left on the side.'

'Oh, come on. You must have had some idea if things were going wrong. Nobody leaves for nothing.'

'You can be a bitch sometimes, Glenda. Yes, something went wrong, but I was not privy to it. She grew moody and went out a lot. I thought she was ill because I noticed a doctor's appointment on the calendar, but she said nothing, and I didn't ask.

You know there's a thing called privacy; oh no, you don't do you. Anyhow, I came in one day, and like I said, there was the note. She had gone, OKAY?'

'Did she leave it to you?'

'Leave what?'

'The house, durr.'

'No, but like you are now when she came across the same paperwork, she turned out to be avaricious and nosy. Tell me, Glenda, are all women nosy?'

'Blimey, how long ago is this?'

'Quite a while, I told you.'

'Did you take Jenny round?'

'Why?'

'Why? Well, I would like to go—because.'

'Because what?'

'Just because. Are any tenants in?'

'Didn't I explain, are you deaf? Now, can you drop the subject and let me mist these plants? This is more important than you and your selfish desires.'

More determined than ever, Glenda pulls faces behind his back. She intends to and will solve this.

'What about the files you have to arrange?'

'I will after this.'

'You're scared, Larry. You can't hide your fear from me and you are scared of something.'

'Lord, give me strength. What is wrong with you? Why must I keep repeating myself? Stop bloody nagging woman.'

'Let's go, and you can prove you are not a scaredy cat. You love being right. So, go on, show me you are a brave little soldier.'

'Damn you.' He spins around and slams the spray gun down. 'I don't need to prove anything, not a damned thing to you or anybody else.'

Glenda's temper boils, and she faces up to him.

'Okay, so this is what you call normal? You tell me you inherited a property not twenty miles away, which you can't be arsed to visit and claim no knowledge of who left it to you.

You're being ridiculous. I mean, this is not an ornament or something where one forgets in the mists of time? You can't rent and you won't sell, so what's wrong, or is something the matter with you?'

'For the last time, I did not tell you.'

'Oh, give over with the pathetic excuses. You must realise, I don't give a crap about the who, but the why you won't say gets to me. You are on your own with no family, according to you, so perhaps your ex-girlfriend, Jenny, did bequeath her home to you.'

The voices beside him mutter. He twitches. 'Leave her to us.' They say. 'Don't worry; you can trust us, Larry, don't get distressed.'

'Glenda, please.' He grasps his ears and shakes his head, trying to end this constant barrage of chatter.

'Ha, don't tell me, you did her in and inherited, and now you are suffering from guilt and won't use or sell the house. Did you love her so much?'

The voices nag. 'Bring her to us; we can help. Go on, do it now—you've done it before.' He curls into a ball to avoid what is coming next—too late. This path is well trodden. He stands so fast his back clicks, he drops his hands, appearing reticent and grins. 'Come on. Let's grab a drink, and I'll tell you the whole despicable affair.'

Cupping her elbow, he guides her out of the conservatory to the kitchen, where he places his secateurs on the table and switches on the coffee machine.

After changing the filter, he pours in fresh ground beans. She opens her mouth, but he interrupts. 'No, no talking; I'm talking now, so button your lip and open your ears.' He smirks and takes the cream from the fridge, adding a generous quantity to each mug of hot coffee. 'Right, are you comfortable?'

At a point somewhere behind her head, he scowls. Did something catch his eye? Peering for a second, his lips move, perhaps whispering but to whom? He faces Glenda again.

'YES, I am adopted, and granted, no outward displays of love came from the family. No affection at all, period. They educated me to a high standard but nothing more. I believed people took children in out of want or longing for their own, whereas, in hindsight, some do so out of a sense of duty or for money.'

'Oh, no, I won't ever accept such cynicism, Larry. I'm sure you're wrong.'

'Believe what you like, Glen, but I inherited bricks

and mortar, not a family, a building, and no, not Jenny's or anything to do with her, and no, I didn't do her in. If you must know she ran off with a professor.'

Surprised and unable to disguise mirth, Glenda's face composes a, so what, shit happens every day, posture, but manages to temper it with a tad of sympathy, 'You jest.'

'No, a damnable science teacher of all things, and why should I joke about something so agonising at the time?'

'Jenny?'

'No, the woman she shacked up with.'

'You mean she's a lesbian.'

Glenda's words spurt out through a shower of coffee. She lunges for something to wipe the tabletop and her blouse, tipping the whole table in her hurry. He keeps his own counsel. Concentrating as she throws the cloth back in the sink, he picks up the thread and continues.

'Thanks; trust you. No, she is bisexual.'

'Did you have any idea?'

'Of course not, you idiot. Why would I want to live with a bisexual?'

'No, given the score, the temptation could be doubled.'

'Yes, like you have any knowledge of this. You infernal women are all the same.'

'Can I ask you something, Larry?'

'Yes, sure, Glen, why break the habit now?'

She ignores his sarcasm and asks, 'Do you recall

when I moved in, you said no kids?' Terror blankets his face, and he splutters.

'No, don't be anxious. I'm not pregnant, but is this Jenny the reason you don't want children?'

'No, I can't make them, and I told you before you descended on me. Don't change your mind now, and no, I will not adopt a child, so don't ask.'

She glances around, taking in the opulence of her surroundings, not able to keep the sarcasm out of her voice. 'Oh, you're so hard done to, aren't you, and no, we, whoever WE are, are not all the same if you don't mind.' Reaching out to him she says, 'Sorry, I am being insensitive, but you must admit, this is kind of funny.'

He swipes her hand away. 'How come... funny? Believe you me, I didn't find anything in the least amusing about it.' They stare at each other for a few seconds until both burst out laughing.

Taking out her phone, Glenda peers at the screen while he sips his coffee.

'Are you expecting a call?' He wipes his lips clean from the cream.

'No, I'm turning mine off too.' She places her phone down. Surprised, he acknowledges the gesture but is grateful for no interruptions.

'In a twisted way, I suppose a certain portion of mankind would think of my pain as funny. Mind, let me tell you, my ego didn't half take a battering. I mean it, Glenda when I say my inheritance has nothing to do with Jenny. The assumption, at least mine, goes like this: the people who agreed to give me a home passed the house on to me, but no, apparently, it came from my birth family.'

'Larry, you can't go back; you can't.' He jerks at the voice in his head. Is this him, or are they back again? No, he mustn't mind them, but it's so close. He checks his shoulder, half expecting a tiny being sitting there. The one that keeps talking to him while he's trying to ignore what it says.

It's time to employ a certain relaxation technique learnt for times of stress. Taking a deep breath, he holds it before exhaling. Blowing out the air in his lungs by pursing his lips to empty them, before taking another breath through his mouth, he begins to relax. His inner voice falls silent again.

Glenda pushes on. 'Is this a family secret? Are you hiding a black sheep?' Without expecting it she scored a bullseye on a raw and painful nerve.

'Fuck off and leave me be.' He says snatching the secateurs off the table and snapping them together, wondering if she is as stupid as she makes out. She's pushing him too far.

The voices whisper, 'Listen to us, Larry; compose yourself. We will guide you. We will sort everything. You have to leave it to us.'

Like the proverbial patsy, Glenda reaches for her coffee, dabs her fingertip in the cream, and draws circles on the surface. 'Ha, so—a secret!'

He bawls, 'Before I afford myself the luxury of finding out...' She cuts him off with a rhythmical and annoying tone. 'How can I forget? You don't let me, at least, not about your freaking research. You are such a weak-kneed fake and a coward. You own what—a mansion, a terrace, or a townhouse—and for years by the sound of what you are saying, and yet maintain this ludicrous stand about having no idea who left the place to you. A house. What a load of crap. Are you sure nobody's buried underneath the patio, or is it Jenny beneath the slabs?'

Her well-manicured eyebrows appear to dance on her forehead, astonished at her daring because she never expected those words to leave her mouth. With the speed of light, he pushes his face into hers, and she spills her drink, worrying for the first time. Is she pushing him too hard?

They row all the time but always make up. Lately, though, fewer occasions occurred to do so. When he's not examining, he's analysing, and it always comes first. Following weeks of disagreements, Glenda forgets when they last made love and is confused. Is her attraction fading? She glances at her expanding waistline.

To date, he hasn't commented on her weight gain. He's so engrossed in his work, that she may as well be invisible to him, but this response is different, and she doesn't get why he won't say. She doesn't want his inheritance. She longs to be told and have a grown-up conversation about it.

Through gritted teeth, he snarls. 'I'm warning you; you'll be under the blasted patio if you don't watch your step.' Pretending to ignore him, she stomps to the sink, picks up a cloth, and wipes the spilt drink. While shaken to the core, she does wonder how far she can push him into spilling all, and with her agenda, she is determined to make him do so. 'Come on, let's make up.'

Her stomach is full of butterflies as she endeavours to bring him round by avoiding catching his eye and taking the stance of a woman demure and subservient. 'Be spontaneous, please and I won't ask for anything else. I'll leave you in peace with your nasty old research, and without any more complaints, scouts honour.'

He pulls a face, turning on hearing something; his face brightens, and his demeanour changes. Staring at Glenda, he drinks his coffee and appears more at ease than before. In a pleasant tone, he says, 'Okay, if I say I'll take you, will you let the subject drop, and I mean never mention it again, ever?'

'Yes'

'Sure?'

'Yes, I promise.' She crosses her heart.

'Right. Let's go.'

'What now?'

'Now or never, take your pick.'

'Let's go then, but I need a jacket.'

Sliding his mug away, he grabbed a bunch of keys hanging on the wall next to the thermometer and said, 'Shift. You don't need anything.'

'Oh, I love it when you take the lead like this.

Triumphant, she beams.

They leave their apartment, and Larry removes the crumpled paper that started the commotion from his pocket. Apprehensive, he skips down the front flight of stairs and passes the envelope to the eager hand of Glenda, who begins to study it in depth.

'Will you use the satnav?'

'Albury Street, yes, if you want, but I think I can find somewhere about twenty miles away.'

'Hang on, it says Union Street on one of the pages. Confused, she swaps the papers back and forth.

'Now the address is Albury, number 47 because the name was altered in the early 1900s,' he says, walking to the car.

'So, you have learnt something about it.'

'Don't be facetious. Of course, I read the confounded thing, didn't I? Now let's go. Did you lock up?'

'I thought you did.'

'Glenda, my papers are...'

'Yes, yes, I locked up. Don't start again. I can't imagine why you think anyone would want your stuff. Oh, wait a min, I left my mobile on the table.'

'Didn't we already establish anything requiring a smattering of intelligence is above you, and you can shove your phone and mine? We're off.'

He moves around his car to the driving side and strokes the bonnet as he passes, a gesture of love. Unlocking the door, he climbs in and lets Glenda in the passenger side. He turns the key and starts his pride and joy, a 2006 Morgan Roadster finished in his favourite Connault green. Revving the engine makes it roar, and he delights in the thrill of the throbbing noise. He slams it into gear and roars off, his face is blank.

Glenda is still smarting at the insult but wishes he stroked her like he does his car, and she flashes a tight smile. Fidgeting without her mobile, she spends a minute or two to program their journey on the satnav. At least with buttons and a screen in front of her, she can pretend happiness.

On the road, Larry's aggressive driving does not abate. While they reach their destination in record time, according to the satnav, the outing is not without all and sundry being subjected to his abuse.

His constant complaints about idiots who use the roads and those who see his vehicle and feel inclined to burn him up annoy Glenda. Revving their engines, they roll back and forwards, to tempt him to race at the first opportunity.

The heel of his hand blasting the horn, followed by a profusion of hand signals, the primary one being his middle finger stuck up in a derogatory manner kept her head bowed in embarrassment before they finally turned into Albury Street.

'Here we are,' he says, slowing down.

'Blimey, Larry, who would believe a house is buried behind this lot?' She says, as he pulls to a stop at the end of the terrace blending into a coppice of overgrown shrubs and privet.

'Is this the one?'

'No, my house is behind the trees, back from the curb. A pub stood on the corner donkey's years ago, through where those gateposts are now.' Waving his hand in a vague direction, she spots the remains of iron gates against a wall. 'The road once went through to Creek Street, but they closed the entrance off.'

Leaping out of the car, he breathes in deeply as if the air is full of fresh mountain goodness rather than the faint aroma of petrol and cut grass hanging around from the nearby churchyard. He makes his way to the side of the house and a gate secluded by bushes; you would have to know about it to find it.

'You told me you never came here.' Glenda stares at his back as she follows him. He ignores her but scrapes ivy from a window to peer through, distracting her. 'How long did you say you've owned this? It's so overgrown, and you say this is your birth family's house.'

They laugh, his smile is tender, and a sense of happiness floods her being, she's pleased that she forced the issue now because he's already happier. The day may turn out better than it started.

'Gosh, Larry, this is a magnificent place. I'm not surprised it won't rent though, it's so overgrown and all this ivy is strangling out of any chance for daylight to break through. Talk about dark and dingy, and those crimson walls look like they are sucking out the last glimmer of natural light.'

Placing her hand to shade her eyes, she peers

through the grimy window again. 'The windows need cleaning too. Let's go in. Where're the keys?'

'Here.' He jangles them before her eyes.

'For someone who says that hey never bothered before, you keep them handy enough.'

'Do you want to go in, or would you prefer to argue out here?

Chapter 3

ALBURY STREET

After admiring the Georgian entrance hall adorned with beautiful stucco plaster cornices. Victorian picture rails and a classic tiled black and white chessboard-designed floor grace Glenda's footsteps as she heads for the door opposite, striding across the room as a child would, by avoiding the cracks. 'Ooh Larry, this hall is beautiful.' She sticks her head through a doorway. 'Do you reckon this is the dining room? Blimey, wait till you cop the colour of the wallpaper in here.'

A sleek black Bombay cat startles them with a meow. 'Where the effing hell did that come from?' Glenda clasps her hand to her throat.

'The blasted thing snuck in behind us, Glen, don't worry, but we better make sure to put it out before we leave. I don't want it locked in.'

He peered around the door. 'No, Glen. I think this is the dining. The other one might be a drawing room, though.'

They entered the room that Glenda peered into through the window, and she thought it was crimson.

'Shit, I swear this room was painted red. How weird. Where is the red room, Larr?' She searches on.

'Hasn't anybody done any decorating since they built this place?'

Larry studies the decor; to him, the room is delightful. The decoration, albeit wallpaper crammed full of roses above the chair rail is outdated, it is his style. Below the chair rail, boasts oak wood panelling.

'Check out this, Glen. Someone has removed the top half of the wainscoting. The original woodwork would be floor to ceiling.'

'Hmm,' she shivers. 'I'm not sure about this house, Larr. Talk about eerie, never mind cold. I wish I'd picked my jacket up now,' she says poking her head through another doorway.

'Blimey, if this is the breakfast room, the décor alone would put me off eating mine.' A depressing shade of coffee-coloured paint covers the walls above the chair rail. Below, the wooden panels are overpainted with a deep brown stain.

She waits for a reaction to her joke, but Larry's mood won't allow sly remarks. Moving on to the next room, she remains unimpressed.

'What another dark, depressing room this is. How old is the house, Larr?' She searches for her mobile to switch on the torch app but remembers she left it behind, 'Bugger.'

'What's up?'

'No phone. I wanted to put some light on.'

'You'll live.' He said, dismissing her moans and smothering a chuckle.

From behind her, he says, 'What's dark? I love this

room because it's so bright and refreshing, and the atmosphere is welcoming. You need glasses, love. Come down to the kitchen; it's late Georgian, but some Victorian influences remain.'

Glenda gawps as he skips down the steps. 'You said you never came, so how come you know it's downstairs?' Again, he ignored her.

Careful to stay a short stride behind and forcing herself not to peer back over her shoulder, she senses a moodiness. The atmosphere grows heavier and more sinister with each tread. A faint but audible sound makes her spin to one side. Nothing or no one is apparent, but she's convinced they are not alone. Somebody whispers, but nobody except Larry is in the room.

Unperturbed and with a youthful spring in his step, he skips down to the kitchen. After a tiring morning, Glenda is exhausted and with the prolonged arguing, decides he may be correct when he says she gets oversensitive. Living with him and his moods, she tends to agree.

This sense of eeriness might be a delayed reaction; at least she hopes so. To break the ominous silence between them, she says. 'Nobody's been here since Victoria sat on the throne. Crikey, this is more of a museum than a house.'

He enters the laundry room, which contains a door to the garden. Through the window, his eyes linger on a well-manicured, walled area.

'Glenda, this is gorgeous.' Standing beside him

and incapable of holding her tongue, she grimaces.

'Come on, are you kidding me?' To Glenda, it's an overgrown patch of tangled weeds and shrubs, most dying or dead. This place has potential, she can't deny, but there's not a soul living who would describe it as gorgeous. It will take months to put right.

'Gosh, take a look at this old cooking range.' She says, focusing through an archway, 'It must be the original, it's archaic.'

Contemplatively, a question sits on Larry's face. 'Yes, over two hundred years,' he says, but he can't understand why she is so derogative because to him it is beautiful and well-tended.

Glenda wonders if he's winding her up as he appears different again, he's like a changeling this morning and more taciturn than the weather, which flounced through four seasons in the last two hours. And when did he develop such an annoying twitch?

'It's still the same, Glenda. This is weird. Let's go upstairs.'

Disillusioned, she gazes around. 'This place is a dump.' The comment is wasted, he has already left the room, and the door closed behind him.

The sound of his footsteps springing up to the next floor belies his years, leaving her puzzling about what he said. Giving the kitchen a final grimace, she turns the doorknob to no avail.

Regardless of how she twists and pushes, the door stays firmly closed. An icy chill hurtles through her body and settles in her bones. 'Shit, Larr.' Glenda's hot breath lingers in the cold air. She rubs her hands together and blows on her tingling fingers before hugging them under her armpits. 'Blimey, talk about cold,' she shivers. 'Larry, this door's stuck.'

Screaming, she rattles the door, slapping the paint-cracked panel. 'LARRY, come and open the bloody door.' Her heart leaps and flutters at a sound from behind and the black cat scurries across the floor. 'Where did that spring from?' Her voice is scarce above a whisper, but at least the moggy may be the answer to what is disturbing her sense of reason. She didn't believe in ghosts before this, but it may be up for discussion now.

A glint of light catches her eye, and a long stiletto-style knife demands her attention. One which came from nowhere, and if not, why didn't she spot it before? 'Oh God, where the f*** did that thing come from?' Her thoughts are a mishmash and uncontrolled like the weapon spinning on the range.

Her head whips around so fast her eyeballs roll as she searches for an answer. Is the bastard playing a stupid and macabre joke? Are the screams in her head as she wrenches at the knob, heart-pounding, blood racing? A heart can't beat like this without giving out. She's about to pee herself out of sheer terror or faint and she bawls like a banshee. 'LARRY! LET ME OUT.'

Anger takes over from fright as she bangs and kicks the old, yet sturdy door. How dare he treat her like this? He's a right pain in the arse. 'LARRY.' Her shriek echoes around the room.

Full of foreboding, like lava through a volcano with the pressure constantly rising, something has to give. Glenda prays she can hang on.

A bloodcurdling stomach-wrenching roar rings out, filling the room, buckling her knees, and sending her sinking to the floor. Slapping her hands to her ears, she twists to peer behind her through half-closed eyes. She doesn't want to look but can't stop herself, and although terrified, she's drawn to investigate.

The spinning weapon drips blood, pooling in a shiny, slick puddle. A foul stench permeates the room, a man laughs, and a woman cries. Petrified, she kicks the door again, a pathetic attempt. She's on the floor.

'LARRY! LARRY. Oh, please, God help me.'

The door opens inwards, and about to walk through, wearing a grin as broad as the Humber Bridge is Larry who hesitates and almost ends up on top of her. 'What's up with you?'

She grabs him, her face wet with sweat and tears, her chest tight, and catching a breath is hard.

'What's up? Come and take a gander upstairs; you'll love the bathroom, Glen. It's got a huge roll-top bath.'

With no sign of the blooded weapon or any blood, and with the sun shining through the window and him ignoring her distress. Did she dream it all? About to go after him, she snatches a peek behind her; she can breathe again, and the horrible crushing sensation abates. Was it all in her head, or there is something beyond any doubt, not right here?

He leaves the room with her calling after him.

'Wait for me. I think they're spot–on. Let's go. I don't like your house.'

'Who is?'

'Those people who said this place is haunted, they are right. Don't leave me; hold my hand, Larry, and what hasn't changed? You said you've never been here.'

He spurns her offer to take her hand and climbs the stairs. Glenda is close to weeping, her voice trembles and she begs, 'What's going on? Don't you believe me Something happened in the kitchen, so come on, give.'

Throwing a sympathetic glance mixed with pity, it hits home to him, she is beneath him; the voices are right about that. 'Yes, the door stuck, and you got spooked for a moment, but, typical of you, you pulled the door instead of pushing.' He disappeared into the bathroom

Glenda, says, 'I did everything. The bloody stupid thing wouldn't budge. You've been here before—you are lying through your back teeth, and who said it spooked me?'

'What? I'm sorry; I assumed you did. What with the door sticking and all the noise and tears. Gosh, I love being here. It's, how do you say, homey. Is homey a word, Glen, because I am so relaxed and at home here?'

'This is what I and everyone else would call a hell

hole. I don't follow you at all, Larr. Open your eyes, man. You're just narked at me because I made you come, and this is your weird idea of revenge. You know more about this grubby townhouse than you're letting on. Spit it out and tell me everything before I lose my stack.'

'Yes, I do know it, my wife and I, a woman a bit like you, lived here after I inherited it. We all do, or so I'm told. I thought then that this house would be our forever home, but well, circumstances. Ha, I have made so many mistakes in my life. I ought to have learnt by now.'

'Who told you what, and who are all of you?'

Larry's lips curl back, revealing pale gums and his eyes black pinpricks. She glares at a face she doesn't recognise.

'What's wrong, Larry, please, will you stop all this mucking about, you're scaring me?'

'On inheriting the house, I unearthed a dark secret. I suppose you want me to put you in the picture but regaling you will not benefit anyone, Glen. We have past the point of no return, but I should tell you.' He peeks behind him and winks at the cat, ignoring them both, and cleaning itself.

'I was blessed with a family, but never knew my birth mother or father, and I missed the comfort and love of one. I thought she didn't want me until I found out she had passed on.

Let's find somewhere to sit; this is a long story. Let's go to the chaise in the living room and go with the flow, Glen, and this time concentrate. I'm sorry, though; the outcome won't change.'

'What outcome, Larry? You can be a bleeding, scary bastard when you want.'

'The saga begins way back with my great, great-grandmother Emily.' Peering over his left shoulder and back, he shrugs. 'Honestly, the only place to start is her and William. You're inquisitive, Glenda, so you must want to find out how and why each generation found themselves put up for adoption; whether by fate or design, I'm not sure. I think they planned it all. Great, great, Grandmother Emily, at any rate.

Let's dispense with the greats; it gets confusing, so I'll say Emily and William from now on. They aimed to try to lose the identity of our ancestors but failed. She always finds the next generation and calls them back to this house. Their home. She can't let any of us go and intends to protect us in death, as she never did her son in life.

'Don't say anything, and please don't stare at me. Let me tell you about my ancestors. Hey, hang on a mo, wait here, sit down. I'll be back.' He indicates she sits on the worn leather chaise with brass nail heads dulled by time and a corner nibbled away by mice. Perplexed, Glenda does as she's told.

An overbearing, fly-spotted, gilt-edged mirror on the wall above the fireplace surveys the room with its blotchy eye and patches. The backing has deteriorated, leaving grey shapes like an abstract of a world map. 'Why, where are you going?'

'I'll show you. Be patient.'

'Don't leave, Larry. Let me come with you?' But he is already halfway through the doorway.

'Stay here, I said. I won't be a minute.' He says over his shoulder. By the tone of his voice, he's in a huff, and she leaves him to it.

It's about now that she regrets uncovering the photo and the following altercation. She must learn to keep her mouth shut. Her mother often told her, "Your big gob will land you in trouble one day." Has that day arrived?

Studying the room and wishing this morning had never happened, Glenda reaches the door in time to see the back of him, striding up the dark staircase two at a time. Should she shadow him? She climbs the first few steps until a scratching sound stops her. Does she check or should she risk his wrath and follow? The thunder of his footsteps on the bare boards carries on. The house consists of four stories including the cellar.

Glancing behind her to examine the stairwell and make sure nothing is chasing on her heels. She doesn't notice the cornice with the tired paintwork or the peeling wallpaper hanging off the walls and dripping cobwebs but concentrates on the sounds from above.

She turns back, she doesn't want more aggro today—and shrieks. The black cat, which followed her arches itself around her ankle, but she kicks it away. It leaps in the air with a hissing snarl and dashes off.

'Bloody thing, you scared me half to death.' The animal shoots through the door.

Larry's footsteps sound louder on his way down, far slower than when he went up. Waiting near the chaise, Glenda wishes he would hurry.

He bursts into the room puffing and saying, 'At first, I thought Emily might be the place, to begin with.' He places the leather-bound box he carried down with a thud. 'But no, I think William is the starting point.'

'What's in that? No, don't tell me, William,' she jokes. His smile looks more like a sneer.

'Where does your morbid fascination with you and bodies in this house stem from?'

'Sorry, I'm just kidding. Don't take the hump.' Plonking beside her, he drags the box closer to his feet, unbuckles both straps and then takes out an old brass key tucked inside his wallet.

'Blimey, is it the family jewels or what?
Impressed and curious, Glenda admires the chest.

'Years ago, when I received the notification of my inheritance, I did start to check my background.' Larry smiles.

Glenda frowns, 'Why did you lie then? You told me you were too busy, and your work comes first. You tell me nothing but lies and then wonder why I'm bothered.'

After drawing a breath, he says, 'I just asked you to focus; this will spell out things if you let me get a word out. It turns out Emily evolved into an avid writer.'

Larry lifts the lid, and the chest reveals books of

varying sizes and colours. 'These are Emilys. I said she took delight in writing and demonstrated this with her prolific penmanship, a hobby shared by Grandfather and Authur Jacob, known as Jake. One also belonged to her descendant, Jasper, and others to his father, and I found one written by my biological father. They all seem to have inherited her desire to pen their consciousness of the world around them, their emotions and causality, or their take on their lives if you want. Don't ask me why because I am clueless, notwithstanding genetics.'

He flicks through the pages of one and reveals the handwritten script inside.

'Oh, Larry.' She reaches into the chest to take one, but clasping her hand, he stops her. 'No, Glenda, you are not to handle them. They are for family only, but because of events, I'll read sections to you.'

'And what events may they be?'

With a trace of drama and mystery, he says, 'No, I won't trust outsiders with what's written within these covers.'

'What about me? Are we family or not?'

'Don't you take the hump this time, you're as near as, but I need you to discern, and I can say without a shadow of a doubt you will never divulge anything I tell you.'

'Do you keep a diary?' Glenda ignores the sham clue. He's being his usual dramatic self. She touches his hand. It's a tender and loving gesture, one she's almost forgotten.

'No, thank the lord, if there is such a gene that makes people want to spew their thoughts, it escaped me. Why people want to slash their concepts and dreams on paper is beyond me, but in a sense, as you will soon learn, I am achieving my dreams, but in a far superior way.'

'How?'

'Wait, and you'll find out.' He scowls, baffled. Will she ever let him talk without interruption? It'll be the first time if she does.

'I undertook a hideous amount of scrutiny on the family with the records available nowadays, and as things transpired, it was not as difficult as I expected.

Coping with the discoveries though is far from easy. Some old newspaper reports from sources such as the East London Observer and other article sources:

The Western Times, 18th July 1889

East London Observer, 19th July 1889

East London Advertiser, 20th July 1889

The Illustrated Police News, 27th July 1889

The Penny Illustrated Paper, 27th July 1889.'

'Victorian. Hey, Larry, the 1880s about Jack the

Ripper's time or the Cristal Palace or something?' asks Glenda.

'Well done, but it's Jack's, time not the Palace. For now, let's kick off this story with William. Now, think, hard, Glen, think about his predicament before you judge him. From what I can tell, this is an overview of his childhood:

William was a shy young boy, bullied at his

private school, not only by his elders but also by his peers. He didn't seem to fit somehow. He tried, but his efforts were always belittled. On term breaks at home, his mother, a frail, timid, woman, fearful of her own shadow mollycoddled him. He was an only child who also lacked cousins. His father, Oswald, a banker was often away, so his companions were the housemaids, who did their duty but hid when he was about as a good servant should.

His maternal great-uncle Tobias, whom he didn't see much of because Tobias and Oswald didn't get on and so he had little time for his great-nephew and rarely visited the house.

Sometimes, though, when Oswald was away, Tobias took his niece, William's mother, out and let William accompany them. On these outings, Tobias always moaned about her husband and often asked her to persuade him to part with some of his cash to help his business.

He would whine that it wasn't fair how hard he worked for some little reward and wanted to know why her husband was always away. Surely banking didn't need that much travel.

His mother was a sad woman who never left the house when Oswald was away unless accompanied by Tobias. She was petrified because terrible things happened to people, particularly women on the streets of London, and she always noticed them more when her husband was on one of his trips. Reports of ghastly murders kept honest folk indoors at night.

William thought about Tobias's disdain for his father and assumed it was jealousy. His father was wealthy, while Tobias was a struggling butcher with no offspring to carry on the business.

One day, his father came home ruffled and as William ran to greet him, he pushed him aside with his black bag hugged under his arm and powered up the Georgian staircase two at a time to be met by his wife at the top, who gasped at the sight of him

She followed him into his bedroom, which was unusual as they slept in separate rooms, and a vocal argument ensued.

Sometimes after a row, William would go and lie with his mother in bed, and she would tell him of her fears and anxiety, not wholesome for a young boy to listen to.

William longed for someone to love and support him. The household consisted of at least ten people, he had never counted all the staff, and they often seemed to change. One, a tweeny, she was nice but disappeared one day. Nobody would tell him where she went, but years later he learnt she was the victim of a savage murderer.

Chapter 4

WILLIAM 1887

'Later in his life, William coexists with despair. He's been duped, his marriage was nothing more than a sham. His wife, Sylvia, turned out to be at best a high-class whore who only needed a husband for respectability. A front for her pastime, and she constantly goads her husband for his gullibility.

Before his marriage to Sylvia, he had been spurned by what he thought was the love of his life, Jane, and on the rebound met and married Sylvia whom he presumed from her lips to be exploited. A woman disowned by her family who fell in love with him as he did her. But she overstepped the line of decency by bringing her diversions to his door, when her affections settled on the family coachman.

Often, he considered how he managed to land himself in such a vile situation as he sat in the drawing room of the house in George Street, LW1. A highbrow locale. The home he inherited from his parents.

'What happened to them, Larry?'

'It's a sad tale. One night on one of his working trips, it is said, Oswald came across a woman in distress and went to her aid. At the time she said she was attacked and escaped and begged his help. A witness came forth and heard them talking. Oswald said he would see the lady home and that he would report the attack to the police.

The woman, scared out of her wits, let Oswald lead her to her door, but somewhere on the journey the attacker leapt out, and it is said, he not only killed the woman, but the body of Oswald lay close by, covered in blood but with no wounds on him and a knife by his hand.

The coroner said Oswald died of a heart attack brought on by the stress of the killer claiming his victim once again as it is known he was taking her home. The killer, though, left the knife behind to implicate Oswald. On hearing the news, William's mother took her own life, leaving a note saying she couldn't go on without him.

'Picture this, Glenda. William, sitting deep in thought. He runs his fingers across the brass swan-necked handgrip before he grasps and opens a drawer in the Chippendale writing desk, which once belonged to his grandparents. They boasted how the maker created the finer details, the curves, and the beauty, with his own hands.

After taking a moment to remember them and how they appreciated the walnut grain of the escritoire, which they wouldn't let him anywhere near as a child. They told him he always broke things with his boisterous ways.

The artistry is wasted on William, who removes a small .22 calibre pistol, another of his father's legacies. The short-barrelled gun fits his hand. He balances the weapon and points at the door. The fact is, if he did pull the trigger from behind the desk, the shot wouldn't even mark the wood, never mind hurt anyone. Incapable of stopping his fancies and left to ponder on the decadence around him. Why should his timidity from standing up to his wife or throwing her out hold him back?'

Glenda sits beside him content to listen.

'Think about it, Glen, William closes his eyes and presses the barrel to his temple; he can't take anymore, and yet it's the chill of steel on his brow in contrast to the lingering bead of sweat that helps overturn his thread of thoughts, something he didn't expect.

'He slams the gun down. In the last few months, the way his luck deserted him, the bullet would cause more pain than kill him. He admitted his fears and cried out. 'Why, why, can't I be a man?'

'Only that morning, Sylvia left the house after ordering his conveyance without permission or telling him of her whereabouts. He daren't ask. She would tell him to mind his own business, and probably add, "Why should it bother you?" With no pretence of shame.

'The vehicle pulled up, and Frank, the driver leapt down, his cloak lifted, flapping in the updraft like a huge bird of prey laying claim to his prize. A promiscuous smirk brushed his full lips, which he licked. The bastard's deep blue eyes catch William's, but Frank affords him only a glance, with no respect for him as the master. He hands Sylvia into the coach.

'Wandering through his much-loved home, the boy in William laments the passing of his parents and wonders if their deaths occurred later in his life, would he be a different man from he is now?

Deserted by his first love, Jane, and his wife, only in her twenties, he found her so engaging when they clapped eyes on each other. He revelled in her shorter stature at five feet four inches, which made him, at seven inches more, consider himself tall and virile.

The trouble began when he learnt his wife was nothing more than a virago and a tramp. A woman who sapped his maleness and forced him into a regression, turning him into a small and inferior being.

'In the kitchen, the cook, on sight of him, scuttles out of the way, never comfortable in his presence. Since he married, he had become subject to malevolent mood swings. Concerned things are not going well, William strolls to the long ash wood table, where beforehand, the cook stood boning a rabbit for dinner using her long-bladed knife. His head leaned to one side, his mind elsewhere. He grasps the whalebone handle, which gels in his hand, and muses, almost ready-made.

Do you get the picture, Glenda?' She nods. He carries on.

'An expert flick took it somersaulting in the air. The Sheffield steel glints, catching the light, and spins, ready for his hand to receive.

A trick taught to him by his great-uncle's

apprentice when William, after the death of his parents, tried his hand as a butcher.

The apprentice, Henry, was a beautiful boy with well-defined cheekbones and possessed a soft and gentle manner, which struck one as feminine

William paused, a punishing flashback to the time his uncle took him in to help assuage his grief before he went out into the world. He deliberated, is this where he forfeited his manhood?

'The boy with the smooth chin, dark brown eyes and a smile at the sight of him. Unguarded eyes, which held more than sympathy. Would this be the beginning of his problems with the opposite sex? No, nothing happened. He closed the door on the memory.

With the knife snuggled in his fist, a sensuous fit as he curled his fingers and squeezed.'

Larry acts out the gesture by holding out his arm and appearing to squeeze an imaginary knife, while Glenda looks on amused. He continues.

'The door in William's mind slid open. Henry's hand slipped into his and led William into the dark cellar the day he broke down, powerless to cope with his lot in life and his losses.

Henry had compassion in his eyes, he held him tight and let him shed his misery on his shoulder. William began to respond when Henry's lips drew close and whispered sympathy, interspersed with kisses on his forehead, his cheek and finally, his lips.

How he revelled in the sensation coursing through his body when Henry kneeled before him and removed his trousers, taking William's member into his mouth.

'Still with his eyes closed, William shudders. Is it the revulsion he feels? It's wrong; he is a man. Men don't do this kind of thing. Why can't he satisfy his wife? Why did Jane turn against him? Is he one of them? No, he isn't. The thought is abhorrent to him, but...

He studies the shank, not the scrimshaw-crafted handle carved by the cook's sailor husband. His untimely demise was a watery grave in the Atlantic Ocean. She often regaled William with the stories portrayed on the whalebone. Her face would soften as she recited them, but the young William must not touch. How things change.

'The artery in his wrist pulsated, beckoning him: Should he? The same as other aspects of his life, the gun idea failed. Would the world be better without him? He wondered as he ran the sharpened edge across his palm, drawing drops of blood.

'In an instant of pure ungodly fantasy, he dipped his finger in the blood and stroked the warm, sticky material between his thumb and forefinger. The cherry red colour fascinated him as he tapped it between his fingers and noticed the colour change, growing darker as it dried.

He examined it closer, comparing the sensation to one while learning to dissect a pig, and the tip glided through the skin with ease. Should he press on? It gave him a weird exhilaration, which he would struggle to explain if asked, and then the scent of blood hit his nostrils and pushed that closed door open a crack more; he fought to close it.

'A battle raged in his head, thinking, I'm sure my wife would love me to do this, he thought, but he had evolved. He had grown sick of bowing to her selfish desires and placed the knife on the table. A drop of blood dripped unhindered.

'The sound of horse hooves clipping along and iron-clad wheels clattering on the cobbles above cut into his melancholy. He leapt up the stairs in time to peer through the window as the driver sprang from his seat and opened the coach door for his mistress. William dashed outside and, for the second time in a couple of hours, witnessed Frank kiss his wife's hand, and to his shame, he thought, why hers?'

Larry winks at Glenda, 'Exciting, isn't it! Now imagine this is what happened next.'

Glenda raises an eyebrow. 'You mean this is made up.'

'No. It's not made up, I studied these diaries in depth and gleaned as much and filled in the gaps.' He continues. 'Trying to prove his masculinity by taking a firm hand with this Frank creature, who is more than ogling his wife., he bawls at the man.

"Make sure this beast gets stabled and strapped; the sweat is dripping from him. What happened? I don't employ you to treat my animals like this. Why is he sweating?"

'Sylvia slipped by but not without bestowing a

caustic comment on her husband in her wake.

"So, that's it, husband of mine. All you can do is shout about a sweaty animal, nothing more. What a pity you can't raise a sweat in anything else." Frank contained himself and stifled a laugh, disguising his humour with a cough.

"You," shouted William, "Fetch the Tripoli for this coachwork; by the number of cracks on these leathers, I think you are neglecting your duties. Oil them now. What the hell do I pay you for?"

'William yanks the reins near the horse's head; the wild white eyes roll in terror as he shies away, but Frank calms him by whispering and stroking his muzzle.

He removed a pocket timepiece, a striking piece on a gold Albert chain, and a clear rebuff to his master because it indicated that it was his time to finish for the day. Frank didn't live on the premises. He worked when required but held his tongue and touched his forelock. "Yes, sir. I'll set about them immediately."

Appearing indifferent, with ease he leapt back into his seat and flicking the reins, said, "Walk on."

The coach lurched before gliding away. William wanted to kick himself, mortified at his lack of action. Why didn't he just sack the fellow? What is wrong with him?

'Chasing in the house after his wife, he heads to her room Confronting her as the outraged husband.

"Where have you been?"

Again, his self-esteem shrinks as she ignores him

while taking pains to remove the ruby-studded pins from her bonnet. She wouldn't take a maid, and he suspected her more than capable of disrobing unaided.

"Don't be tiresome, William. I am taking a rest. Please leave me. I am quite exhausted."

'With clenched fists and his nails piercing his skin, he despaired, ready to lash out and smash things but impotent to do anything. He loathed himself for the useless, pathetic, weak individual he was.

'In one of their many disagreements, she told him to take a mistress or two, as other fashionable gentlemen of the district do. He, though, was not like them. He assumed that if he gave his heart, it was for life.

"William, I told you I need a rest. Leave now or else." She sorted out a hairbrush with a silver stock from the tray on her dressing table; grabbed it and balanced the weight in her hand. Sylvia launched the weighty missile directly at his head. He ducks, crouching as the brush flies above him, crashing into the door.

'I think Glenda, this was the turning point, because he says the strangest of feelings possessed him as he retreated with his head down, his fingers still bleeding from the cut in the kitchen. He realised he liked the colour and the texture, if only, and then came the light bulb moment. One of them must go, but it won't be him.

'He says he fought with his feelings and tried to think straight telling himself he must make things work. In his way, Glen, he still loves her, but for her to dally with the coachman was an indiscretion too far.

'Frank, well, you can imagine him laughing as he stabled the horse, remembering the wonderful time with his boss's wife. They suited each other well, and perhaps she hinted that given time, he would climb into the master's shoes and his bed, and his reply could easily have been something like, I bet your sop of a husband wouldn't mind me in his bed with him, the way he gawps at me.'

'The condition of the harness and carriage was good, as was the horse. His employer had tried his hand at being masterful but guessed they laughed at him when they were together.

'Squinting again at his timepiece, a gift from his mistress, Sylvia, and clicking his tongue. It started as an annoying and deliberate move, but became a habit, highlighting the gift of the watch and the diminishing respect Frank held for his master. This was not unnoticed by William.

'After waking from her slumber, William slipped back into his place, beneath her thumb, without a struggle. He pretended to make amends by offering her a night out at the Avenue Theatre on the corner of Craven Street and Northumberland Avenue.

Arthur Roberts headlined this little venue along the Thames. Sylvia remembered seeing him before and enjoyed his performance. William was not a lover of Pantomime dames, but the pretence of treating his wife must be kept up, so he would accompany her.

'Maybe he thought time together may help their marriage and she may become amenable and learn to interpret how damaging her behaviour is to their marriage and him or maybe it was all planned.

Sylvia proved hesitant to go, she didn't want a night with her husband, but she did fancy a trip out. He sweetened the invitation by telling her about some business he must attend and said he would join her later and he arranged transportation. That was when she warmed to the idea because transport meant her lover.

'William told Frank he would need him to be on duty the following Wednesday, May 4th, to take his wife to the Avenue Theatre. He said he would try to join her for the second act after he finished his business. His employee seemed smug and took out his pocket timepiece, clicking his tongue. This time, William admired the piece and for the first time, wondered how his coachman could afford a gold fob and chain.

'Whether he pretended politeness, unnecessary for a man of his standing to a man in his employ, or to dismiss the torturing thought this may be from Sylvia, well used to spending his money, he asked,

"My, what a good–looking timepiece. I must be paying you too much.'

"T'was a present, Master," said Frank, with a self-satisfied sneer, and swivelled the chain before pocketing the watch.

Did his smugness portray more? William was

more tortured than before but would not ask from whom he received the gift, for in his heart he knew the benefactor was familiar to him.

'May 4th birthed a warm spring morning, and loath to leave Sylvia to the lusts of the coachman for the entire day, he sends him off on an erroneous errand but instructs him to come back in time to collect her for the theatre

"He must attend to urgent business" he said, "impossible to postpone."

William left for his appointment at three in the afternoon. His philosophies, though, revert to the pitiful, pathetic man he now is.

'Afterwards, he often, pondered, what would have been the result if he cancelled his meeting and went straight to the Avenue to join her in the coach, or if he dismissed the driver like he wanted to, and drove it himself? Now he will never find out.'

'Why, what happened to her?

Glenda can't resist piping up, annoying Larry.

'Keep the questions for later, please, and pin your ears back. This is William's story as he told it, but he endured another side too, and I have faith you will come to make sense of it. Now, can I carry on?'

Glenda nods, beginning to enjoy the close contact. She can't remember the last time they did anything together. She would be happy if he only told her horror stories.

'He, and I mean, William, broke down at his wife's disappearance, or out of dread?'

'Why? Did he do her in?' Glenda's eyes gleam with excitement.

'Shut up; I'm coming to it. Now where... oh yes, the blubbing episode. Where she went is a mystery, but two police officers arrived on his doorstep and were also baffled but held onto their theories. This may be her body or part of it, found in the filthy waters of the Thames on May 11th in Rainham.'

'Wow, she is dead. Did he kill her?'

Rolling his eyes in exasperation, Larry says,

'The police arrive at William's with the typical greeting, "Morning sir, I'm Inspector Worley from D Division." The senior of the two sported a bushy beard and handlebar moustache, accompanied by a colleague, Sergeant Badham from H Division Whitechapel.'

Larry examines the page by running his finger under the line of print. 'Here's what happened next, according to William.'

The Inspector opened with, "A gruesome find of body remains turned up in the river, a female, do you think they might be your wife, Sylvia?"

William was aghast at their questions—no lead-up or by your leave and he answered.

"Why would she be in there? Why do you say such things? We planned to meet at the theatre." They questioned him in earnest about his wife.

"We believe someone also reported your housekeeper as a missing person, and as I understand, your coachman too. What do you have to say, and why did you not report these missing people.?"

He nudged his companion, who took a notebook and pencil from his top pocket and licked the lead point, ready to take notes.

'William told them in his words what happened.

"I didn't find her at the theatre and will confess to my surprise. I caught a glimpse of them when they left because it was I who ordered the brougham for 3 o'clock in plenty of time. I didn't want to appear anxious, but when she didn't turn up after the first act, I came out to search for her. Outside, other carriages lined the street, parked with drivers either loafing about or chatting to each other, but not mine."

"Why didn't you go with her to the Avenue?"

"My business, I had a meeting in the city. I'm a banker with important matters to contend with, and you can check."

He explained his disposition as unfavourable and how he wanted them to try to come to terms with their differences and with sadness in his eyes told them, "She, though, didn't bother to turn up, and I realised my efforts to pursue matrimonial bliss came too late."

"What are those conflicts?" The inspector said, raising a sceptical eyebrow. William fidgeted under the scrutiny and decided he must tell the facts.

"My wife, erm, my belief is that my wife is carousing with the coachman. If this is a full-blown affair, I am not sure or, I hate to say, it's a result of boredom with me."

The sergeant butted in, "Where is this said, paramour?"

The senior of the two reminded his colleague by his mannerisms that he would be the one to ask the questions. The sergeant stepped back.

"I am not able to say, but..." William was in despair and wiped his eyes. "I think they ran away together."

"What makes you think they did?"

"I searched her wardrobes and found her best dresses, hats, and jewellery gone. Money too."

"Why didn't you report her missing?"

"In my own stupid way, I confess, I hope she will return."

"You thought she shared her favours in an affair with the hired help, and yet, you say, you want her back. Come now, do not tell us these stories."

'Unashamed and weeping, William admitted, "I love her and want her back. You don't seem to grasp; we are talking about my wife."

'To an extent, his sudden emotional outburst shocked the officers, but they remained dubious. The senior officer nodded at his colleague, who scribbled in his notebook, 'to be convinced.'

"What happened when you couldn't find your conveyance?"

"I took a cab and offered the cabby a generous tip if he would hurry. You can ask him. I never came across a surlier sort, middle-aged, but he did as I asked because he grasped that I wanted to check my wife's whereabouts in case she may be at home, but as usual, she disappointed me.

Angry, and baffled on my arrival home because I found no signs of her. I stayed up all night, but she didn't return. I wondered what to do. I checked her dressing room, but I was too late, she had taken her things. She had left me and run away with my coachman. None of this makes sense though. What can his class offer a woman of substance?"

"Where is he?"

"I already said, I have no idea. The man doesn't live on the premises; he rents a room adjacent to the stables. I went over intending to catch them, and, to my surprise, I found my coach and stallion already stabled. The stable boy told me Frank left to pick up his mistress. The boy said he must have come in after dark and sorted the beast, but as far as I can tell, he seemed to disappear afterwards."

"What did you do next?"

"Asked the boy where he lived, of course."

"Didn't you have an address?"

"No, as I said, he didn't live in, so why should I bother about his abode?"

"What happened?"

"Well, I visited his lodgings behind the building where I rent the stable."

"And?"

"And what?"

'The officer regards William, thinking he's slow in the head.'

Glenda jumps in. 'How on earth can you say that?'

'Pin them back, sweetheart; it will become clear.'

Did she note a hint of sarcasm threaded through that endearment? She's not sure.

'They carry on with questions,' says Larry.

"So, what happened next?" Asked the officer.

"Nothing. The place was empty. All his clothing and anything personal was gone. I questioned the boy about Frank, and he said he hadn't seen him in the last day or two. I asked him to think, one day or two?"

"He said the last time he spoke to him was last Wednesday morning, and that's when I realised, they had left together. My nightmare turned into reality, and I admit, the thought was unbearable. My wife and a stable hand, an employee. So, I didn't tell anyone expecting she would regain her senses and come home."

"What did you do next?"

"Well, I wandered around in a daze for the day, praying to wake from this nightmare."

"How long, where did you go?"

"Round and about. I don't recall."

"Covering your tracks, you mean, after you butchered your wife and dropped her corpse piece by piece in the Thames."

Both officers know anyone can toss a body in the river anywhere west of Rainham. The current takes the unfortunate body befallen by villainous acts. Many are washed up on the riverbank. Others are taken out on the tide to sea as fodder for the fish. Still more are too drunk to realise the riverbank is not their road home.

'At this point, William leapt to his feet, kicked the seat out of the way, and dragged his fingers through his hair. A muscle twitched in his cheek and to his eye like a wink. He rubs his nose hard as if something had crawled up his nostrils before shrieking.

"You are insane if you think I would do such a thing. Do you believe I am so sick of mind to perform an atrocity so disgusting and degrading on any person, never mind my wife? Leave my home now and find any evidence and the proof you need to arrest me."

"We will. What did you do next, and why didn't you report her missing?"

"How often do I need to be embarrassed like this? I already told you, and more than once, of the shame. What kind of fool puts up with the treatment she dished out? At first, I told the servants Sylvia left to go abroad on holiday, but no, I should not have done so, but I..."

William broke down sobbing, embarrassing the two men. Eager to contain himself, he slumped in his seat, eyeing the whisky decanter on the bureau, and drummed his fingers on the desk. The officers gave him a moment.

Facing them, William asked. "What makes you think this is my wife's body in the Thames? Can you not identify it?"

Again, they eyeballed each other. The elder one cleared his throat. "Er, um, no. We are not able to identify the body. We can say, she is a female in her twenties, the same as your wife. Does your wife bear any birthmarks or scars on her torso?"

William stumbled on his next words.

"She, she is a female. What do you mean, what sort of marks?"

Was this some kind of ploy to find out how much information they possessed?

"She bears a birthmark, pear-shaped." William touched his abdomen to point out the position of the mark: "Next to her navel."

The officer nodded, glancing at his colleague, who noted William used the present tense. The officer carried on. "I'm hesitant to say but I'm afraid only the torso is available. No head or limbs."

Heaving, William's face blanched, and he vomited. Both officers quickly stepped backwards. The sergeant misjudged the flow as a spout of thick carrot-coloured liquid splashed across his shoe. Shaking his foot in disgust, and tried not to reciprocate.

'They prepare to leave, and Badham turns to William, "We are sorry to bring this news to you, but we are not able to identify the body. We do need you to try to make a formal identification. This is a murder case, whoever the deceased is, she belonged to someone. We will return when we unearth more."

"Torso, no. I cannot, and I won't do it. Talk about ridiculous. You cannot force me, not against my will." His body involuntarily trembles. "Does this corpse–or body, whatever–have the birthmark?"

'Wiping his shoe clear of vomit, Badham is aggravated with William and shows no sympathy whatsoever for his sensitivities.

"I'm loath to tell you that you are obliged to identify her." He emphasised, "You must want to discover if this is your wife's remains or, more so, not her?"

They take their leave, both a tad concerned about the state of William.

"Did you catch his expression when you told him about the torso?" Said the sergeant as they left the room, still within earshot of William.

"Yes, I did, and what about the tears?"

"Would you give any credence to this coachman story?"

"Call me daft, but I think he's genuine. I mean, come on, he's begging for her to return. Would you want your wife back if she ran away with a hired hand?"

"I wish. I mean, if I were moneyed, I would send her off with him."

"Things still rough then? How long now, eleven months since we last worked together?"

"Yes, sir, and yes, things are still the same. Hey, I don't want to talk about my wife. What about this William bloke?" Said the sergeant shrugging.

"Honest, until we find out otherwise, I think he is the genuine article, and the coroner found no birthmark."

"Shame, me too, but I don't put too much stock on the birthmark." The sergeant snapped his notebook closed and pocketed it.

William checked the broadsheets daily; he didn't ask why, because they couldn't tell him anything. Riots ravaged the streets in Haymarket, Boston, USA, and the Oshea divorce case began on the 21st of May. Nothing about a body or anything else to give clues to his wife's whereabouts.

More remains turned up throughout various locations in the city, but they did not belong to the torso in Rainham. He waited for the police, but they didn't return—not until June 11th, when a parcel of limbs landed on the shore of the Thames three days before. The same sergeant grilled him.

"Can you come and identify these for us? We think they may belong to your wife."

"No, never," said William, you can't make me."

"Do you understand what I am saying–if this is your wife, this is homicide? A murderer is on the loose."

William said, "How ludicrous. I could say what I want if I was the murderer."

"True, but would you perjure yourself? You must come. Your duty demands it."

The police forced a wretched William to view the body parts. He held his handkerchief to his face, trying to cover his disgust, and shook his head. Why should he gawp at something dismembered and submerged in water for so long?

"You are inhuman," he said and retched.

"Can you aid us in identifying either as your wife or not?" They pushed him for answers, but he shook his head and left.

In July, a man mudlarking on the Thames fished out another package. He hoped for a profitable find, but the police thanked him for handing in the third bundle of a torso, no head, and he received not a coin for his pains.

This parcel did reveal some evidence: a two-inch length of gold chain hooked on the canvas that held the torso. Did the killer miss something? Is this at last, their first clue?

They ascertained the body at about five feet, four inches and in her–mid to late–twenties. They introduced the few links to William, who, horrified, couldn't say anything for a minute. Recovering to a degree he stammered, "I think I have seen a similar chain. If so, you must find the coachman, Frank."

"May I ask why?" asked Badham.

"He showed off a timepiece and chain with similar links, and I wondered how he might afford something so expensive."

"Where do you think he got it?"

Dragging a seat close by before his legs gave way, William sat down and, appearing like a despondent child, spoke, informing the police he thought his wife gave him the timepiece.

'You can guess how it went down, Glenda,' said Larry.

'Go on, tell me. Don't keep me in suspense.'

'They said, "Well, the motive to rid you of both is staring us in the face, don't you think?"

"Don't be preposterous," said William. "I love her, but you must find this Frank, the driver. I'm begging you; I need to find out if-if…" He couldn't continue.

'William demanded they comb the area for him. What had happened to him, if these remains were hers? He may be the murderer. He begged them to explore all avenues and discover the truth, even offering a substantial reward for any information. He declared he couldn't go on without obtaining answers about what had occurred on the day Sylvia vanished.'

'What did happen then, Larry?'

Glenda's natural curiosity is now making her an excellent listener.

'The writings in these pages piqued my suspicions. At first, I thought them too far-fetched, although, I'm not sure if anyone read them, and I appreciate why everyone ignored them if they did. You will find out why if you let me finish. I said, at the start, Emily might be the beginning, but I realised William is. So, up to this point, this is the background to William's sorry tale.'

Larry studies Glenda; is he expecting her to say something?

'Go on, tell me the rest.' She said, enjoying being beside him.

He twitches and smirks at something over her head. She spots the gesture but pays no mind.

Chapter 5

EMILY
17th July 1889 Union Street

'Now back to Emily, Glenda. At this time, she's a spinster in say her thirties. Don't forget that a woman was considered past childbearing and on the shelf in her early thirties. I'll start with her in a hansom out alone apart from the driver, and at night on the 17th of July,' says Larry.

'A bit specific with the date, Larry.'

'It's a diary. That's what they are about: dates and days things happened. Now, do you want to hear this or not?'

'Yes, go on.'

'Right, now remember the date and think of Emily gathering her skirts together, expecting one more corner and then home after a long, long day.'

'I can try to remember it, but it means nothing to me.'

'It will. Now remember, I said she was out late when a collision on the road stopped them, and a horse needed shooting. Carriages were held up waiting for the knacker man to remove the carcass after the horse was shot, it had broken two legs. Jameson had arranged for the other drivers to help drag the dead horse off the road and right the carriage so they could continue their journey. Well, the gun firing had upset Emily and she presumed she may need to send for her physician. She hated upsets.'

'You talk as if you meet her every week, Larry.'

He stares her way across the room to a dark corner and smirks.

Glenda catches his eye movement, but nothing is in the corner, and she asks herself, Why the smirk? He carries on.

'Well, imagine her, she's almost home so she's checking if her reticule is still on her knee, maybe searching for her sal volatile. Muddled and a little disoriented after the earlier ordeal and arranging her bonnet when a scream rings out in the night air, and the brougham jerks, thudding over an obstacle in the road.'

'Good imagination, Larr.'

'Shut up. Ask yourself, did the horse squeal? Did a man cry? Was it both? The driver, Jameson, already worried about the earlier incident calls out. "Ma'am, are you all right?" while he's straining to stop the stallion from bolting.

When, at last, the stampeding beast comes to a jarring halt, he leaps down, grips the reins hard and calms the animal by whispering and blowing up its nostrils. When he's happy, the horse is calm, he opens the door to assist his employer.

Thrown from her seat, Emily is on the floor in an embarrassing heap with her headdress askew. The decorative plumage on her hat is wilting and tickling her cheek, all so close to her gateway.

"Ma'am," he says, finding her on bended knees, distressed and desperate to regain her dignity.

"Are you hurt, ma'am?"

"What happened, Jameson?" A beautiful, well-groomed Bombay cat jumps in and starts grooming herself, ignoring her mistress and the commotion around them.

"Has a wheel broken? Are my parents all right?"

'Hang on, Larr, I thought she was alone.'

Larry's face flushes purple, and he sucks in a breath about to explode.

'Oops, sorry, I'll let you finish.' She pats his knee.

Larry continues. 'Jameson gasps, tense, because Emily's parents perished in a similar wreck a while back and he wonders if she is having a relapse. He tries to calm her, praying she will be well.

"We are involved in another incident, ma'am, this time somebody ran in front of us, and I couldn't stop. Stay where you are, please."

"No, I must find out if I can help, my parents."

"No, ma'am, remain in your seat." He oversteps his mark by patting her hand, but he is fond of his employer. She suffered a while back when her mama and papa passed, but against the odds, she managed to stay strong, and now, earlier this same evening she showed such concern for the animal who was put down, never mind for him, knowing his love for horses.

Jameson stared at Emily, "We have suffered one

shock this evening and it is more than enough," he said, "So I would prefer you to stay and remember, ma'am, your parents are not with us now; this is not their accident, they perished a while back."

'Emily shakes her head. "No, of course not. It's the shock, I suppose. It has brought all the fear and trauma back, even though I wasn't with them.

A small group of men gather from a local pub on the corner, all anxious to discover what disturbed their drinking. A scream rang out above the din of their voices. Not the usual quarrelsome arf—an—arfers hitting the cobbles—but blood-chilling, they said.

"Please stay where you are, ma'am, while I check what must be done."

"No, please don't fuss."

A police officer rushed to the scene, blowing his whistle for assistance, without knowing what would confront him. The crowd pushes forward, pressing in on all sides. He fears he may be alone in the middle of a drunken brawl and grips his billy stick, ready to swing if the need arises.

"Move over, come on out of the way." He cries, suspecting he sounds more authoritative than he feels. Jameson hands an insistent Emily out of the carriage, where she can see the prone body of a man on the road.

'A pathway opens as the crowd parts, noticing the gentlewoman. Bystanders shake their heads in unison as blood pools around the unfortunate soul, spreading out and seeping into the cobbles.

They all agree nothing can be done. Onlookers nod, remove hats, and bow their heads. In muttered undertones, they all agreed, "Aye, he's a goner."

The police officer edges towards Emily, still holding onto the nervous Jameson who wants his employer to leave. Emily presses a handkerchief to her face, sprinkled with her favourite perfume, lemon verbena, to help mask the noisome night air.

After a summary glance at the inert body, the constable, a conscientious chap, motions the sign of the cross with his right hand and apologises to no one in particular. "I did train in a monastery at one time and old habits, as they say." He can't stop a little chuckle.

Turning to Emily, he says, "Cobb, ma'am," she stares with vacant eyes.

"My name is Elijah Cobb, Ma'am. I'm sorry you had to witness this. I will send one of the men for the horse and chair to take him to the hospital, but I don't think we can do anything for this poor creature." He gawps at the prone figure lying face down. "Do you live far from here?" he asks.

Still shaken, Emily stares at Jameson, the scene reminds her of the accident her parents suffered and a policeman explaining to her what had happened. He talked to her as if she was a child, but she knew exactly what they were saying. She shakes herself.

"No, this is my home." She looks towards a detached house set back between the end of the terrace of townhouses on Union Street and the King's Head public house.

Cobb gazes at her home, mostly hidden by fauna, swinging it back to the lady next to him in the unfashionable attire.

This neighbourhood once boasted industry and a high-class clientele, with houses owned by sea captains and shipwrights. Not so much now since the naval yard closed and the foreign cattle market opened.

Cobb thought it unusual to find a gentlewoman in the area, and she did possess the air and grace of a titled woman.

'Emily said, "Lift him but be careful. Take him into my house and send someone for a surgeon, or Dawson." She faces Jameson, "Oh, goodness me, is the horse all right? Can we do anything for him? Perhaps a rub down?"

"Yes, ma'am, he's a trifle skittish, but not hurt. The man, though, I am sorry, his injuries appear critical."

"Pick some men to help you carry him in, Jameson, and call Agnes, and you must summon a physician, or better still my own, doctor, Dawson, and then we can partake in a cup of tea."

'He flinched, praying no adverse effects were developing from this night. She had enjoyed fair health since her parents perished in the carriage, which overturned and went down the embankment, and he intended to keep her well.

"Are you sure about carrying him inside, ma'am,

with so much blood?"

"Do so and quickly," she said. "My conveyance was responsible for running him down, so I must be the one to help."

"He appeared from nowhere, ma'am. There was nothing I could do to avoid him." Jameson stumbled on his words.

"Oh, no, goodness me. No blame is attached to you. I take full responsibility because we would not have been out at this late hour except for my ladies' meeting and that awful accident. Goodness, two in one night."

'Two hours later, in Emily's bedroom, doctor Dawson, who understands Emily well, snaps his bag closed and studies the woman. She has been in his charge since her father sent for him to diagnose her problems as a child.

Now she's a woman and one considered too old for childbearing and, in his opinion, weak-minded. Emily displayed a smattering of the symptoms, as her father described them to Dawson, enough for him to diagnose her as a type of schizophrenia characterised by delusions and her unpredictable or silly behaviour. He believes she suffers from a form of the illness called hebephrenia, but milder compared to others with the same condition.

This illness tends to start during adolescence. On occasions, a cause materialised to take her away for specialised treatment, but this was at the request of her parents.

Her father, a naval captain, found difficulty coping with his only daughter when he came home on leave after long trips away and with his regret at not having a son.

Her mother always agreed with her husband's opinion. They must send a servant for the family physician and discuss her going into "that." Larry riddles two fingers on either side of his head.

'Oh no, not the air quotes.' snorts Glenda

'What?'

'Nothing, sorry. I hate those stupid air quotes when you said, "that."'

'Oh, stop it. I meant treatment in the hospital.'

'Slapping the book on his knee, his silent glare says so much. Glenda emits a theatrical "sorry" to calm the difficulty, and he continues.

'The said treatment at times involved restraints and hydrotherapy, and always strong alcohol as a sedative. Her parents left Emily an orphan and with no other relatives in the world after the deaths of both in a mysterious tragedy.'

'Why mysterious?' asks Glenda.

'The authorities never resolved their findings, and bizarrely after their deaths, Emily's health did improve, and she suffered no episodes for a long time.

'The doctor had recommended that her father install a spacious tub, innovative back then, and copy the methods dished out in the sanatorium. Icy water to shock, hot water to relax, and to keep her incarcerated if deemed necessary. Sometimes a few hours a day or week proved beneficial.

He staked his reputation on the cure and gained quite a list of wealthy patients willing to settle his fees rather than the private caregivers. The night of this accident, though, Dawson struggled with advising her to take a medicinal glass of sherry or not.

He glanced at Agnes; the maid come nurse. The one he advised Emily's father to hire some years before. He made a coughing sound to gain her attention. He sought her advice and wanted Agnes in his confidence, unsure of the best way to cope with the night's misfortunes. Emily decided for him.

"Well, Dawson," she said, removing her bright yellow gloves, not complimenting her ensemble, which in his mind is a hideous red. Over the years of studying Emily, he honed his skills to recognise her peculiar ways and learned that her dress sense deteriorated when she was stressed. On the day in question and by the gown she chose to wear, others may be deceived into thinking she may have what they called 'an episode' building, but this is one of her favourite dresses and it pops out of the closet on more occasions than is fashionable.

Dawson walks to the small table in the alcove beside the ornate fireplace, set ready to light, and lifts the cumbersome, starburst-bottomed decanter, more suited to a ship's cabin than a lady's bedroom.

He removes the stopper and sniffs the neck, twirling the liquid and taking in the aroma, before filling the sherry glass to the brim and ogling the second empty glass. His eyebrows quiver. Dawson wanted to partake of one but decided not to take a tipple. Who can tell, someone else may require his skills?

He replaced the glass stopper with a clink and handed the drink to Emily. "Here, sip this my, dear. We don't want you getting upset. I trust you can accept it when I say it's in God's hands to decide if he wakes. The blood loss is heavy from a gash on his head, and I'm sure he's suffered a depressed fracture of the skull. Head wounds tend to spew out copious amounts of blood, never mind his other injuries. He should go to the hospital. You must not nurse him here, my dear."

His chief concerns were for Emily, not this new injured patient. A repeat episode of one of her turns may harm his growing reputation. After basing his successes on her treatment and publishing papers in elite medical journals, he received invitations to speak country-wide at university conferences.

Stifling a sob, she tells him, "I must. My vehicle ran him down, so I am to blame, and I will not put the poor man in one of those places. You must listen, and you will obey me in this."

Her steely glare penetrates his air of confidence. Although fond of him, she still blamed him for her incarcerations away from home. She continues, "It's up to me to nurse him and give him the best care money can buy. I owe it to him." She said. Adamant in her protestations.

The cat leapt onto the bed, but the physician shooed it away with a flap of his hand. Emily is beginning to look flustered, unsure what to do.

Dawson tried his powers of persuasion once again. "My dear, this is not your fault. Accidents happen. Do not assume responsibility. You are not indebted in any way."

Her hands and lips tremble, not a reassuring sign. After being stoic for a long while, she appears unsure and backs away from Agnes, who waits for her to state her requirements. Emily, though, picks up her black Bombay cat from nuzzling around her hem and rocks it like a baby, clueless for anything else to do.

"Shall I sit with him, ma'am?" Agnes tries to take the cat from her wanting to help remove her mistress's headdress, but Emily slaps her hands away, obstinate in her refusal of help.

"No, I will stay with him, and don't fuss," said Emily, who shuddered.

Her memories disturb her. She hasn't felt like this for a while now and has a decision to make.

She remembers the last decision she made, the one that dramatically changed her life. Is this going to be the same?

She hugs the cat, which starts to struggle; she is held too tight. Agnes stands immobile, waiting.

'Pitting her mistress, her number one priority, and her loyalty to the man of medicine who recommended her for the position because of her outstanding nursing capabilities, Agnes is troubled but waits for direction from either of the two, Dawson or her mistress.

'With an air of authority, Emily decided. "I will not need the tub filling, no. I am composed, and I will stay with him. Thank you, but I am responsible. You go to bed, Agnes."

'Unsure, Agnes flashed a meaningful plea to the doctor, who, familiar with her plight, nodded, it was a gesture to allow Emily to have her way.

Dawson didn't believe she would be sitting too long with the man who was dying from his injuries. Instinct and training told him he may well not live after such trauma. He already resembled a ghost, drained of colour and covered in bruises.

In his estimation, the man has three fractured ribs, a fractured cheekbone, and an open fracture on one leg. His right hand, it appears, was already damaged by a deep-set slash across the palm, and despite being healed, his fingers are deformed and curled inward.

He lets Emily persevere with her mercy mission, hoping not to overtax her. He would ensure Agnes took over if the need arose. The man may live, if he does, he will arrange for competent nurses.

His priority is Emily, and to ensure she can cope with her philanthropic and idiosyncratic conduct. Emily came across as a woman for her causes, a righteous woman, but she laboured under this weakness.

At least this night's catastrophe may aid in stopping her from becoming self-absorbed and slipping into her delusional ways.

Between Agnes and himself, they professed they kept her out of the asylum for a long time now. The cold baths shocked her out of her peculiar behaviour, as the warm ones helped to reduce her tantrums. They did make an accidental discovery from her incarcerations, as she scribbled in her diaries.'

Larry's eyes move to Glenda, pleased because she is keeping her mouth shut, and he can't help thinking, It's about time too. 'This next part I gleaned from her writings five years later,' he says.

Chapter 6

1893
Five years later

'Emily pulls the embroidered bell cord in her sitting room, reflecting as she recalls the last few years. Reading her exclusive book, her account, in which she records all of her news. This time it's so significant, so enormous, she is not equipped to believe what is staring her in the face, and all the while waiting for her stalwart nurse and companion, Agnes, to arrive.

As Agnes approaches, Emily stands shaking and says with a trembling voice, "Agnes, please come in and close the door behind you."

This simple request places Agnes on her guard, watching for symptoms that may predict the possible onslaught of an episode.

"What is wrong, ma'am? My, you are dithering. What's happened?" Agnes presses Emily down in a lavish gold-coloured, satin-wing-backed armchair. She planned on putting her on the chaise to rest, but the chair was more convenient. She kneeled before Emily and patted her hand.

The caring maid agonises. Is this an attack? She hopes not, because she hasn't suffered one in years. Not since they carried the battered wretch in and none expected him to make the night through, but here he is with his memory partially restored. His name is William and he's still in this house five years on.

Grasping the maid's hand between hers, Emily says, "Agnes, I, I, have something to tell you before William finds out for I can hardly contain myself."

"Tell me what, ma'am? Don't get in a tizzy. You can tell me anything. Do you need a bath drawing?"

"No, don't concern yourself; I do not need one. No, no. I promise."

Her face lights up. "Agnes, I can't believe it. Please be happy for me, only, I don't know how to say this." She looks at a worried Agnes, who urges her on with a look.

"This is so significant; I will just say it. Agnes, I am with child."

On a shuddering breath, Agnes sobs. "No," she tried to rise. Shock registered on her face, but Emily clings to her. Agnes's head pivots to the ceiling, her expression fearful. Emily recognises the question in her eyes. The one she is scared to ask.

"Yes, Agnes, William is the father."

Stunned, she covered her mouth with her hand and said through her fingers, "Oh, Emily, ma'am. No, this can't possibly be. Oh, my goodness, I pray you are wrong."

"Yes it is true, I am not wrong, but don't say anything. Please. You must have guessed by now that we love each other. Who would think what gratitude can do? William came into my life while I was at my lowest ebb, and him knocking at death's door."

"You say he isn't aware. You will tell him you must, and I pray he will do the right thing." Said Agnes.

"I'm not sure and I'm quite nervous about telling him. Of course, William loves me, but he never once mentioned marriage. Regarding children, I remember we talked once during his recovery, and he said he didn't want children. He may hate the idea, and if so, I must take steps to protect my baby." Her face takes on a dreamy, soft allure.

"Before I tell him, I want you to deliver a document for me to the lawyers after I sign it. Also, I want you to countersign for me, and, Agness, I would prefer this delivery to be by your hand and yours only."

Emily rose, took a thick envelope from the French polished bureau and slowly removed the contents—a monogrammed and embossed sheet of writing paper already filled out. She perused and signed it in front of Agnes, who silently waited.

"Sign here, Agnes. You can write, can't you?"

"Yes ma'am." Agnes signed her name beside Emily's, who used the blotter to stop smudging and replaced the document in the envelope. She opened a small drawer and took out her father's signet ring inscribed with the family seal. Something she was never inclined to use before but now feels she must.

Thoughts of her papa's treatment over the years were never far from her mind and they come flooding back as she contemplated what he would do to her in this predicament. What about Mama? Would she disappear like she used to? Where did she go?

Pausing, Emily reflects on what now seems like long periods of punishment, torment, and no love. She loved her mother and papa too, but in her heart, she understood they didn't respond in kind, they didn't love her.

The memory of the day of the carriage accident, which claimed their lives, and if truth be told, came as a relief.

"Stop it, Emily." She spoke aloud.

Alarmed, Agnes cried "Emily ma'am, stop what, I don't understand?"

'But Emily carried on with her reverie, where I gather the last time, on her arrival home after her treatment her parents didn't even greet her.

She overheard their coach driver one day as she passed instructing the stableboy to ensure the buckles and harness tack were tight and fastened properly, or it might cause a mishap.

What made her wander past when he had finished checking, and loosen the straps he worked on, she doesn't say, but she penned this.

"I tried, Papa, and I did everything you asked of me and experienced ill for what I consider no reason. The last humiliation I endured, where they stripped me naked and left me to be ogled at by a lewd porter who carried in buckets of ice to freeze the devil out of me, tipped me over the edge. When he squeezed my breast, I knew it had to stop.

Honestly, Mama, Papa, when I overheard one of the nurses talking to another, she said my parents never visited because my father always tried to keep you, mama, out of this place. Why should he?

Things jumbled in my head. Did I not commit those wicked acts he accused me of? Did my father feed lies to Dawson to protect my mother?"

"Are you all right, Miss Emily?" Agnes gently touches Emily on the shoulder, bringing her out of her retrospection, and she warms the stick of wax over the oil lamp, making sure not to contact the flame. Dripping the melted wax on the envelope, she pressed in the ring.

"Dear Agnes, I am sure this all seems rather dramatic, but I do not want some nosey clerk reading my instructions. Trust in others is a rare commodity, outside of you, Agnes, my most trusted companion. You always cherished me, didn't you."

'Pressing the sealed package into Agnes' trusty but quivering hand, she said. "This needs to be delivered to the solicitors at the far end of the High Street. Remember, Agnes, not to my family lawyers who can be such gossips. In case anything happens to me, I have made provision for the child, but I am positive this is all unnecessary."

Holding onto her maid's arm, Emily gently squeezed. "I don't need to ask for your silence. This is only a precaution, for I am confident this will never come to light."

With a nod of assurance, Agnes takes her leave.

After collecting her cloak and wishing to ask Dawson for advice, he didn't attend the house anymore since Emily's health improved, and his patient list expanded. This benefited him with new ground for his work and less time for old patients.

In the meantime, Emily waits, balancing on the corner of her chair. Her hand slides over her stomach. Never in this world or the next did she think the blessing of a child would come to her, but she is indeed going to have a baby. She accepted their love must be so powerful to make her wish come true. A baby, heaven forbid, society will frown on her. To procreate before marriage was a grave sin. The order may not be right, but she will be a mother. She must work on William as a husband before too much time passes.'

Emily rises from her seat when William walks in, and seeing her looking so content, he beams. He has a surprise for her, but she forestalls him.

"William my, dear, I need to talk to you, and I assure you, this is important if you can spare me the time."

"What is the matter, dearest? Am I tardy? Did we make plans?"

Full of concern for this magnificent person, he considered asking for her hand for the love she had showered on him over the past years, a loving home and a reason to live. William wanted to repay her by making her his wife.

"Sit down, William, please, for I am at a loss about how to say this, beloved. I think you had better take a seat."

"You concern me, my dear. What troubles you? Come, you must tell me now." He stands before her.

Emily broods, gazing at the floor and back into the eyes of this most cherished of men.

"William, I believe I am with child."

William's benign, loving face blanched. Within a matter of seconds, his features transformed. His whole manner turned from indulgent to horrified. He gasped. Hit by a sledgehammer to his being, he ventures, this is not true.

Memories hurl back, smashing his senses. What he thought were nightmares turned into reality. Above his eye a scar from five years before throbbed red and puckered. An indelible jagged streak ran across his forehead, indiscernible under his hairline until now.

A rage not felt for a long time stampeded through him, tempting him to hate, but no, this is his sweet Emily.

William turned and crouched into the foetal position. A howl escaped from his clenched teeth, and his fists thrust heavenward.

Emily floundered. What should she do? This most unexpected reaction confused her. He looked shocked, even terrified, but his face and demeanour conveyed a story of their own that of a horror story.

Believing that at her years and single status, she would be beyond being able to conceive, and while not horrified, the stigma of being an unmarried mother did shame her. What would her father say and do now if he were alive? She gave silent thanks for his demise.

With all her dreams pinned on this most wonderful man, Emily wouldn't beg. Not at first. She prayed for him to experience the same toe-tingling flush of wonder.

On reflection, his set jaw terrified her. She can't be wrong. This is her precious saviour, and does he not love her? She adjusted her approach, ready to implore him if necessary. "We are a family now, please, William. All I ask of you is that my child, our child," she said, touching his hand, "is born in wedlock and will bear your name."

Chapter 7

RISE OF THE RIPPER

William's features paled, his eyes were lifeless, and his cheekbones grew prominent. He stared at Emily before easing her back into the seat. "Emily, oh Emily. No, you can't. I must not father a child. Trust me, and I will not do so, and as for giving one my name, you do not conceive of me what you ask of me. To think, tonight, I truly wanted to ask you for your hand, but now, no, it's all wrong."

He stood before her, hunching his shoulders. A thousand expressions passed through his facial muscles, though none she could reconcile with.

'I don't understand, William, why is our child so abhorrent to you? You tell me daily of your love for me, a child, which is part of you and me is all I could dream of, apart from your name for him or her. Can't you see us with a little one, William?'

"Emily, you have brought the veracity home to me in all its stark reality. The rendering of what to you is a ray of good news reminds me how foolish I think I have been. What possessed me, I will never work out."

Emily's face lit up at his words. Recalling the positive, he wanted to ask for her hand. "Yes, we can marry, William."

Once again, Emily rises, wanting to embrace him, but his demeanour changes and his face morphs as his flinching facial muscles seem to go into battle with other vying for expressions. Which way does he go? How can he simplify and mitigate?

"Sit down, Emily, I need to talk to you about something, and I swear, I never wanted to keep things from you, but now what I have fought against for so long, I believe is true and I must tell you."

"Tell me what, dearest? You know you can tell me anything but please think of our child. It may be just the shock which has upset you momentarily."

"I pray that is so, beloved, but I have no reason to think my prayers have ever been listened to or answered before this, so why should they now?"

"Don't say that William, dearest. You know God works in mysterious ways and I believe he has with me. I prayed for years for a child and when I gave up hope, here it is, my prayers answered well almost." She reaches for his hand, but he turns away.

"You are making me afraid, William. Please do not shillyshally."

Keeping his back to her he speaks. "For months past, I have fought with nightmares, or what I hoped were nightmares and not recollections."

"Oh, my poor William. Why have you not said before; we must send for a physician?"

Emily is willing to fix on anything now. She is sure the outcome will be favourable. Didn't he say he wanted to ask for her hand?

Clasping her hands to her knees, she prepared to take in his forthcoming speech. Steeling herself to receive disappointing or sad news. Is he wed? Well, if so, they would deal with it. Perhaps he keeps a mistress, if so mayhap a little indiscretion may be allowed as long as he never brings any home to her door, or he may over-imbibe, though no evidence is apparent for any of those traits. She waits her nerves taught. "Please look at me, dearest and let me help."

"Argh," William moans and paces the room, slamming his fists to his head and raking his hair with his hands. Tormented, he begins to shake as a person with the ague.

"How can I do this to you, Emily? It's all true, I cannot deny it and I do not think I can live with what I am going to do to you, my love. I fear I am about to break your wonderful innocent heart." He turns to face her, stretching his arms out, but she remains seated.

In a motherly tone, while holding his gaze, "I have told you many times; you can tell me anything. Now come, you are frightening me, William. Please hurry, my love, and tell me."

"This is not easy. Oh my..." his body shudders and he drops to his knees as though in supplication before her.

"Emily, I warn you, you may never forgive me, and I can never repay your kindness. For me to do this to your adoration breaks the heart I once disowned before meeting you. Oh, Emily, what am I to do; why did you bring it all back?"

"Whatever I brought back was unintentional, William. Could it be you maintain a wife?"

Her heart, once bursting with love, palpates with fear. What is she going to do if he is married?

"Once, I did marry once, yes. A lifetime ago now." He slumped and took her hand, tears welled in his eyes. "Why did this happen now, when your love lifted me so high and with all you have done for me?"

"Tell me please, William. I can forgive you anything. Do you maintain a wife? If so, you can divorce? In monetary terms, I am secure, as are you. I am fearful of the scandal, but we can move. All I want for our child is your name, William."

"Emily, this is so much worse than scandal for you, my love."

"Us, William, us..."

"No, you, my love. When I think of everything you showered on me, including your love. When I sold my family home, yes, a sumptuous one, and took charge of my inherited fortune. Without you, I would never have thought to utilise the money as you showed me. The charities, the effort and time you give to those tragic wretches. Those forced to live off immoral earnings. Can one really call their existence living? With children having to pick up the scraps from mothers' trying to feed them by whatever means available?"

He stumbled sobbing and found containing his emotions difficult. Thrusting his forehead into her hand, he lets her perfume play havoc with his senses.

Emily always exudes a pleasing fragrance. Tenderly, she strokes his hair and whispers, "Tell me, William, tell me. All will be well. I guarantee it."

He removed her hand, stood, and turned his back to her. Pausing, he fought with his conscience. The one he discovered when he won Emily's heart, and one she instilled in him. What can he do? About to ruin this piteous woman's life, and nothing can soften the blow. How can he do it to her? Why did he have to remember now?'

'What did he say, Larr?' Glenda peers over the book Larry is holding, but he snatches it away.

'Wait, in time, I will answer your questions.'

'Larr' Glenda whines, 'Can we do all this later at home because I'm starving, never mind cold? Aggravated she waves her hand under his nose; she is bent on going. He dismisses her. 'No, as I said before, now or never.'

The hair on the back of her neck stands. The tension begins to rise again. Someone is watching her; she turns, but nothing and nobody is present. She decides this place gets creepier as she snuggles into Larry's elbow.

He shrugs her aside. 'You're squashing me; move over. Right, so, William is about to break his sweet Emily's heart, so concentrate. I'll make this easier for you. Think about their circumstances before you make a judgement. What would you do if faced with this?

William, stuck in a difficult position struggles with his decision. Anything he says will mean the end of all their plans. Pain etched on his face. Visualise him, Glenda. Pacing the room back and forth. He stopped to face the wall, focusing on the panelling, cradling his head in his hands and shoulders slumped, before focusing back on Emily, he said.

"Do you remember when I did the decorating work in this room, Emily?"

"Of course, William, you did such a splendid job bringing colour and warmth to this room. Removing the top wainscoting made the room so much lighter. To think, I would never have entertained the idea of wallpaper before, but why bring the subject up now, this is not the time?"

"It is the time. Do you call to mind when I insisted on doing the work myself and wouldn't let you in until I completed my task?"

"Yes, and this is my favourite room because I remember you wanted to do something for me, you said, to say thank you, but I never found thanks necessary. In retrospect, it is you who have given me so much."

Emily took in the flowery-patterned wallpaper above the chair rail and below the oak panels. The colours of every item in the room complement each other, creating harmony in an atmosphere of peace, and dare she think—love.

She adored how such a warm and loving aura emanated from the few decorative pieces, but in her heart of hearts, this room is her favourite because William chose the decor with her in mind. He said that all of the beauty reminded him of her, and called her, "my wonderful Emily."

William's beautiful turn of phrase always calmed Emily, and her thoughts began to wander. Lowering his voice, she found it hard to take his words on board and was convinced she misheard when he said, "Do you recall several years ago, my love, the days when the Ripper roamed the streets of Whitechapel?"

She couldn't understand why he would ask such a peculiar and disturbing question, yet he presented an air of solemnity.

"Of course," she said. "But he's gone. No murders have been attributed to him for years now. Why would you mention him?"

"Yes, over five years now, I also presumed him to be gone. Did you never think or wonder what ever happened to him?"

She shrugged, her eyes glistened with unshed tears, confused and shaking her head.

"What if I tell you I knew him, Emily."

"No, William, that is impossible, how could you know him, your mind plays tricks, I think. Surely you mean, you know of him.

"No, my sweet, it has returned to me, I believe in full. It began with the headaches and nightmares, little pictures of things kept coming into my mind and I can tell you now that yes, I did know him. Emily, I tell the truth. He was a man who suffered at the hands of a brazen wife. Cowed and emasculated by a whore who spread her favours. Reviled and beaten by her, unable to keep up with her avaricious ways. Frightened to be a man, and too stupid to leave."

"How ridiculous, William. He was a fiend, a beast, nothing less. How could you ever be in the company of such a man?"

"Yes, they all believed he was a fiend, but may I ask you, my darling, do you think I am one?"

"One what?"

"A fiend."

"Why such preposterous questions, William? Of course not. You are being absurd."

He paced the room, chewing on his knuckles. Watching him, Emily grew more afraid. She doesn't want to go away again, but her father isn't here now. Has she done something wrong? Those horrid episodes stopped after her parent's demise and William came into her life. The thought of returning to that most dreadful of places made her entire body tremble.

While fighting with his conscience-stricken past about knowing the ripper, William focuses on the woman, who has become his life and bows his head.

"Believe me, Emily, I swore I would never call on any deity again, but what am I to do?" He smashed both fists into the patterned wallpaper.

Emily squealed and leapt from her seat, unsure whether to approach him. She glimpsed at the clock; Agnes should be back by now. Oh, where is she?

It's only when blood trickles down the wall that her sense of reality returns. "Oh, William, I'm here.

Let me help you."

She rushes to him with her arms outstretched, bursting with love and wanting to cradle him to her breast but he staggered back and thrust his hands in the air.

"Stay away from me, Emily. Leave me alone and let me explain to you. Try to absorb what I am about to tell you. This is, I believe, the only way."

William stoops down, and after manoeuvring, he removes one of the oak panels. He peers at her over his shoulder. Frozen, all Emily can do is wonder what he's doing. She tried to wet her lips, but her tongue stuck to her palate in her dry mouth. She may vomit with anticipated dread.

He turns to face her, holding a black bag like the one Dawson used to carry. He holds it out as if he expects her to say something. Emily, as often when confused, is stuck for words. William pleads, with a tremor in his voice. "Do you recognise this?"

She's puzzled; what interest can an old doctor's bag be to her?

"No, why should I? What do you mean? Is this of importance to you, William? Am I supposed to remember? Tell me, and I will if you want me to. May I ask how you found it?"

Poor Emily is more confused than in a long time, William demands her full attention. Should she recognise to whom it belongs—maybe someone of importance? This isn't Dawson's. Her memory was never one of her strengths, but his brown case proved to be the bane of her life.

For a time, she was well but still remembered periods of bewilderment when they sent her away. On occasion, they tied her to a bed and forced strong alcohol down her neck. She doesn't want to go back there. Her one desire is to stay with her William and their child. But how did he know the wooden panel came out?

"Oh, my sweet, Emily. How do you remain so trusting and unworldly? You're so naive, my pet. When I came round from my long recovery I grew to love you. I also adopted your problems, dearest, but did any of this make an impact on you?"

He shakes the bag and turns back to the hole in the wall. "Beloved, I am the one who put this in here."

"Stop it with the games, William. I'm not sure what you want me to say. What about our child? He or she is the most important thing. What's all this got to do with anything else?"

'William breathes deeply; Emily is trying his patience. "I didn't find it, my love; I made the place when I decorated this room, and it was me that hid it. Do you follow me, Emily? It was I who placed this," he shook the bag. "Behind the panelling."

"No, this is cruel. I never thought you would torment me thus, William. I discern nothing you say. Why, if you wanted to hide something, why not use the safe or the bank, she can hardly recognise his features, she never thought to see him so angry."

William's face contorts as he struggles to get

through to Emily, he must remain calm and retain a grip on the man he is, William his saviour. His face relaxes and she recognises him again.'

Larry gestures, throwing his arms in the air, and says, 'William's face contorted, Glen, so much that she couldn't recognise him.' Although she's puzzled, Larry's demeanour demands Glenda's silence.

'As his features relaxed, he smiled at her, and she recognised her William again.

"Emily, you make this so difficult for me. Let me think how I can help. Take your mind back to the night of my calamity. Do you remember?"

"Of course, I can never forget the wretched horse trying to bolt and all the blood." Tears stream down her face. "Why the need to bring this up now and remind me of such horrors? William, I think you are determined to upset me tonight. This is a shock neither of us expected, but you are taking things too far."

"Think back, Emily. Did you never once think to enquire of your driver what happened the night of July 17th, 1889, when I ran under the horse?"

"Why what happened? He said you appeared from nowhere, he was powerless to do anything to avoid trampling you."

"Yes, Emily—nowhere, you never asked, did you? With my mind lost for months, I remember to a point, but you never once asked from where I came or why I ran into almost certain death."

"I suppose the shock made me not want to recall, but I remember the whole ghastly episode. They said you wouldn't live. They all said so, and I accepted that. You hung on day by day, and by the time you were well, I didn't need to dig into your past.

You told me on our first night together that we were meant to be. I never thought love would reach me, but you did, and now you are determined to torment me. Why, William, WHY?"

William struggled to keep calm, he must for his Emily, but the man he was unwavering in trying to pull him back. Emily sobbed, covered her face with her hands, and shook her head. She didn't accept a word of it.

"Because Emily, the head wound that frightened you with so much blood knocked my senses away. Some months back, I began to suffer those dismal headaches. You were so kind and loving and would soothe my forehead with unguents and love, but those headaches began to bring pictures to my mind and nightmares to my sleep.

Do you recall the day you cut your hand on the wine glass, and I tried to help? You made light of it at the time because you thought I was going to faint at the sight of blood. It wasn't the sight, my love; it was the scent. Remember, I had to leave the room. The scent took me back and reinforced my memories as a butcher. Being among the carcasses, ugly and hanging from the ceiling, and amongst them a face. A feminine face that cajoled and urged me on.

The aroma of your blood took me back, Emily, and I began to remember more and more of my old existence. My fancies said they were a result of the accident, but Emily, the nightmares returned in the day while I was awake, and I came to realise they were indeed memories. Oh, my love, I have been so troubled, but I," he twitched and seemed to tremble before regaining his composure. "I am he."

"Who? What are you saying, William dearest, you are who?"

"Did you not question why there was so much blood?"

"You suffered a head injury as well as others, and everyone said profuse amounts of blood flow from a head wound."

"My darling, oh, how do I say this? It is I; I am the monster."

"What are you saying, William? What is all this absurdity?"

"While running for my life that night, I called on the entity people that believe will help, and I implored Him to stop me. But He didn't attend me or care for me, so why should I bother?

"I am the one who disposed of another whore from Whitechapel. When she helped a blind boy, I stood in the shadows and her strident tone rang out, and I realised if HE didn't put an end to my thoughts, no one would, I am he, Emily, I am Jack the Ripper.

Chapter 8

EMILY'S DOWNFALL

That night, her voice sounded so like my wife's, and it came to me, I must rid the world of her and her ilk. Oh yes, they blamed me for the others, Annie, Rose, and Elizabeth, but no, I will not hold my hand up to them. My last one, until my reappearance was called Mary Kelly, and yes, I was responsible.

Alice McKenzie, the one they said I didn't do because they believed it was done by a left-handed killer and not a right-handed one, or I left the area or something worse. Well, it was I who did it. The time in between Kelly and Mackenzie, I was recuperating, Emily, and on the 17th of July, I slipped back into Jack for my debut and my finale."

"What do you mean, William? How can you slip into Jack; what are you saying?" Emily gasped and crossed her hands over her chest, she found breathing difficult. "No, don't say these terrible things to upset me. Don't lie to me, please. The Kelly girl fell victim to Jack the Ripper; tell me that's so, please, William."

"Yes, that's correct. The last alleged one of Jack's victims, and where my misfortune occurred." He held his right hand in the air, flaunting the evidence, his curled fingers.

"What do you mean? I remember you told me you

confronted misfortune. You rescued a woman from a robber who stabbed you."

"Is that what I told you? It slipped my mind, but yes, I suppose it was an attack of sorts. They tried to blame me for the deaths of all those so-called seamstresses, but no. I like to believe I was more selective in my choices."

"Seamstresses, what are you saying and why are you trying, and, I am sure with some deliberation, to confuse me, William?"

"Let me put it this way. I believe the expression seamstresses is a "nom de plume," which works for me as their turn of phrase to say they exist. Those women you wished to save are ladies of the night, Emily, and the irony is I set out determined to wipe them from the face of the earth. Don't you find fate odd for throwing us together?"

A bemused Emily plucks at her skirt, her mind spiralling unbridled and further away from any understanding. "You loved me once, William. You told me only I would do for you."

"And I still do. Every word I speak is true and comes from the deepest parts of my being. I must tell you, Emily, I thought another, and I were fated, too. Alas, and I asked myself many times, how did I misjudge things so badly?" He shook his head.

"I came from a first-class home—a privileged, rich, and varied life—aside from losing my parents until I married. From then on, I struggled to continue with my existence. I realised my mistake early on.

Talk about blind."

He paused, taking in Emily's stunned silence and although desperate to reach out and tell her not to distress herself, he didn't dare. He had to complete his sorry tale.

"I met a young girl, an attractive young thing who caught my eye on a visit to an art gallery. She wandered through admiring the paintings and stood out amongst the other visitors. I plucked up the nerve to talk to her, and soon she told me her name—Jane. Her knowledge of the exhibits she perused fascinated me.

"After frequent interesting chats, she disclosed that she also painted. She admitted not to the standard we viewed but still thought of herself as an artist.

"All this happened before my marriage. Jane and I stumbled across each other in the gallery, and I mean literally. She stepped back from a painting to get a better picture, she said and walked straight into me. Over the following months, I fell in love with her. Can you believe this?

"We travelled to France for two weeks, all correct, I may add, with separate rooms. I gave her my heart, but she changed. Jane disliked Paris and expressed a forceful desire to leave. I wanted her to stay. I even asked for her hand."

'Emily tried to digest all he said yet remained silent. Her mind by this time was at breaking point.

"Jane confessed she married once, but she was now a widow. Her husband met his demise in a dockyard accident.

I was heartbroken for one widowed so young, but I reasoned, that time heals, and said nothing mattered because I adored her.

"She told me she held my heart but lied and left me in France. I swore never to love again and made plans to travel home. So wretched and incapable of facing anybody and in need of licking my wounds. I travelled for a while and met a damsel, and I may say, one in considerable distress. Her dress, speech, and manner all pointed to her being well to do, and against all I vowed, I gave my heart for a second time to Sylvia, and this time, life promised to be perfect."

Glenda interrupts, 'Larry, this is enthralling, but I'm freezing. Can't you tell me at home?' He didn't pay her any regard; he just carried on.

'William said, "Sylvia confessed to belonging to a wealthy family, and my guard slipped. She said they had severed contact with her, but she hoped to put things right between them. I said nothing. The recklessness of what I did, Emily, haunts me daily; I asked her to marry me."

"I can't say I'm not disappointed in not being your first love, Wiliam, but why are you revealing this to me now?"

"I must, beloved because this is what you want. This is my story. Please, Emily, try and grasp what I'm saying. Sylvia agreed to my proposal but wanted the wedding before I was to meet with her parents. She believed they were more likely to take her back into the fold if she took a husband. I thought her predicament was strange. What did this beautiful, gentle woman do for them to abandon her? After the debacle with Jane though and in my eagerness to put a ring on her finger, I lost my good sense. The marriage took place before the end of the month. I never did get to meet her family.

"Her story was nothing more than a tissue of lies, Emily. Her persona was nothing short of a masquerade, and she was no more than a high-class doxy. By then, though, I was in love with her. I tried to transform her and our lives, and in contrast, ended up hating her.

"My life evolved into misery. I failed as a man, ridiculed from the start. On our wedding night, she laughed at my inexperience. Before this, I thought of myself as a sophisticate. Sadly, I never satisfied her. The day came when she told me she was with child. Not mine or she hoped not."

"Oh, my darling. What did you do, and what about the child; where is it?" Emily reached out to William who backed away, balling his fists, and seemed to shrink into himself.

"I told her of my happiness; we would be a real family, but she derided me. Oh, Emily, I can't tell you; I just can't. This is so hard."

"But William, you said you must."

"She laughed at me saying, who said it's yours? Who would want you for a father? My picture of a rosy future shattered. My dreams squashed like a cockroach under her dainty foot. I learnt, well, I think I always knew, she played me false with a person in my employ, my coachman. This was the lowest point in my life, yet I also held the solution in my hands. I do mean it in the literal sense. She must go. In the end, I devised a simple plan. I didn't need a driver; I can handle the carriage and that way I would rid myself of them both."

'Emily's confusion begins to increase becoming more evident. "Are we dispensing with Jameson, William?"

"No, my darling, not him. I am talking about Frank, the man I hired before I moved here. I planned well, Emily. The man standing before you is the same one you want to give your child my name. I managed to persuade Sylvia by reinforcing my promise not to interfere in her life, and to ignore her indiscretions. I allowed her to perform her seamstressing. I went so far as to tell her the driver would take her. All along I wanted to ensure they were together. Yes, and give them the prospect to be intimate."

Poking his finger into his sternum in rhythm with each word, he said, "I planned for them to travel together with enough time to become involved. Call it a parting gift. I said I would join her at the Avenue Theatre, which is close to the Thames."

Once more, he appraised his curled fingers, not out of regret or disgust but as one proud of an achievement.

"What deed, William? What is this deed you speak

of?"

"You must take heed of me, listen and most of all, hear what I say, Emily. This is of the utmost importance."

Emily glances at the sherry decanter. Should she partake in a glass to aid her anxiety? She hasn't trembled inside like this for a long time now.

William continued. "My plan necessitated them being together. I also required an alibi. To do this, I arranged for him to drive Sylvia to the theatre, saying I would endeavour to meet her later. I assumed he would take her to the house. She rented a house where she took her paramours, but never the most intelligent of women; she forgot to secrete the bills. So, I shadowed her when I spotted the address on one of the bills. A place set back from others, quite a little find for a bitch on heat."

"William, mind your language, please."

Ignoring her plea, he says. "On the night in question, I covered my tracks making sure someone would remember me on the other side of London, where I said I had some business. Afterwards, I took a cab and paid the cabby well to move with haste so he wouldn't ask questions. I found the cad and her together and finished them both off. I hit him over the back of the head with a two-foot-tall bronze statue of the naked Venus. Appropriate, I thought, under the circumstances.

I find it regrettable now that he will never find out who struck him, me. The eunuch he so despised, he never thought of me as a man. I dispatched him to his father, the devil. Emily, it transformed into an obligation. I tied a curtain cord around his neck, pulling it tight. He would not be waking up. A pity, but at least that evil bitch learnt who her dispatcher was, with my eyes inches from hers, watching her fear with me reflected in her pupils as they dilated in recognition before she screamed. I strangled the life out of her."

Emily cupped her pale cheeks in her hands. "No more, William, please say no more."

Misery masked her face, but William carried on.

"Our time together flashed through my head, but, to my dismay, her end came too soon. Would she survive? I doubted she would, but to make sure, I smashed her on the head with the same slut-like ornament. I even planned my escape. I didn't need to remove his garments; he had thrown them on the floor. I dressed in his coat and headgear and drove the carriage around the back of the Adelphi Theatre because no one would think anything strange about a parked coach and horse.

"Many young scamps congregate to stay with the vehicles if the coachmen want a drink, which is against the rules, but who would tell? I paid a boy to mind the horse and swore to give him double when I returned if he stayed and didn't run off. I also stressed that if he ran away, I would find him, and he would run no more.

After discarding my disguise, which I left in the

carriage, I returned to my seat in the theatre and rested knowing they would be together forever—not in the manner they planned but... Next, I took a cab home after pretending to search for her. I paid him a handsome tip too so he would remember me. I told him he must hurry as my wife, Sylvia, was missing and then I made my way on foot to their sleazy love nest and dealt with them both.

"My dearest, I won't upset you with too many details. Afterwards, I returned to the theatre to pick up the carriage and drive home. The darkness cloaked me from prying eyes, and with Frank's clothing, I was invisible, because nobody would bother about a coach driver. At the stables, everybody slept, and I had to work fast. I planned it all down to the smallest detail, Emily, from the canvas sheets and knives to the cleaning equipment. I left nothing unplanned. Frank's body caused me no problems.

After dismembering him, I dropped the various limbs in cesspools, ever mindful of the time, because after midnight, the night soil men come to clear them of the contents. I was smart and selective by using those pools seldom emptied in Whitechapel. No one would find him, and the specimen piece of shit deserved nothing less than ending up in it."

Emily roused herself. "Oh, William, please... mind your language."

Sniggering, he said, "My love, are you not listening to me; you must try to hear me out, Emily. Bring your beautiful mind back to me, and now, my love."'

Larry's timbre lowers at this point as he studies Glenda fidgeting beside him and motions to zip her mouth.

'William's adrenaline raced, or was it Jack's, Glenda. No, Glen, it's rhetorical.'

"Next," said William, "came Sylvia's turn. I admit I underwent periods of purgatory with her. Cheated out of my manhood; I wanted her to stoke the flames of Hades. She must never come back, and so I planned to dismember her too. Oh, I liked the planning, Emily. I used the same procedure as I used on Frank."

"I feel faint, William. Please stop." By this time Emily feels she doesn't recognise the man she loves, the father of her longed-for child. His whole look and character were changing before her eyes, he waved her fears away by flicking his hand.

"On the first sheet, after tying the limbs above the joints, which helps eliminate blood loss, blood coagulates slowly. Something I learnt and prepared for as a butcher's apprentice; therefore, I was limiting much of the mess.

I removed her arms and legs and found each twist of the weapon joyful. And last, her head. I savoured my plans for her comely face and breasts. I stropped the steel on the leather for ages, so the sharp edge slid through her skin, and I enjoyed this the most. The whore I united in holy matrimony with would serve no more.

"I thought about the baby she said she carried and

eviscerated her. I sensed no regret because, if the child matured to become like her, I would be rendering mankind a service, and if, lord forbid, the child turned out like me, I would be doing women a greater kindness. So, Emily, boy or girl, what chance would a child of ours have?

"After wrapping her headless body in the canvas and making a tidy bundle, I slipped her into the Regent's Canal below the lock at Limehouse Basin. I intended the package to wash down the muddy Thames and out to sea but remained confident that if any of her did wash onto the shore, no one would identify her.

"The damned housemaid stuck her oar in and reported her missing; a woman I never liked, so I dealt with her too, but I answered the questions the police officers plied me with. I played the gutless husband, which, I acknowledge flowed with ease, because it was brought home to me that I had mutated into a specimen of contempt. I think I kept them guessing.

The knowledge I still held her limbs in a chest up in the roof space added a dash of piquancy to the scenario, but the Thames called them in for a dip too. I dropped them in from the riverside near the Avenue. The stink from the water matched the stink from her.

"Her torso turned up in Rainham. It did worry me, but I did my best to cover my tracks. I tried not to think about it too much. The police said they retrieved a body and I assumed they thought I murdered her, but couldn't prove anything. I thought about everything, from clearing out her best dresses, shoes, and hats as if she had deserted me, to removing her perfumes and cosmetics. Also, I told them money and jewellery were gone too, and as an extra safeguard, I kept this." He smiled while removing a velvet pouch containing a gold watch from his waistcoat pocket.

'By this time Emily is lost in a world of fantasy. She doesn't understand what's real anymore and says, "How lovely, William, but what happened to the chain, my love? This link is broken."

"I deliberately snapped the links, Emily, to ensure suspicion fell on the coachman. I worked out Sylvia bought it for him because he showed it off. I broke the chain and hooked a part in the corner of the canvas containing Sylvia's remains. An inch or so, nothing much, but if the police were to ask me anything again, I may shed some light and help them as the links are unusual."

"Should I call Agnes to bring us a pot of tea, William?"

"My poor darling, you must concentrate."

"How about a sherry?" She points to the glass decanter.

"No, Emily, LISTEN, come back to me and try to focus. This is the reason we must not marry or become parents."'

Glenda notes the sadness in Larry's voice as he relates the sad tale of William and Emily. He carries on with William.

'"They asked me when someone hauled the final

parcel from the Thames near Temple Gate with the chain still attached if I recognised it, and I told them of a similar one and where I saw it, whether they believed me or not didn't worry me.

"They offered no evidence and keeping me under surveillance proved fruitless. No identification meant no justification to generate more harassment. I did hold onto her head for a while, though I wondered how best to deal with my prize trophy.

"One night, I found myself in Whitechapel, which is not a place anyone should boast about being. But the alleyways and passages beguiled me.

"Women, not unlike those you and your charity help, hawked the alleyways and passages. Using their bodies in the alleys, either against a wall or anywhere for a coin.

"This made me wonder if Sylvia began on those depraved cobbles and eventually the area obsessed me. I waited until the answer came to me in a vision. I got away with killing once, or I should say twice, with him. So, I thought, I can rid the city of them."

Emily's lips mouth the word killing, but William is lost to her. He almost gloated as he said.

"Actually, three times. I had already disposed of my housemaid. She went to live with her sister in Ireland; well, her correspondence said so, but in all honesty, as I said, she had followed her mistress, every nasty malicious part in the sewage-filled torpid water of the Thames.

"Afterwards, with no time to hide them away,

Whitechapel is such a busy place, I left them in situ. No dignity in it, but dignity in death should be absent for street scum. I reckoned if they left me alone with the victim I would do better, alas, an impossible request, but I stopped a small number. Oh, the fuss, Emily, what a palaver I created."

Once again, he took a moment to contemplate his redeemer, Emily, who offered him no ill and did no wrong.

"I arrived home each night engulfed in dishonour and guilt, but no matter what I did, the lure of the Whitechapel streets would not let me go.

"I returned often to rid them of the filth and degradation, but Emily, I will profess this to you, and to my dying shame, I developed a deep passion for what I did.

"My wife still played in my head, urging me to be a man, and for a change, I judged that I was one. I gained the power to do what I wanted. I didn't use them like other men. I wanted to stop them from producing more street vermin who would mature to perfect treading the same worn-out pathways as their mothers."

'His words began to seep through Emily's defence mechanism, making more sense as he explained his mission because he sounded earnest in his delivery.

"You say you kept her head, William? No, it's impossible, and where are the possessions of those you talk so unconcerned about murdering, the way you would invite them to tea?"

"Again, Emily, my love, when I completed the decorating and sent for my belongings, I chose a day you went out visiting. I erected a false wall in the roof above, a hidden divide, but behind are the trunks holding the lamentable remnants of their lives."

"No, William. It can't be true; you are not the Whitechapel monster, not him, no, and yet you say that bodies lie in my house. Deceased human remains scatter my floors!"

"No, Emily, no. Clothing and personal trinkets. I am confident no one can stumble across them here. You said you never venture up to your attic. They are safe unless you choose to tell. I am safe.'"

'Are you saying, Larry, it's this house?' She stares around the room. 'You already said about the wall so are you now saying that Jack the Ripper lived here?' Her excitement begins to stifle Larry's enthusiasm. He'd already guessed her reaction would be like his wife's.

'Wow, the newspapers will love this. Is it all true? Wait till we put this on social media.' Glenda slaps his knee, inspecting the room with new eyes. 'Hey, Larry, we'll be famous all thanks to Jack. Who would have guessed?'

'Don't overexcite yourself. I'm not finished.'

'Oh no, did your aunt, whoever, however many times removed, nurse a fanciful pipe dream and turn out to be nothing more than a storyteller?' Doing his best to ignore her while inside he seethes.

'Grandmother, Emily told William she never

detected a trait of anything bad in him saying, "Tell me this is not true. Please? Tell me this is one horrible delusion I am having. I would prefer it than give ear to this."

'She said she would go away again and suffer the treatments if he assured her of the real truth. William tried to convince her, swearing she single-handedly stopped him. She took him with her to peruse those impoverished creatures, to talk to them, and to offer alms and optimism. She provided so many of the destitute women aiming to free them from their drab existence and the depravity they suffered with her money. He helped and learnt to pity them too.

He often dwelt on his misadventure with her horse was it bad luck, or the answer to his prayers, and he did pray. He emphasised the fact, Glenda. He did, and he said Emily symbolised his salvation and the saviour of no end of women.' Glenda tries to look impressed as he continues.

'Emily fidgeted her face conveying utter misery. Her hands trembled, and she avoided catching William's eye. He stalled. Is he about to lose her? He begs her to let him finish what he called his piteous story; he was impatient after this long time to reveal all. Devasted, Emily said no, not willing to bear his revelations.

'All her life, Emily thought she was different. Convinced her father didn't want any children, and her mother only wanted her father. They gave her material things, fancy clothes and jewellery, but she never suspected they didn't want a child.

'They allowed her a puppy once, and she loved him so, but her mother would not allow him in the house and banished the mutt to live in a kennel in the back garden.

One day, Emily thought her mother had hit the little dog with a stick, but they told her she imagined it, not only by the maidservant but also by her father. Emily loved Rags, the first real companion in her young life. No one questioned where she plucked the name from, leaving her assuming they took no interest in her or her little puppy.

'One day, she went to play with Rags but couldn't find him. She searched for her mother to ask after him but couldn't find her either. After calling his name and searching everywhere, all to no avail. She cried. Vivid memories of the day haunted her because the same day was the first time her father sent her away. Her father faced her, "You are a wicked child. You have tortured a little dog for your enjoyment, and now you have killed it."

'Emily swore she didn't, saying how much she loved him and would never hurt him, and she cried, 'Ask Mama if you don't want to believe me." Alas, her distress didn't affect him. He grabbed her, dragged her to her room and locked her in.

'After six months at sea and home on leave, he was restless and short-tempered. This time his anger exploded, and he sent for the family doctor to pack her off to the sanatorium. A building she learnt to harbour a hatred for, where they strapped her down when she cried about her treatment and her lost dog.

'She remembered, on the same day, she never saw her mother. She had time to think about her mother, who disappeared during these awful times. Where did she go?

'In the institution, they said Emily ailed from hot blood and they would cool her down, which they achieved by strapping her in an ice tub, and she overheard one of them say in passing. "She's just like her mother."

'But Emily didn't register it properly because, to her knowledge, they had never met her mother.

'On these occasions of immersion, she worked out the memories of her episodes were during her father's leave, and her mother seemed to go away a lot. She began to accept that life could be more comfortable if she didn't complain.

'The doctors said Emily suffered tantrums and hot blood and would need specific treatments and medications. They told her she did terrible things to her pets and other animals from the same street. Her kitten they noted disappeared too, yet Emily recalled nothing, neither owning one nor indeed any of the supposed abominable acts. Did she kill it, and if so, did she empty her mind of these atrocities, or did someone convince her she did?

She remembered one day after someone called at the house. There was shouting between her father and whomever the caller was. Her mother was upset and began to scream and beat her father on his chest, and he whisked her away. No one told her where they had gone and tried to tell her she was mistaken in what she thought she saw, and then she got into trouble for eavesdropping.

'This thought gave her a dilemma because she remembered other aspects quite well. Like her father beating her, saying he must for her benefit. Emily accepted all he told her, longing for his love, and when he presented her with what he described as her devilish acts, Emily agreed to please him and suffered her fate.

'Why was her mother never around during these times, and why did they only happen when her father returned from the sea, always bemoaning his lot in having a daughter, she never did find out, but it played on her mind. She begged for his love and would settle for anything, but he sent for Dawson and locked her in her room until he arrived.

On his initial call, after meeting with her father for a while, the doctor left the room, smiled at Emily, and took her by the hand. He spoke as if she were a naughty girl throwing a tantrum, stating she must grow out of her childish ways for her father to find her worthy of his love.

'As a child, she distrusted him and pleaded with her father to relent. She swore her respect was paramount, yet all to no avail.

'Over subsequent years, the physician, Dawson, showed her kindness and a declaration to help, with what she never did find out. Why would she not begin to believe the terrible things her father said? As a respected Naval Captain, surely her father would not lie.

'Against all her instincts in being a well-brought-up young lady, she put her ear to his study door, needing to find out why he sent her away and where her mother went during these times.'

By this time, Emily was lost and depressed in her memories until William's voice dragged her back to the vileness of the present.

"Emily, are you listening? You must, my love, you must. I am an educated man, but I ask, why did these most heinous crimes give me so much pleasure, and yet each subsequent morning, I woke horrified and loathing myself? To my shame, I developed into an addict, akin to the call of the opium dens prospering amid the Docklands. One too robust to discount. The only difference was, I lusted for blood. Time passed and I emerged ever more destructive and revelled in my cleansing.

"One whore named Catherine, such an ironic name for a person of her standing because Catherine is of Greek origin and means pure. Well, she died a miserable death at my hands.

"No, don't stare at me, please, Emily. Let me tell you everything. I want you to appreciate what I am saying, and you can only do so if I tell you everything.

"I soon wearied. Killing is exhausting, work and I did reconcile what I did as work. I asked myself, Was

I doing God's will? After resting, I went through Eddows' belongings and came across a mustard box with a folded pawn ticket inside and bearing a name; one burnt into my brain, one that took me back to the woman I once adored, Jane Kelly.

Somebody had scribbled an address on the back, and I needed to check if this was the same girl, while questioning why this whore should be in her place of residence. I couldn't settle until I unearthed the truth.

"The address turned out false. But I still wanted to find out why the Eddows' woman wrote her name on it and if she might be my Jane. I squandered so many nights searching the dank paths and passages of Whitechapel, becoming more inured to them.

"I became obsessed, until one night in November when I saw her accompanied by a short stout man outside the Queen's Head public house. Older yes but her identity was no longer in doubt, Jane Kelly was on the arm of a man, Jane, the girl who stole my heart.

"I carefully tailed them along Commercial and Dorset Street, through the arch, and into Miller's Court. All the while, I noticed someone else appeared to be tracking them too. Intrigued, I wondered why this should be so. What purpose did he have?

Passing by, she talked with the short man, and I remembered her voice. A touch coarser, I admit, but I recalled it well, and it convinced me of her identity. I waited. The man who followed them left at the stroke of three of the clock and I never did find out whom or why he stood waiting. My fixation now was only on unearthing Jane's abode.

Heavy footsteps broke the limited silence in the quadrangle. Taking leave of a doorway, I took a gamble and peered around the archway, wondering if Jane had accompanied him, but no. I did though discover her abode. I almost laughed aloud; she lived at number thirteen. Unlucky, they say, and it proved so in this case too.

I knocked and whispered her name. She let me in, how my nerves tingled. I was so nervous but horrified to find she didn't remember me. Can you imagine how I suffered? The girl I once loved and who stole my heart did not recognise me.

Fantastic as it may seem, I didn't realise her real name was Mary Jane Kelly. Not until I read the headlines in the newspapers. Another thing happened in her room. I lost the best use of my fingers. I wanted to do her justice, but I made a mistake. Well, I made two mistakes with her, one in loving her and the other in my heedless disregard for what my uncle taught me in my youth.

My father wanted me to follow him into banking, like him. At the same time, I bore an obligation to my uncle for the time he cared for me while adjusting to my life. I feigned an interest in his work as a butcher, except one of my mistakes struck home painfully. I forgot the golden rule he taught me: never catch a falling cutting tool. I will not regale you with another lesson I learned but it surrounded a young man named Henry.

Jane, the silly girl, put up an almighty fight. To quell and stop the screaming I found exhausting. I dropped my knife in the melee, and much to my dismay, I checked its fall, and in doing so, I cut my tendons. A mistake to haunt me ever since, and one I won't repeat. She fought for her life." The whimper of her croaking cries in a feeble attempt to call out stay with me. "Why, why?"

"I put my fingers around the throat of a girl I once idolised as tight as possible. They felt comfortable and the right size. I placed a kiss on her chin and stared into her eyes, so different from the last time I held her, and said, My lovely Jane, it's me. Why did you leave me?

With scarce breath in her, I swear I made her remember me before she breathed her last. The flicker of recognition came, and she whispered my name through her bloodied lips. I was content to finish her. Even though spent, I completed my task. My problem started when I attempted to separate her arm at the shoulder. The tip of my blade glanced off the bone and pierced through the other side, catching my hand and causing more damage."

He tried to flex his hand in front of Emily, but the fingers on his right hand remained stubbornly curled. "You see, Emily, I was once right-handed but now only for my pen."

Emily stared at him and his hand her face wrinkled in fear and understanding.

"Let me warn you," he said. "I was mad as hell, so

I spread her for all the world to gawp at and repaid her well by taking back the most precious thing she had. I gave her my heart once, which she threw aside, so I stole her treacherous heart to bury, close to where I kept my case, hat, and, yes, my wife's head.

"I left and behold someone shouted murder. It was not an unusual cry by any means for the location. By this time the area was familiar to me, and I made my way to Aldgate station. I wrapped my hand in a square of rag I picked up from her room with her heart, still warm, enclosed amid the folds of cloth. I sensed no pain, not until I buried the treacherous organ in the undergrowth beneath my feet before making my escape.

"My almost useless fingers stopped me for a while. I tried to regain my strength and believed I was ready the night Alice woke up the real me. Her voice was like Sylvia's, so similar and scary, and the sound of her rekindled my desire to continue in my work.

"You may find this odd, Emily. My first night back, shall we say at work, was also my last, because beloved, the same night, after discarding the bag, I ran into the path of your carriage.

I am still unsure whether I wanted to die. Call it fate or accident. I sensed peace in the churchyard when I rested amongst the headstones. Countless have fallen into a state of disrepair and crumbling with age. This serenity was what I longed for. The dead suffer no earthly troubles and pay no regard to the condition of their stones.

"They should have seized me back then, so I would not be here now. I was the beast fresh from a kill."

'Think, Glenda, he's revealing all of this to Emily.' Larry pauses, contemplating what to say next. What do you say, but he doesn't take long.

William says, "I swear to this day After I left the churchyard, I don't remember running into your carriage, I remember I needed to scrub myself clean, also a symbolic cleansing. I was heading for the King's Head across the road. I could use the stable to clean myself. I did contemplate taking my life and asked myself, can I rid London of the filth? Is this a mission from God, or am I a walking devil? Undecided, I made to cross the road, and you, Emily, my angel, my guardian, tell me that is when you crushed me beneath your horse and carriage wheels.

The blood though, was not all mine. They made a huge mistake. I was coated in a whore's blood. Emily, when you took me to your bed, did you find me a brute or a bogeyman, my love?"

Cautiously, Emily backed to the wall, horrified, speechless and desperate to escape.

"No, Emily, please do not consider me bad, not like that." He hides his face, lifting his forearm. "Your love of me saved more women of Whitechapel. You changed me, but Emily, I cannot father a child. She, my wife, taught me as much."

"No, William, you mustn't say such things. Tell me if you don't want me and if you used me, say so, but please don't give me a tale. All I ask is for you to give our child your name, please. I won't hold you to marriage if the act is repulsive to you, but I cannot bear a bastard, and you must not ask me to."

"Which name, Emily, Ripper? Is this the name you want for our child… I longed to save men from loose pawing, women, any women, and to my knowledge all of them. Above all, those like the bitch I married. She is the one who led me to the brink of the abyss, beat me, and degraded me by bringing men home, saying if I couldn't support her, they would. She pushed their coins in my face to teach me. Yes, I was afraid of her. She said she would make a man of me but ridiculed my efforts, and I stepped over the chasm. She created the Ripper, the creature I came to be."

"No William. I don't believe it. Nobody can make you into something you are not, and you, my love, you are not him."

"When Sylvia told me she was pregnant, she rubbed my nose in the fact it may be anybody's but mine, and if I were the father, she hoped her lineage would be stronger and the child would take after her. Sylvia sealed her fate and became my first victim. I couldn't take the chance and let a woman like her rear a child, never mind mine. I studied myself, my weaknesses, hatred, and my strengths, of which I am sure I lack any."

He shuddered and took Emily's hands, gazing into her tear-filled eyes. "What if this child is a son and follows in his father's footsteps, and what if...?"

"What do you mean? No, no, you are not him. In my heart, I would sense it." He picks up the bag holding the tools of his trade back in his Ripper days when the populace believed the Devil roamed the Whitechapel Streets. William opened it and removed a knife with a long, thin spine and carved whalebone handle, which he ran along the palm of his hand, already blooded from the wounds on his knuckles.

Emily, fearing he meant to do harm to her or to take the child from her body, screamed, but no one was home. Agnes had not yet returned.

"I must remove our son now to save virtuous women like you."

"Please, please, don't do this, William. She may be a daughter. I pray for a daughter, please, please." She begged. William dropped his gaze to the floor and kept it down, as it would be if it were the most interesting floor in the world.

'Emily began to think he was considering her and their child until he faced her again. Emily didn't recognise him. His lip curled, and his pupils constricted as his goal became clear.

His features contorted as he said, "I must. You don't sense the beast lying in wait inside of me. You kept him at bay, but that's all. How can you stop the evil monster if I enjoy the delivery of a son? I am so sorry, Emily; I must take this child. Don't think of this," he waved his arm dismissively at her, "as such. Think of how you will still be helping man and womankind."'

"Yes, I am," she said, realising the broken pieces scattered around the floor were the remains of a Wedgwood vase, a gift to her mother from her father, and one she treasured.

Blood bubbled from his mouth, his gaze burnt into her soul, and his hands clasped hers, still clutching the hilt. "I realise now. I will not let you go. Not now you are like me. You have killed me for love. We are the same, Emily. You will never desert me and now as I lay in front of you and before my last breath, I vow I will never leave you; I love you, Emily."

Emily denied her love, withdrew the weapon and slashed at his dying body until exhausted.

When the results of her handy work permeated through her brain, she threw herself across the bloodied corpse, pleading for his forgiveness, begging him not to leave her.

'Agnes returned after her errand and came upon the scene. One she described to the police as a bloodbath. Emily was kneeling beside him crying, covered in blood, her hair tangled, and her garment torn. Fragments of the vase were scattered around the floor, with one shard protruding from Emily's arm, which didn't appear to affect her as she held out her bloodied hands to her trusted maid. With one hand still gripping the thin-bladed knife, Emily implored her to understand what happened.

'The aroma of fresh blood mingled with Emily's perfume as she tried to convince her William was the monster, Jack the Ripper. But she also said she killed him to protect her and the baby. Emily panicked and showed her the bag with letters and blades, but Agnes couldn't stay. The ramifications of the sight she saw were too much. Her poor mistress—her friend, this is too far, but she dare not deny this incident.

Racing out to hunt for a police officer, her face took on a mask of fear and disgust as she reached the end of the street, a hysterical mess. Her skirts swished around her ankles as she ran. Impotent in uttering a word, she tripped and bumped into an officer on the corner. He caught Agnes and demanded she tell him, but all she did was point behind. He clasped her hand and walked back, with her pulling against him, refusing to move, desperate to run away.

He tugged her by the arm, demanding she tell him what had occurred, to put her in such a state and tried to soothe her fears. People turned their heads at the spectacle.

Agnes stalled her relentless sobbing, beaten. The constable blew his whistle to alert other bobbies as he dragged her along, with her still begging him to let go. Agnes reluctantly takes him back to the house.

On arriving at the house on Albury Street, this house, Glenda, the policeman's stomach churned at the horrific display spread before all. Deep in shock, Agnes witnessed something far more sinister. In the gloom in the corner of the room stood the image of the dead William. His composure presented a scene of peace, yet his face flickered between love and evil as he overlooked where his body rested on Emily's

Persian rug.

'Agnes ran from the room and never returned to this house. The spectacle turned her head. Emily, though, had been savvy enough to put the black bag and its contents behind the wall panelling, which she replaced as before.'

With great pride, it seemed to her that he took his time to emphasise, 'Because it remained undiscovered for years.'

Chapter 9

THE TRIAL

'With no one to stand for the defence of Emily and no one to aid her apart from the charities she chaired to help fallen women and her family doctor, her counsel held the opinion the case would be difficult but not impossible to obtain an innocent verdict. Emily was a person of high quality, but like a flower blooming in a garden surrounded by contrasting colours and scents, displaying elegance and supported by beauty, she now stood unattached. A cut bloom, left to wither. A sad reflection of her former self.

Her counsel read out Agnes' statement, chuffed by the proceedings: Agnes, her maid, said she witnessed Emily with the knife in her hand, yet the police recovered no such weapon. This begged the question, where was it? He thought this would be his best line of defence, but didn't realise how his words would backfire on him.

'Next, they called on the family physician, Doctor Dawson, to provide background on Emily's medical condition. Eager to safeguard his reputation, he leaned towards what her parents told him about the terrible acts they said Emily performed rather than give his professional opinion.

He told the court. "As a child, Emily's pets soon

perished and in horrible ways. The bodies were mutilated beyond all recognition. Emily has no recollection of hurting them. She said she wouldn't hurt them, while her father said it was no other."'

Glenda fidgets.

'What's up?' Annoyed, Larry enjoys his part in telling the story and doesn't want her to disturb him.

'Got a numb bum, and thinking of those pets.'

'Yes, ok, it's a long time ago. Let me explain it all, and if you behave, I'll rub the numbness away later.

Dawson gazed around the court before he carried on. "On my advice, after many repetitions of these unexplained incidents and finding that time in the asylum helped, Emily's father hired a maid named Agnes Warpole, a trained nurse. This was in the belief that she would befriend the child and induce a calming effect."

"Calming effect, was the child uncontrollable then?" asked the defence counsel. A reptilian-looking man and ineffectual at his job.

"I personally never witnessed uncontrollable behaviour, but I let myself be guided by her father."

"And where was her mother during these incidents of mutilation, Doctor?"

The prosecutor stood. "Objection, the mother is not on trial here, her whereabouts are unimportant."

Defence countered. "I am trying to establish that Emily may not have been responsible for these actions or said actions."

"Overruled." said the judge, carry on. You may

answer, Doctor."

Defence counsel repeated, "Where was Emily's mother during these incidents"

"That, sir I cannot say," said Dawson.

"Come now, was she not herself admitted to the asylum?"

Gasps rippled throughout the court, and Dawson coughed.

The prosecutor straightened his paperwork.

Defence counsel then asked, "And what was your diagnosis of Emily?"

"In my opinion, sir, Emily suffers from a form of Hebephrenia and a weak mind, which manifests itself in delusions and peculiar behaviour."

The prosecutor stood to ask...'

The defender sat down with a smug smile.'

'Can we have a cuppa yet, Larr? I'm spitting feathers.' Pleads Glenda.

'You wanted this, Glenda. Where was I? Ha, yes, the prosecutor:

"Odd, what do you mean by odd?" He turned his nose up, sniffing as if talking to a child.

Dawson countered. "Well, I mean in the way of disordered thinking and inappropriate or silly conduct."

"Do you think the butchery of an innocent man is inappropriate?" Fired the prosecutor. A murmur ripples through the gallery. The judge declared order.

The defence stood waiting to cause an effect before asking, "What, as a man of medicine, do you believe is her prognosis?"

"In my opinion, we can expect a deterioration of the mind, and the defendant," the doctor nods at a smiling Emily, who sits like she is presiding at an afternoon tea party. "She will need a prolonged plan of treatment.'"

'Imagine, Glenda; a lull falls on the courtroom. Everyone expects him to continue, but suddenly, the prosecutor butts in. "Where, doctor, where will this treatment take place?"

Dawson said, "In the asylum, his voice almost inaudible in the room."

Blinking, the judge rouses himself from his boredom. "Speak up, man, speak up."

"Erm, in the mental institution, your honour.'"

A scattering of gasps fills the public gallery. Emily appeared unconcerned and serene and sat casting smiles at the ladies acquainted with her charity work.

They gawp and gossip about the downfall of their one-time friend as they whisper to each other behind decorated fans. Some say they knew she was odd others remember incidents from years gone by, all wanting to top each other with their recollections of Emily and her family.

'The counsel asked, "Do you, Doctor, as a man of science, have any idea what brought about this malady?"

"I don't think anyone can say what brings these episodes on, and as they say, there, but for the grace of God."

The prosecutor stood and said, "We are not here for homespun homilies, thank you, Doctor."

The judge loses his patience. A grumbling noise came from behind his bench. With lunch on his mind, he said, "Doctor, will you please answer the question to the best of your ability?"

"Yes, my Lord." His nod aimed at the bewigged elderly man with haughty, piggy eyes, who was far more interested in lunchtime arriving than listening to a case, which in his mind would deliver an obvious guilty verdict.'

'Who wrote this?' asks Glenda.

'I'm gleaning this from the diary. For the record, Glen, now I think about it, this must have been written during her incarceration or while waiting for her trial. I think it's a good account, so she must have been lucid then, now listen.

"I said before," said the doctor. "I cannot say when or why this malady struck. I can say after one spell of demanding therapy in the rest home," he coughed again, not desirous of using the word asylum while his reputation was on the line. "Her parents perished in a mysterious carriage crash, and Emily, against all expectations, began to become more stable."

At the mention of her parents, Emily tried to stand in the dock but was pushed back into her seat. The court grew silent, and Emily wiped her eyes, but some thought it odd because her smile beamed out to all once seated.

The prosecutor sneered, "And why would this be so, Doctor?"

The judge interrupted, "Erm, why do you say this accident was mysterious? What made it so?"

Dawson looked towards the defence counsel, who shuffled his papers, stood and spoke to the judge.

"Ha, well, the carriage was travelling at speed when a problem occurred with the harnessing. On taking a tight turn, the harness failed resulting in the carriage hurtling down the embankment and into the Thames, where both perished. On examination, they found no faults or breaks in the leatherwork. The coach driver tried to blame the apprentice. They all assured the police the harnesses were secure, so the verdict said death by accident."

"Carry on." The judge began to mutter under his breath.

Turning his head away from the prosecutor, Dawson faced the judge. "Sir, as to the question of stability, in my honest opinion, I do not know. I do believe the innovative care given by myself and the nurse, Agnes, is the chief reason for her stability and not the death of her parents." The judge eyed Emily who smiled at him.

The prosecutor's next question threw the gallery into turmoil, one of shame and embarrassment. "Do you think, sir, the defendant's pregnancy had anything to do with her sudden behaviour change? Is this woman here?" His forefinger stretches towards Emily, who smiles. He faltered before saying, "Is this woman here with child?"

The defence objected, and the judge threatened to clear the court before allowing the question to stand.

Disconcerted, the highly respected medical man tried to attract the attention of the defence counsel, who was sitting with his eyes fixed on the floor. A woman in the gallery fainted, and her friends hustled her out in haste. The prosecuting counsel said, "Come now, Doctor. You are under oath. Is Emily Vincent pregnant?" Gasps rippled around the public gallery.

"Is it conceivable?" He scans the gallery and eyeballs the jury before facing the doctor. "Would her condition have anything to do with her sudden decline?"

The prosecutor pointed at Emily, his finger straight and commanding notice, not as the conductor of an orchestra with a baton. He was accusing as he pursued the waving motion with stabbing damaging words and did not waver until each one pierced Emily's character. He managed to shred her reputation beyond all recognition.

Dawson lowered his voice as if he were uneasy using the words pregnant and unexpected in the same sentence in front of the court.'

In Victorian and into Edwardian times, to talk about an unmarried, so-called respectable woman expecting a child would send the moralistic reeling into fits of the vapours. The old Victorian adage of, what goes on under the bed sheets, should stay under the bed sheets, mentality was still rife.

'The doctor's answer was cautious. "It is possible, Emily's err, the defendant's unexpected condition may generate severe alterations in her mental faculties."

"Would this, and the fact this woman is without support from a husband, a woman who occupied her life reforming fallen women and now finds herself in a similar position, cause her steep decline into one of a murderess?"

The doctor would answer no more; he lowered his eyes to the floor and pressed forward on his hands. Leaning against the mahogany witness box, he despaired. Dawson gauged in all he said that he had done his best for Emily. The court charged Emily Vincent with the murder of the man named William Warren. The courts also considered her sick of mind for the vile mutilation and swearing she killed the so-called Jack the Ripper.

The prosecutor took his turn after hearing the information and stood looking pleased. Pausing, he kept all waiting for his next, in his mind, brilliant diatribe; he's noted as saying:

"We must consider the killing of William took place in Deptford, yes, only a train ride from Whitechapel, which would put him, if he were the so-called Jack the Ripper and still living, in the correct locality. The bigger question at hand, though, is why did the murders by this so-called Ripper stop for over five years?"

He glanced at Emily, "As the defendant says, if he

was the Ripper, then one might ask, why for over five years, were no more murders attributed to him? Is it not more logical to believe this so-called Ripper departed from this mortal coil over five years ago or, at worst, moved abroad and continued his reign of terror elsewhere?"

He faced the bench, decisive in catching the eye of each of the twelve, before calling upon them to think about the story Emily concocted, holding his arms out as though to embrace them.

"It must be obvious to all," he said. "You cannot believe her." He shook his head from side to side. The jury was hooked, nerves on edge as they waited. Head bowed and resting on the podium, he said, "The elusive Jack is no more."'

Larry spins around and throws his arm out, pointing at Glenda as though he is the prosecutor accusing Emily, and says, 'And she is nothing more than a liar and a murderer.

The jury's verdict, with only the minimum of deliberations, was guilty without a doubt and the murder weapon. They believed the nurse when she substantiated their claims with her testimony, and she held her mistress in the highest regard.

'The fact Agnes swore under oath to the officer on the scene when she said, "I walked in the room, and Emily was still holding the knife in her right hand while crying over the bloodstained body of William, who in death was smiling," meant nobody gave any credence to the simple-minded Emily's story. So,

Glenda, because records from the constabulary showed no pieces of evidence of murders perpetrated by the rogue since the death of Mary Jane Kelly some five years earlier, the court, convinced of her lies, committed Emily and her forthcoming issue to the asylum.

'Also, those of the opinion Jack was right-handed, and the last callous similar attack was of one Alice McKenzie, but the consensus of the experts said the murderer was a left-handed person. Only the facts of her mental state and expecting a child saved Emily from the Gallows. The doctor admitted, under pressure, that Emily was insane. He pleaded prison would be too harsh and thought she would fare better in the sanatorium.

'He hated to do this, and it may cost him his growing reputation from his other patients afflicted with a similar complaint since he was using Emily as an example of a cure for her malady, but he hesitates to say other, after the horrific scene he witnessed at the house.'

.

Chapter 10

ASYLUM

'They say, Glenda when they sent Emily down for the first time, it occurred to her where she was, and she falls into rants of insanity and delusional speech. She swore she lived with and loved this man and fell pregnant by this William, whom she now calls The Ripper.

In due course, her child, a boy she named Jasper, took his first breath in the asylum. So overcome with love for him, she found peace in her mind for a short while, and they let her keep her son with her.

One day, with her mind more settled and appearing lucid, she played and chatted with her child.

"Oh, my darling boy." Emily chuckled as her loving fingers stroked the infant under his chin and called, "Agnes, Agnes, where are you?" Emily is once again unaware of her true surroundings, which are in her cell. The mental institution is her home until the courts free her if they ever do. With her mind unbalanced and her delusions ripe, she believes she is in her own home with her baby and Agnes, her nurse and companion. Again, her cry rings, "Agnes, where are you?"

A warder enters the room and grins at Emily. She is fond of her and more so since the baby came. Emily is an easy inmate and doesn't give us any trouble now.

"Yes, Emily, what can I do for you?"

"I want you to witness something for me."

"What sort of thing is this, my lovely?"

"My Last Will."

"Oh, my, and what do you have to leave to anybody?"

"It's not for you to ask. I want you to witness my signature. Can you read and write? I am making sure of some security for my son."

"You are doing an excellent job. He is a fine boy."

The warder glanced at the child, kicking unaware in his crib. "The authorities are kind in letting you keep him here, so you remember to behave properly, my girl."

"I do recall the case. Thank you, Agnes."

"Now, Emily, please pay attention. I already told you; I am not she. Now, think Emily—I am Rose. I can put my cross next to your name, but no more."

"I have thought long enough. I want you to lodge this with a notary. My wishes are for a first-rate couple to adopt my beloved son, and he must never find out who his real parents are. It will be unbearable for him to reach adulthood with the stigma of having Jack the Ripper as a father and an insane murderess as a mother.'"

Rose, the warder, was a rare specimen of the times, one with empathy and sympathy who hated her job. She was an everyday dogsbody caught between a jailer and a cleaner. She tried her best to keep aloof from the piteous situations she dealt with. She kneeled before Emily, pity etched on her brow.

"Don't say such things, lovvy. You are not mad, you are ill, and you are doing so much better now the baby is here."

"I understand, but duty requires me to consider him while I am doing well. Please tell me you will take this note to Doctor Dawson and my maid, Agnes. Oh, you are Agnes." She suddenly pulls back and stares at Rose. "No, you are not, are you? You are my jailer. Am I deluded once more?" She sobs. "I am sorry, but can you deliver this to the doctor? He will appreciate what to do with my son. He has always treated me well since I was young. Am I still young, nurse? You are a nurse, aren't you?"

Rose sighs and says, "Yes, dear, don't worry. I will put this in the hands of the doctor myself, so don't you mither, and yes, you are young, as young as you want to be."

"I don't want to be too young; I didn't like it. Only with William was I happy and he's dead. It's a terrible shame because he never even saw our son. Somebody called Jack killed him." Emily sobs again.

Lifting the kicking boy from his wooden crib, the warder slips him into Emily's arms. "You cuddle this little chap, and I'll take your letter." She smiles as Emily turns her attention to the child, and Rose takes the document to the office, where the personal effects of the inmates are kept.

No doctor or maid will be waiting for Emily's

return; her mind is beyond redemption. Her so-called friends never set foot in the place to offer comfort from the day she arrived from the court, and none will.

Larry says, 'These are the last of Emily's words. I gleaned the rest from the clerks who took down the details of their mission and from police reports, Glen. So, bear with me.

'In earnest, Emily began to add to her journal for her son's sake when he is old enough to read, and yet she still assumed she lived in her home with Agnes. Often, she asked her to find a tutor for the boy. For a while, she called all the nurses Agnes, and they played along with her, negating the use of alcohol and restraints or the baths.

'In her cell, the staff took little heed of her rambling. Her insistence on the authorities to move Jasper into the doctor's charge was either dismissed or ignored. This gave a weary Emily the necessary impetus to begin the final tumble of the downward spiral into madness. Once again, they return to the resort of restraints and sedation.

'The administration ordered the destruction of any letters and the diary, but Rose thought it wrong. After glancing through them, she placed them with Emily's effects to make sure they would move with her son when they removed him from her care into the baby farm. His usefulness to the turnkeys was over. Emily is insane, and sanity will never again visit.

'Alas, in life, the twists and turns are constant. The baby spends the next four years of his childhood locked away in the district's workhouse, an institution where the workers are void of sentiment and rigid in routine.

'To say he was lonely and unloved is almost a contradiction. One could never be alone with up to four or five children in a bed and between ten and twenty in a small room. Unloved, yes, but only when he was removed from his mother, who had wrapped Jasper with her love.

Bribes in the penal system were commonplace, and the baby farm, attached to the workhouse, was no different.

Normal practice meant a member of the board of governors would liaise between the higher echelons of the aristocracy and the privileged class itself. A trusted citizen of the community and feasible to believe, intimate with the Matron, who helped to ease any inducements in which to line their own pockets through delegation and ample rewards. Donations. Larry starts to make air quotes with his fingers on either side of his head but remembers how Glenda scorned him.

Donations by the Regal and influential fathers, gentlemen of standing and wives, who were unable to account for the correct passage of time to produce a child when the father battled the oceans on sailing vessels at the time of the child's conception.

These anonymous pillars of society were never named when a significant contribution appeared. A go-between would sweep any such problems under the proverbial carpet.

On receipt of a proffered donation with anonymity guaranteed, if the amount is generous enough, a child could be lost with the greatest of ease in the labyrinth of their corrupt system.

Matron resided on the premises under the direct control of the governor. Her varied duties included the welfare of her workforce and the supervision of the whole female department. She looked after their moral conduct and assisted in teaching and supervising the dietary requirements of the very young and old.

Her priorities were to enforce the observance of establishment rules on the inmates.

Another task was to delegate and supervise any considerations on offer or favours of guilt, as those knowledgeable ones, or suspected ones, called them. These were often watered down and filtered by the devious members of the workforce. Most of them were uneducated. Some criminals, lots were drunks, and few were capable of caring. Anything from food to a gift they would snaffle, therefore, few reached the intended.

Unfortunately, children were the easiest prey as whipping boys for those judged by the hierarchy in this dreadful place, untouchable by agreement. The administering of corporal punishments, though against the rules, was no barrier for those black-hearted carers who resented being in that place as much as the inmates. They, though, received payment as a reward and took pleasure in the beating of Jasper and others like him, it was a favourite pastime.

'Emily departed not long after her child's removal, and some said, foaming at the mouth, though none would admit it when questioned. The last words she spoke, as a sane woman, to a person in the room were about a man detected only by her. She called him William, and as she conversed, her physique changed.

With an air of respectability, her voice was that of an educated woman, all fronted by a broad smile as she said. "I will be with you soon, I assure you, my darling. We can start again. I am so sorry, my love. I sent our son away. I'm sure it was for the best when I suggested the doctor look after his interests. But soon, we can guard him together."

So many tears rolled down her cheeks in this period of her life, and here was another as she sniffed before saying, "Forgive me, William. I know I ruined our lives, didn't I, but soon, beloved, I also know, we can be together and tend our son."

The incident unnerved the superstitious workers, who surmised that witnessing this extraordinary transformation would portend evil in their simple minds.

They swore a ghostly apparition walked around the room and described him as a man with a cape or, long coat and tall hat.

'In their self-perceived wisdom, the governors ordered the matron to discount tales, declaring, "We don't need ghost stories. Insanity is more than enough to cope with inside these walls." However, she was also fearful and didn't dare tell anyone about seeing a cloaked figure wandering the halls until much later.

'The administrators contacted Emily's family lawyer; the only contact given by the court. The parish authorities' primary concerns were to inaugurate a hunt for relatives to take charge of the funeral and collect her meagre possessions because if there was no one, the only choice was to surrender Emily's remains to a pauper's burial.

'A week later, a clerk arrived with the last will of one spinster of this parish, Emily Vincent. They found it in its original envelope in a box, among others, filed in the same manner at the office where Agnes lodged it.

After dusting them off, they learnt with some astonishment how wealthy she was, and yet with her vast wealth, she made only two personal bequests: To her maid, one Agnes Walpole, and the other to one Isaac Jameson, her former coach driver. The clerks searched for them to enable them to discharge their duties. They found no beneficiaries for any of the properties. Emily's instructions were plentiful regarding how to dispose of them, barring one, at the expense of the estate, and until further notice.

"A puzzling thing," they said, "for a dead woman to write."

'The investigation began and ended with Jameson, who succumbed to an influenza outbreak in January 1894. A terrible epidemic raged throughout the world. He left no heirs.

'They also tried to contact the doctor who stood for Emily in court, hoping he may know of Agnes' whereabouts. That search also proved fruitless, the doctor succumbed to Typhus in 1893 while visiting his family in Worthing, not long after appearing for Emily as a witness. The outbreak killed up to two hundred people. The headlines in the local newspaper reported: A sad ending for him, such a well-respected doctor.

Agnes recovered after suffering a breakdown following the dreadful scene she witnessed. She had moved to the country and was soon employed as a companion by a wealthy gentlewoman of sound mind and nobility.

One day, her employer asked her to take a parcel to the church fete. Agnes, who enjoyed walking, suddenly came to a staggering halt as a picture entered her head, she stared in fright at the brown envelope. Her eyes glanced at the immense Norman building, a place of religious worship, and her mouth dropped open.

This simple errand triggered the memory of the envelope she delivered for Emily, her previous charge, some years before. She staggered, losing her grip on the parcel and almost fell grabbing the church's iron railings to steady herself. Recovering, but pale and shaking, she hitched her skirt and ran most unladylike back to her Ladyship in absolute terror.

"No, I can't believe it," she cried, startling Lady Beatrice, sitting at her leisure in her favourite wicker chair and reading a book in the orangery.

"What is it? What is the matter, Agnes?" Beatrice stood, holding out her arms for her dearest friend to run into, all decorum and sense of position gone.

"What on earth has happened, what is wrong, my dear?" Genuine in her concern.

'Agnes, her staunch companion, had never acted this way before. She had told her about a traumatic ordeal she endured and the effects she suffered for a considerable while but never talked about it in detail.

After listening to her tale, Lady Beatrice urged her to make herself known to the local police, where, after scrutiny, they ascertained Agnes was a wanted woman. Solicitors had initiated a search for her as a beneficiary in Emily's will.

Questioned with the utmost vigour, Agnes still had symptoms of being traumatised by the scene and didn't want to relive the images flooding back. She also despaired because if Emily had never asked her to take her envelope, she might have stopped her before she murdered William, and then she wouldn't have to regret her weakness in dealing with the aftermath.

As Agnes retold the tragedy, it brought the horrors of that day back to her.

'However, the family lawyer denied ever receiving the document, and this troubled Agnes until she recalled it was not to him she took it but couldn't recall where she delivered the bulky envelope to.

Eager to help recall events, Agnes said, "Sir, how has the child fared?"

"What child is this?"

"Why, Emily's child. Oh no, don't tell me she lost the baby. Oh, poor Emily."

'Puzzled, the solicitor wiped his brow, he was not acquainted with the blessed event of any child. He flicked through his paperwork, hunting for a mention. What was he to do?

Leaning back in his well-worn leather-bound chair he tried to appear calm. "Erm, we have no record of a child. I think you are mistaken."

"How can that be possible? said Agnes. "Everyone involved must have known. The case was a sensation at the time. All knew of her condition, her pregnancy being the reason she escaped the Gallows."

'With inordinate urgency, the lawyer dispatched a clerk to attend all the remaining solicitors' offices in the area and not to come back empty-handed. Fortune favoured him as the letter materialised in an office on the high street.

The swing door opened on a boy who stood in a daze and was roused by the young clerk eager to start his search by clicking his fingers, startling him out of his world of imagination and dreams. The anxious clerk directed him to search, and the dozy assistant earned his eureka moment when he stumbled across the documents.

On returning to the office, the reading revealed a different side to Emily. Yes, Emily was a woman of substance, but why did they not have records of any child? Agnes reminded them of the uproar, but they believed that once the guilty verdict came in and Emily was incarcerated, no one bothered to check if she delivered the child.

At her age and with her state of mind, no one expected her to have a successful birthing. Regardless, if she did, the authorities said somebody must have paid fees to keep a child. Where would it be, except in the workhouse? The parish would not give a coin for one's upkeep if someone else had the funds to pay.

'In a dilemma as to what to do, the solicitors contemplated the legal options. Who would pay the administration fees for a child, and where were the records? Something was amiss.

The most reasonable recourse would be to launch another search, this time for the missing child. This also left unanswered questions, such as why the child's birth was not recorded. All anyone understood at the time was Emily may be lighter of a child.

The only record is the document Agnes delivered to a firm of solicitors. Apart from the two personal bequests, she bequeathed her entire estate to him or her. The lawyer's firm addressed the governors at the asylum with a strong letter demanding they question staff about the death of an inmate, Emily Vincent. They wanted to know; did she deliver a child, and if so, what about its whereabouts?

A reply came three days later, stating that only days before Emily's incarceration in the asylum, the daughter of the Matron back then grew concerned for her mother's safety and had reported her missing. The governors excused themselves saying that no written confirmation of Emily's admission was found. It was the Matron's job to record these events, and she perhaps hadn't done so being more concerned for her mother's whereabouts. They asked for patience while they sought information.

The law firm decided this must become a police concern and they questioned staff, not only regarding Matron, but they also required the details surrounding the death of Emily and her child.

'Don't forget, Glenda, it must be obvious; this isn't all written here. Having read these diaries so many times before I put them away, I can almost be a part of it all as it happens. So, bear with me.'

'I think you missed your calling, Larr. Never mind science; you ought to have gone on the stage.' She claps and settles in to listen as Larry picks up the tale.

'Police officers began their investigations by interviewing the former matron's family, convinced her disappearance was unusual, and how they feared harm might have befallen her. The eldest daughter, a mother herself, had sobbed, recounting the night her mother disappeared. She recalled the terrible events years before, when the most horrific murders plagued the city, and how her mother was last seen with a man near the entrance of an alleyway before stepping into a carriage and disappearing.

Inspector Reid from Whitechapel was drafted to supervise the case of Matron's disappearing mother. He drew a blank saying that someone must have seen something. But nothing was found.

He began to worry. What if this is a repeat of the past? The never-to-be-forgotten events when the serial killer named the Ripper haunted the streets. Then he began questioning the staff about Emily's admission into the asylum.

'With pertinent files collected, collated, and examined by the police and lawyers, nothing emerged until a warder overheard him saying they were searching for one Emily Vincent.

'It came about one morning when Rose was on her way to the Matron's office and she happened to overhear the new Matron, deny all knowledge of Emily when questioned by Inspector Reid.

"You must retain some memory, Matron. Not all your, shall we say clients, escape the gallows because of their condition."

"What condition?" Exasperated, the Matron cast him a withering glare. "I think you need a word with my assistant, Sister Lucy, she has been employed here these past ten years. She may recall. May I remind you that I am new here? Let me find her and if her duties permit I will send her to you."

'Matron left the room, and a startled Rose, listening unseen, scuttled off into the first opening to hide, leaving Inspector Reid to take advantage of the time she was gone. He rummaged through the drawers in Matron's desk until footsteps clumped along the stone floor. He stands away from the desk.

Matron arrived trailed by a stout woman with a

sour face and wearing the garb of a nun, a not-too-clean habit. His mind ran at a tangent—a long-term employee, probably bearing a grievance because she was overlooked in taking on the position of Matron.

"Sister, do you recall an inmate, one... what's the name again, Inspector?" asked the matron.

"Vincent, Emily Vincent, Matron, she was, I believe, in a delicate state."

"They are all in a delicate position," said Sister Lucy, with a grin, revealing black, rotten teeth. "Why d'ya think they're 'ere, and I can't remember the name of each inhabitant inside t'walls? Nor should I be expected to."

Reid thought, here's another uncouth northerner. Having problems with their policing abilities in the past, he suspected Sister Lucy, for all her outward appearance of piety and habit-wearing, may not cooperate, and he had no time to waste.

"Are you trying to be perverse, woman? I can bring in men, and we can go through all your records and find all your dirty little secrets and cause more havoc to this hellhole than already exists."

Surprised by the sheer intensity of his voice and embarrassed at her chastisement in front of Matron, Lucy shoulders past her new adversary and stops in front of a wall panel. With a grunt, she pushes a lever above an unlit fireplace. The wall slides open, and she reaches in to produce a considerable-sized register. Placing it on Matron's desk, she puffed with the weight, slapped her hand on the leather cover and laughed. "Yer can examine all ye want and hell's flames t'yer," before hightailing it out of the office.

Nobody kept exact records for several reasons, so, searching through them would reveal nothing. This was a common practice at the time. They were either in receipt of sufficient reward for not doing so, too busy or couldn't write.

After a futile search through the names and dates in the register, the inspector left the office. Hidden nearby in a doorway, Rose took her chance to chase the frustrated inspector heading to the door. She called to him, "Mister." He either didn't hear or chose to ignore her.

"MISTER."

'Alarmed, he spun around. After all, he is in a nuthouse, and who knew who was behind you?

"What do you want?" Reid backed away a step, but she had a kindly face and wore a wraparound uniform, with an apron but whiter than most on view. "Are you one of the warders?"

"Yes. Are you looking for Emily?"

"What makes you ask?" said Reid.

"I overheard you. I was walking past. Honest, mister, you mentioned the name Emily, and we don't have many Emily's in here, so it stuck in me mind."

"What is the family name of this Emily you talk of?"

"She called herself Emily Warren, but Warren was not her real name. I wer' told by the others that she just took it on. I think it wer the gobshite's name, the one who left her in the club."

'Reid peers through the central doorway at the clerk, who travelled with him but feared entering the building. Reid told him to remain where he was, but now he gestured for him to approach, and as he did, he snatched the clerk's document bag.

"Hang on, Inspector. What are you doing?"

"Where are those damn papers? The committal ones, I want them now."

The clerk dug them out and handed them over, appearing embarrassed as the inspector shuffled through them. The name Warren rang a bell. He found the documents and began to read: On this day of our Lord, 13, April 1893, Emily Vincent, spinster of this parish, is committed, at her Majesty's pleasure, for the unlawful killing of one William Warren.

Ecstatic, Reid shoves the papers into the clerk's face with a laugh. The search may be at an end for Emily. "Hey, I think this is what we are after."

The clerk needed to pee, his feet ached, and his mouth was drier than an Arab's flip-flop in the desert, was hoping this woman knew of her and asked, "May I?"

Reid nodded while the clerk studied the document. Reid turned to Rose. "Did this Emily Warren bear a child?" He waited.

She twiddled her thumbs. "Yes," she said. "She delivered the child in here."

"Did it live?"

"Yes, a boy."

"Here in this place, she kept the child here." His unkempt eyebrows, more like a monobrow, separate as surprise registers on his face. Rose glanced behind to scan the corridor and make sure nobody could overhear. She may lose her job, and she had a family to keep since her husband brought them up from down south and then ran off, leaving her with three little mouths to feed and not for the first time. Why she let him back is a mystery. Will she never learn? "Ssh, don't tell, mister. It's more than me life's worth. Sometimes, if things keep 'em quiet, we leave 'em be, because anything making our job easier is welcome. When she birthed him, she wer' a different person altogether. No issues at all, so we let the babe stay with her."

"Him—a boy?"

"Aye, that's what 'him' means."

"Where is it, err, he?"

"Well, she got 'erself in a screw after a while, and we couldn't pacify 'er, so the baby went where they all go, to the baby farm. Emily thought she was a nob with money. She wanted him adopted out, but he ended up in the farm, though, he may be dead now. Terrible places they are."

"Are you sure about this?"

The clerk intervenes. He fidgets; the need to pee is urgent. His irritation at waiting was evident to the Inspector and the empathetic warder, who were close to discovery but not close enough.

"Yes, mister. I'm sure she is the same person and a

wonderful mother. At least for the short while, she wer' sane, but she committed a dreadful crime. Is she the one?"

"Yes, my God, woman. That's her, I swear. Where is this baby farm and the birth certificate?"

"Oh Lordy, don't ask me to say more, I dare not."

Reid thrust his hand into his waistcoat pocket, pulled out a shilling, and mused. She's done him a huge service, well worthy of a coin. He hands it over. Making sure no one was watching before she snatched the coin from his palm, pleading, "You won't tell on me, will ya, mister?"

"If we need you to swear to this in court, will you do so?"

"Eeh, no, I'm orf. Don't you tell, mister, I don't want to lose me job." She scampered off, slipping the coin into the pouch in her apron and tapping it with reverence.'

For all her protestations and promises to keep shtum, Glenda interrupts, 'Hang on, Larry, is this THE inspector Reid? The real one, the one on the telly in Ripper Street?'

'Well, he's not fake, unlike him.'

'And you are recounting the story of a child, your great-grandfather, or whatever you reckon. The one born in an asylum to a madwoman and Jack the Ripper.'

'How eloquent you are at putting things, dear, and yes, I am indeed betraying the truth.'

'But hang on...'

'What?'

'You are... no.'

The realisation is almost too much for Glenda to take in. The ramifications compound and begin to give her doubts about sitting in an old house with a descendant of a monstrous murderer beside her. She shudders, and Larry, who cannot stop his lip from lifting in a supercilious smirk, carries on.

'The men resume their work in their respective offices' triumphant. Reid said, "So we should consider the ramblings of a so-called madwoman and not be so quick to dismiss them in the future."

Chapter 11

JASPER

Each morning, on waking in the baby farm, a building attached to the workhouse proper, Jasper finds himself squashed under the fleshless arms, legs, and bodies of his fellow inmates who share the same bed. The reek of stale urine doesn't trouble him, with not understanding any differently, and being too young to remember when he arrived in the place he calls home.

The boy is almost five years old and has no idea what a mother and father are, and the accounts of certain inmates make him believe he is better off without them.

The room he inhabits measures ten feet by fifteen and houses up to twenty young children, but only five straw-filled mattresses and one single iron–framed bed. The number of children in the room changes daily for various whims.'

Night staff consisted of individuals with little to no experience, drunks and mothers desperate to earn money, or trainees available to take up the role. Their responsibilities included preparing ailing or weak children for burial or transportation to the mortuary if they believed they might not survive the night. Even in death, they treat the children as unwanted trash.

The staff slept if the night was quiet, or sometimes they would disappear and reappear before the start of the next working day, often smelling of booze. The first task in the morning was to empty the slop bucket kept in the corner and used by the older children and the staff member if they chose to spend the night there.

Except in the most inclement weather, the high barred windows in the wall close to the ceiling remain open day and night but are inaccessible for viewing. Even so, the fusty, stagnant air sits heavy with no circulation to stir the stale atmosphere of the cell-like room. The children are never let out of the room for exercise or fresh air that is, not until they are moved to the workhouse proper.

Jasper grows into a clever and sturdy little chap, skilled at taking food, if it can be called food. Watered oats for breakfast and maybe a thin vegetable broth for dinner with dried bread in between. Twice weekly, low–quality meat was added to the broth, and he learnt to take it from those incapable of fending for themselves. He sleeps in the nurse's empty bed when she decides not to turn in. If caught, he took his fair share of punishment without complaint or tears.'

Punishments, including a stroke of the cane, often called the stinger or tickler, or being forced to drag the slop bucket to the nearest pickup point in the hall to be collected by the adult inmates to empty. Woe betide them if any was spilt on the floor. Either penalty and more were dished out without feeling, as though normal for a child under seven to deal with.

Even though Jasper detests this task, in one way he doesn't mind because it gives him the chance to leave the room. Also, as he struggles, he sometimes sees a woman in bizarre clothing watching him while he tries not to splash the filth over him. He often looks for this woman because she always flashes a smile his way, but, always on his second glance, she is gone; she vanishes. He sensed comfort in the smile and assumed she was only in his head. He desperately needed some comfort.

'Bear in mind, Glenda, all this was in breach of the Child Act of 1834, wherein the workhouse and baby farm: No child under twelve should receive the cane, except by the schoolmaster.'

The beatings were more applicable to the newcomers than the resident children, who were well-versed in keeping quiet. They developed various skills to avoid unwanted attention from the carers, a misnomer if ever there was one.

New admissions, who, for whatever reason, still clung to cherished memories of mothers and fathers, were the ones least equipped to understand how things altered so much. They longed for the old days, regardless of how dire their lot was before.

Those born or deposited soon after their, as a rule, unwelcome births didn't expect anything but maltreatment. The Draconian baby farm was a place that conditioned them. At seven years old, when they moved the surviving children to the workhouse proper, their labours compounded in intensity and were unrewarded for the most, but they settled in with less fuss.

Children such as Jasper, born in the confines of the workhouse system, where the chain of utter despair and depression linked the asylum, baby farm, and children's homes together, were uncared for. In such cases where the children are alone in this world, those whose parents were dead, unfit, in prison, or insane, including drunkards, were made the legal guardians of the board of governors. This left the lives and livelihoods of the majority, held and manipulated by the hands of said guardians, to dispose of as they wished, rented out for work and sometimes sold.

Not a day went by without the nurses sneering at the likes of Jasper and his ilk. They relished the joy of reminding them of their base-born beginnings. Jasper, a little bastard born of a madwoman, could only contemplate existence in the workhouse.

The familiar cry to each one singled out for torment, derision and coerced into a chore or act against their will was, "You won't never leave here, boy," dogged by verbal threats of, "They will sell you off to some foul tobacco-chewing fiddler, and if he gets bored with you, you will be back here and slapped in the army to repay your keep."

Most revelled with sadistic delight in tormenting children to ease the monotony of their days. They impressed on those such as Jasper, considering their breeding and himself, born of an insane murderess, that he would amount to nothing all his life. They all faced transfer to the workhouse, which would happen aged seven, where they could be farmed out to work.

Doubting anywhere would be worse than where they were, Jasper anticipated going if he survived the horrors of the baby farm. One day, in his innocence, Jasper asked a nurse, "What's a bastard?"

She rewarded him by snatching him by his ear and washing his mouth out with a block of brown carbolic soap. Later, the same day, she swished him with a bunch of stinging nettles to remind him of his place and her power.

This was a common punishment from the heartless nurses wise enough not to physically brutalise their charges and leave identifying bruises in evidence.

Intent on not crying as the nettles stung his back and legs, a woman in the corner caught his eye. Fashion meant nothing to him; even so, her clothes appeared rather outlandish. Her rosy cheeks were wet. Was it for him she cried for? He hoped so.

On inspection days, which were a duty, rather than to unearth anything underhand, if they ever observed the rashes, the staff blamed them on the ever-present lice. They also savoured the delight of knowing that an order to scrub down the hapless lads, their skin already aflame from the stinging leaves, would follow. The boys dreaded the rash and tried hard to conceal it with the scant clothing they wore, fearing what would come next—the stripping and the freezing tub with the carbolic and scrubbing brushes.

One morning, stretching his arms and fingers with his back arched and groaning, after another cramped, lousy night, the horror of a new day dawned on Jasper as he climbed from the mattress resembling a battlefield, with eight other arms and legs akimbo. A wet patch was visible on his nightshirt. He's not to blame; even so, he will make sure enough bodies are between him and the bedwetter next time. What did he do to deserve this? This question often tormented him.

Dulled eyes in small, encaged faces turned in anticipation toward the direction of the noise of keys grating in the lock of the ironclad wooden door. Their curiosity is instant as the door swings inward, grating on worn hinges. Something is happening. Those bored ceased to pull out their hair, and the fitful became alert because this was new and exciting.

One day they may get a glimpse outside their prison, where they sit cooped up like unloved pigeons, who due to the lack of nourishment and nurture would never win a race and left to wither in confinement were too feeble to overcome the monotony of their daily regimes.

On this memorable morning, an unfamiliar nurse entered. Her hard features, tangled, greasy hair and swollen lips seemed more fitting for a failed boxer. She drew in deep on a clay pipe gripped between her teeth. A cloud of foul smoke billowed in her wake as she walked.

As small, stout, sallow looking, well-dressed man carrying a case and trying to ward off the fetidness of the airless room by holding a handkerchief spotted with a tincture of garlic to his face for protection from the unsavoury odours, was swamped in her smoke trail.

"Him," said the nurse, pointing at Jasper. The boy feared he had somehow broken another unknown yet stringent rule and was terrified she would spot his pee-stained nightshirt, and he backed against the wall.

"My God, woman, don't you ever bathe these children or wash them down?" The man's eyes raked around the crowded room, wrinkling his nose in disgust.

"It's early yet; yer shud come later if you want 'em bathed, an' I mean later in the month, ha ha ha."

'The youngest of the nine surrounding children whimpered for attention. One, a sickly toddler and not expected to last the week. At least after his demise, they would gain more room for a short while before another took his place.

"Clean and feed him. His new governess will collect him later." Said the man, frantic to leave, he shook his finger at Jasper. "Remember," he said, "He is the heir to a sizable fortune, including properties, so make sure he doesn't take any unwanted guests. I am placing him in your personal charge, so don't make any mistakes."

He wriggled in his jacket and began to scratch his neck. The thought of lice upset him and made his skin crawl. Post haste, he left the room, pulling his collar high, afraid the beasties could jump. Surprised, the hard-faced nurse's eyes swept over the boy, still with his back against the wall, and drawled venomously,

"Well, what's he doing here then?"

The man didn't bother with the courtesy of facing her when he said, "None of your flaming business just make sure he is clean when the time comes."

Prompt at 4 o'clock on the same afternoon, a tall woman, wearing a dark blue gabardine dress, her attire clinical except for an over-large white, wide-brimmed headpiece acting as a shining nimbus to her coarse features and repugnant face, presented herself ready to collect the boy. While apprehensive about moving from his only known home, Jasper looked forward to learning about and experiencing the world outside.

Scrubbed till he gleamed, picked over, and fed, which consisted of a double portion of the skilly and toke, watery porridge, and dry bread for breakfast. No lunch would be forthcoming. Jasper was dressed in the workhouse uniform used for inspection days.

The charge nurse released the boy into the care of the starched woman in blue, who, without a glance, walked away, expecting him to tag on behind. The same woman had interviewed and engaged a couple, Jasper's new housekeeper and tutor, sanctioned by the lawyers and provided by his estate, the one he will inherit on his majority.

The woman in blue positioned her headgear back in place after it escaped from her pin. She liked the brim to hide her face—one only a mother would love. She couldn't give a flying fig for the boy; her jealousy was too hot. Why should this brat have the lot while she was doing the bidding of others? She considered she chose his guardians well. The woman, nothing less than a lady of the night and the man her bawd. An educated yet failed tutor, and a drunk.

She met them at the bawdy house where she once worked, not as a prostitute but as protection for the woman. No one wanted her for any release. This job in the social care system was a blessing. She dressed the couple in decent garb and thought how well they scrubbed up and could pass for an upstanding couple ready to raise a young heir to a fortune, and she would take her cut.

From being the bastard urchin son of an insane murderess and a murderer, Jasper overnight gained a certain stature as the next of kin of a wealthy woman.

The letters and journal saved for him by Rose were delivered to a lawyer via the police station, who seized them for investigation with Emily's other belongings. They briefly glanced through, deciding nothing of importance, and passed them on to her family solicitor, who agreed to hand them to the boy in person, per Emily's written instructions.

The lawyers themselves needed to make a favourable impression on the boy, who, regardless, may take matters further about his abandonment in the baby farm, if someone urged him to do so. To avoid this, the notary must hand them to the lad in person when he was home and settled.

They took him to this house on Union Street, this

one, Glenda. The street's name was changed in the early 1900s. This is the one his mother valued and wherein his perceived fortune lay, and yet in a short time, he would spend the rest of his miserable childhood wishing to return inside the walls of the farm, where one expected nothing and received nothing except punishment, a status quo he didn't think he would miss.

Jasper never thought he would miss the toke and skilly or the sore–ridden skin of other bodies pressed against him for warmth and comfort. It's in this house that confusion reigned with his ill-treatment. Not knowing from one day to the next which rule would apply, each designed to break him.

At first, his life transformed beyond recognition. He lived in disbelief at the choice of plentiful and delicious food, laundered clothing, and warm water, which delighted his young skin as he washed. He wouldn't allow either the housekeeper or tutor to wash him. He loved to feel his clean hair, which began to grow in abundance, and his body cleared from his many sores.

Life touched on bewildering for him. Visitors from the solicitor's office came to call sometimes without warning. Jasper soon learned of his housekeeper's sudden transformations if she expected them at the door. All the airs and graces of a faux lady came to the fore, and she afforded him such kindness, which he found disconcerting.

His tutor practised the same duplicity. His duties

were to educate and teach him to become a gentleman, and he stood as a prime example of etiquette, bringing a smile of satisfaction to the visitors, who would leave believing all was well, but things were not well when they were alone.

On the solicitor's final check-in, he delivered the chest holding all of Emily's letters and diaries. The housekeeper tried to take them, but the solicitor ignored her grasping hands and handed them to Jasper, stressing the importance of the contents, saying, "Your mother's wish was that I give you her notes and writings to keep safe for all time, so she can believe she is close to you, and in time you will come to regard her in the same way as she did you, with great love and affection."

Jasper, who had never owned anything before, kept this treasure to store by his side. No one read Emily's words to her son. Those who had skimmed through found nothing worthy of investigation. No one grasped the full significance which he learnt and digested over time as his reading improved. The only task his guardian was to fulfil and although basic, Jasper's ability to grasp the fundamentals of English was quick.

After filling out legal requirements, the notary, mindful that all was well and with the foundation of his guardianship laid, left with the idea that the boy seemed content and happy. Satisfied, he allowed them to continue their lives together without interruption.

The housekeeper then turned true to form. She was

nothing more than a drunken fishwife with none too fussy morals. Men visited the house. Foul-mouthed brutes who warned him. "You open your mouth, boy, and we'll do for you."

This new life was a learning curve and Jasper regressed into a lonely and scared child. He never bargained on the terror alone in the dark and longing for the human contact of his companions in his bed. Even though most nights he had slept between urine-stained, stinking sheets, the small arms and legs of his companions wrapped around him had brought comfort and warmth.

He began to dote on his mother's letters and read them often because they demonstrated the extent of her feelings. They fed him snippets of belief, like, when offered, he only needed to reach out and embrace love, but from where he brooded in his dark, lonely room. Jasper already adored his mother with an all-consuming passion from her diaries, which became the only source of comfort in a room where he longed for company.

One day, he fished out a piece of paper tucked in one of the diary's covers behind a piece of the lining that had worked loose with the many times he handled it. A curious note, written by a mad woman, said that his father was Jack the Ripper, an unknown man. This intrigued him more each day and set him on a mission to discover more.

Emily had written the letter as a will, which she asked the warder to sign, but neither signed, dated, nor witnessed it. This was the one Rose did not destroy when instructed to by the administration. It said Emily wanted them to find Jasper a home, but his parentage must never be disclosed.

The message was not meant for his young eyes, and it hurt him badly until, during his tender years, he grew to understand he was not meant to find out from where he sprang. So, the question arose: Why did his mother write the letters and diary to help him unravel his beginnings?

'This is something that puzzles me still, Glenda. It seems contrary because if Emily wanted to keep our ancestry from us, why did she write everything down, and I mean everything?' Glenda shrugged, and Larry continued.

'These diaries Jasper treasured more each year, and as his understanding matured, loneliness festered, and he kept them to himself, unlike the books in his extensive library, which included his favourite, well-thumbed one, Bradshaw's Handbook on Railways. A book that released his desire to escape and travel, yet it did not stir his heart as his mother's words.

After years alone with threats and crying each night before sleep, he began to think he was losing his mind the night a woman materialised in his room. She came on the night he was suffering after a severe beating.

He wondered if he knocked his head like he did in the baby farm when sometimes he upset a nurse and she would bang his head on the wall or throw him to the floor, and his senses emerged disturbed. He even laughed at his musings—a melancholy, mirthless sound. Disturbed, yes, he'd agree, but the woman was somehow familiar.

This same woman began to return night after night, and one night she came in the company of a man dressed in a long cloak and a tall hat. They talked to him and soothed him; he didn't care if they were real or not. When they said they were his parents, he accepted this as fact and when they assured him they would protect him, he thanked them.

The boy made a huge mistake in telling the housekeeper of the visitations. He doesn't remember why, guessing it may be a foolish thing to do, but he wanted a reaction, which he got. She beat him severely and locked him in a brush cupboard, bruised and hungry with the words, "You are insane. You are as crazy as your mother, but I'll cure you and knock Beelzebub out of you, albeit I die trying," ringing in his ears. She called her husband to thrash the lies, the devil, and the madness from him. He set about the task with relish. The boy learnt to keep quiet and the only people he talked to were the ghostlike apparitions of his father, William, and his mother, Emily.'

Larry is lost deep within the tale and senses a kinship, which sends shivers down his spine. Yet he fears the consequences if his analysis isn't finished in time. Glenda's voice reaches him. 'Let's go, Larr. This is reading more and more like a horror story.'

He laughs, ignores the plea to leave and continues.

'Don't you understand yet, Glen? Emily killed my great-great-grandfather, Jack the Ripper.'

'I don't understand, no. What are you saying?'

'Same old problem, Luv, you never catch on. You seem unable to grasp even the simplest of statements. You have made my life hell these past few months and this morning you went too far. You destroyed my filing system, which will take an age to systematise. You implied you needed to dig into my past, so now you will heed me for a change.'

'What!'

He cuts her protest off with a snarl and pauses, glaring at her before beginning again. 'Grandmother Emily was a wealthy woman.' His voice sounds full of pride but his face. is expressionless.

'They visited Jasper each night, and he begged them to help and take him away, saying he wanted to join them, but they only comforted him with their presence until the day he turned fifteen. This birthday, in one way, was no different from others. No one presented him with gifts or celebrated them. Even if they had, it came at his expense. It also reminded his guardians that only twelve months would pass before he reached sixteen.

They often discussed what would happen then because, as stated in Emily's will, their charge would take responsibility for his essentials as well as his staff and education would be for him to decide. Although, responsibility for his finances would not be his until he reached twenty-one.

Each year became a significant source of unease for the couple. Left to their own devices and living well over the years, they planned how to treat their charge. Should they ease up and befriend the boy, or tighten their regime giving him no opening to say anything?

A third option was available, but, they had not reached such depravity yet, it was still a consideration.

Another concern on the horizon was the solicitors, who would start poking their legal noses in the pie once more when the need came to explain the options available to Jasper.

Three months after his birthday, and even with his accumulated wealth, Jasper still had to ask for every penny for his personal needs, and he needed a shaving kit. One morning, he rubbed his forefinger and thumb around his chin, annoyed at the growing fuzz. He sensed being half-boy and half-man and disliked it.

Before this, when he had to leave the house, his tutor, who throughout the previous years groomed the teenager with a mindset of control and fear, took him out. This time, to his surprise, believing he had trained Jasper not to divulge anything about his care fearing the worst if he did, he said he may go out to buy a razor, adding, "You better go to the barber for lessons before you try a straight edge around those baby cheeks."

His tone was mocking when he grabbed the boy's chin. Jasper jerked away. An angry leer followed, allowing Jasper a moment to focus, had he misheard?

Going out by oneself was unheard of, but he took the opportunity. He asked for money, which the tutor doled out by placing coins in a purse with misgivings asking for an account of all spending for the day when he returned.

Jasper left the house with, "And keep your mouth shut, Master," following him, chased by a rollicking laugh.

Standing on the street before his home, a hitherto unknown euphoria overcame him; he was free. A gentle breeze brushed against his face and neck enveloping him in a refreshing calmness as the late summer sun peeped over the rooftops.

He headed off towards the sound of the whistles, which often tugged him to the bedroom window that commanded a view of the pillars of smoke as they puffed from the tall chimney to pollute the sky. Each one that powers away offers hope, escape is possible.

'Once on the platform, the sheer magnitude of the engine facing Jasper captivated him. The iron monster pulsated like a beast at rest, waiting for the pressure to build and drive the gigantic wheels towering above him forward.

Before this, when he was taken out for any necessary appointments, Jasper never absorbed any of his surroundings. His guardian hurried him along, and he kept his eyes downcast, with no time to take in and enjoy the sights. The thought of the awesome thrust needed to power those enormous wheels overawed him, and the horsepower of the massive machine and boiler bellowing out volumes of steam so powerful he could walk through and bathe in thrilled him. When he breathed in the intense, oil-laden aroma it was now all new.

He only wakes from his musings when a platform porter urges him on saying, "You better climb aboard son, and hold the carriage door open for him to step in." The kindly voice roused him out of his reverie. A guard at the rear of the train waved his flag and blew a whistle as he leapt onboard, his signal to the driver to set the fire-eating monster in motion.

Relishing his own company, Jasper waits to arrive at Cannon Street Station. This, he understood from studying his book, was the required stop. The train chugged across the sinister, torpid, stinking Thames as he gawped through the window.

Where the smoke avalanche from the buildings lining the riverbank broke in the breeze, as the train crossed the bridge, it offered some exciting glimpses of the huge spreading city.

Thrilled with the excursion, Jasper forgoes the purpose of his outing, and instead of catching the next steam engine back, he rides north, hoping his coins will last. On departing from the station, he walks a while, basking in independence, before riding again until he reaches Camden Town. Next, he went to Kings Cross and took notes of the stations he visited to compare with those in his book.

September 12, 1907, proves a defining time for the young man, a crossroads in life.

He loved the railway and realised how far he travelled in such a short time. He dreamt of the day he could do so without resistance from anyone. He was dying for his freedom and yearning for his majority to take ownership of his life.

This freedom, due at age twenty-one, would open a sample of life never experienced, but he hungered for more. His heart set on his sixteenth birthday when a range of duties would pass to him. He planned to persuade the solicitors to give him full autonomy. For now, he plays their game. His governess and her man think they are winning by grinding down his will and forming him into a fearful puppet to dance in whatever direction they pull his strings.

Jasper's mind is unburdened for the first time, and he revels in the world passing by. A blink of light like a beam hits him and drags his eyes to the barbershop window, stopping him. Displayed in the window, encased in an open box and fitting snugly in its moulded tray, is an ivory-handled straight razor whose lustre appears to glow and spawns previously unfelt emotions. This is the image in his head as his beard annoyed him. It fits the picture perfectly, and he must own it. He was about to walk in when a female, ready to pass him, made it her purpose to brush against him.

He glanced, and she smiled, but the thought of a hair-free chin was far more appealing than a woman making cow eyes at him.

A ginger-haired, rotund barber poked his head from behind a curtain. "Good morning to you, young sir. What can I be doing for you, this fine day? Is it a shave you'll be wanting?" His pleasant Irish twang sounded reassuring. Jasper fingered his cheeks, hating the growth, yet the cordial greeting induced him to relax.

"Yes, and a trim. I would also like to purchase one of your best razors—the one in the window if you please."

"Righty-ho there, sir."

Jasper puffed out his chest, noticing the pronoun young, dropped.

"May I enquire of you if this is the first shave? If so, a little instruction will not be amiss." He chuckled to himself. "Now, hark at me, tripping mesen up with me manners. I apologise. Do you have a father or?" his eyes take in the well-dressed teenager. "A valet to show you the ropes if you are inclined to shave with your purchase?" He retrieved the box from the window. "This is the most expensive one in the shop, sir, and begging your pardon for me mentioning, I trust you can pay."

Jasper examines the prize, and on the face of the blade read, Sheffield Steel, Rodgers and Sons, Cutlers to Their Majesties. The cutthroat lay across his palm, well-balanced in his hand. He closed it on the pivot, then flicked it open, hooking his little finger around the hook tail as he studied the workmanship. Now he will learn how to manage it.

"A shave first, and if you please with this?" Jasper passed the razor back to the eager hands of the expert.

"Aye, well, sir. The first thing to do is give the steel a proper stroppin'."

Taking a leather strip from the wall, he swipes the razor across it several times. "You'll be needing one of these and the brush, sir. The boy will make up a pack for you. Now lend me your ear and remember to pay the greatest attention. You don't want to damage them fair features you have." He grinned, showing a gap from where he lost a tooth.

"Make sure to keep the edge well-honed," he said, treating Jasper with the utmost respect. "Now what we do first is use a nice hot towel to soften them bristles and open the pores, or if you prefer, we can just use soap."

Taking a badger brush with an ivory stock, he filled it by swirling the soft bristles in a soap dish. A youth with a face covered in pimples stepped from behind a curtain, carrying a tray with steaming towels, and guided Jasper to a chair.

"Erm, what do you suggest?" Jasper thumbs his chin.

"I think the hot towels for your first time, and if I may say, you will enjoy the sensation."

'The shave is a sexual experience for him, from the towel to the swift slide of the razorblade across his face, with alternate hot and cold towels swaddling his cheeks. He's intent on the barber's instructions and to stop his mind from returning to his washroom discoveries. The barber stresses him to take extra care on his first attempt.'

Glenda can't help commenting. 'The dirty little wanker.'

'Shut it, Glenda. It's acceptable behaviour, these days.'

'What's that mean?'

'Please! You will find out if you just shut it. Now where was I, oh yes, with the barber?

"Be careful." He says, forgetting his position as he polishes the blade with his apron and places the razor in a leather pouch, which he passed to Jasper, indicating to the assistant to hand over the package. This time, staring hard and in a solemn voice, 'Will you be paying now, sir, or do you have an account it will go on?'

'Handing over his purse, he tells the barber to take the required money. Confused, he does so. A smile of approval creased his face.

"A good day to you, sir." He said handing the purse back.

"I expect we shall have the pleasure of your company again." He flashed a smile, but his appeal in the young lad, who had paid, diverted as another customer entered the shop.

'For an inexplicable reason, as he fingered the pouch containing his purchase, stories of his father, William, come back to him. Was he Jack, and if so, did Jack the Ripper's blood flow through his veins?

'The thought excited him as well as nauseated him. Not a father to be proud of, but Jasper, from old newspapers, read all he found about the murders. They fascinated him. What if the story was true?

Engrossed in his reflections, he didn't even notice the woman who pressed into him on his entry to the barber's shop, or her approach him, not until she spoke. Her voice held a pleasant, lyrical lilt, which made him smile.

"Ha, now thee is a handsome specimen of a man, now the peach fuzz is all gone, and are ya old enough to use ya weapon?' He peered at the pouch, fingering the outline of the razor, but she pointed at his manhood, not what he held in his hand. He flushed, his naivety evident, but undeterred and unashamed when she had the gall to take him by the hand; he didn't resist.'

"Come on, ducks, I'll show you how to use it if you have a coin for my time."

A wry smile reaches Larry's lips. 'Who would think it, hey? Not yet sixteen, lucky sod.'

Glenda, unimpressed, interrupts him. 'Larry, what's going on, please? Are you sure about all this, and what's it to do with you and us?'

'I will reveal all soon, Glenda. Be patient.' His voice is that of a storyteller relating his tale.

'The boy had inherited not only his mother's belongings and property but also her love of writing, and he kept a diary with his thoughts, wishes and accomplishments written in it. His only companion, apart from a couple of cherished books he dug out. Oh, and his ghostly parents.

He writes about the day a woman named Phyllis,

older than him, and experienced. Funny name, Phyllis; don't you think Glenda; why would anyone saddle a child with it? She led him to a room situated in a tenement, all hush-hush. He jotted down, "When she touched me, blood raced through my veins."

"You're so young. For another coin, I'll be your teacher." She began to fondle him. His instincts took over; he knew what to do as the warmth of her body accepted his manhood, and he surged into the depths of regions hitherto unknown to him. The sensation set him on fire, a primal need to cry out burnt within. Her face showed no reaction, disappointing him when he was in paradise.

With her skin the paleness of light-coloured stone, he was in ecstasy when, to his horror, her face transformed into that of his mother, who smiled and left. Emily's face transformed into his father's, who mimed sliding his finger across his throat, a deliberate act.

His eyes dilated to pinpricks; a sense of glee filled the room, and a glint of mischief passed between them as he gestured his approval to his son before fading away. Jasper almost lost momentum as he cried out, and a moment later rolled away. Not a word spoken, nothing! Phyllis wriggled to the edge of the bed and gave him an account of his effort.

"That's better, ain't it, love. We'll make a man of ya yet. You can kiss goodbye to your boyhood now, can't you, me little cock-sparrow. Now thee's had thee pearly shower with a woman and not in no jerking session. Don't distress yersen. I ain't suffering from any of Venus's curses. Now my lovely, now you understand what to do, you'll do better next time."

With her back facing him she began to readjust her clothing before placing one hand on the bed and shifting.

The small amount of light penetrating the dingy bedroom, from the dirty window with ragged curtains, caught the tip of her nose. She waited with her palm outstretched demanding payment. Grunting, he knelt on the bed behind her, reached for his long coat, which he threw on the footboard, and fingered in the pocket for his new razor. Phyllis turned her back and continued to dress.

The crude remark regarding his premature ejaculation began to rankle him. What is she? Nothing but street trash. A slut. He was willing, yes, but his virginity was gone. He didn't want it to be like this. Oh yes, a most pleasurable experience—one to repeat. But he felt dirty, and this is when the crossroads came before him, but with no signposts available to help.

The path he chose would stamp him forever, and beyond any doubt, it came to him in his bones—he was Jack's son, the one William so dreaded having, and he was here to step into his father's footsteps.

The odour of her assaulted his nostrils, the rancid room she dragged her clients to, now seemed seedy as he turned and grabbed her by the long tresses of greasy hair and pulled her head back, slicing across her oesophagus in one sweep of the razor-sitting so sweet in his hand.

'Halted in his work with surprise, she died quicker than he thought she would. He laid her back in the prone position on the bed, one he believed she was well acquainted with. He sat for a while. Placing his head in his hands, he felt the sticky blood on his cheeks. Jasper gazed at his palms, red with the whore's blood. How dare she bleed on him?

Anger welled in him as he began to slash the bed, ransacking the room and spilling cheap trinkets on the floor. Kneeling to examine the baubles, he spotted a box under the bed. Intrigued, he opened it. Inside, he found a collection of postcards. Sneering, he leered at the blood-soaked bed.

"Ha," he said aloud. "So, you liked these well enough to save them and all signed by different people. Oh, my little whore, you can have twice as many now," and he sliced them in half, completing the dulling of his new shaver.

He lifted the ewer of water from inside the cracked bowl, which contained only enough to rinse his hands and arms. He used the towel, hung on a rusty nail, which left a zigzag crack across the wall, to wipe his face, neck, and hands clear of splatter. When satisfied, he left without a backward glance.'

Foremost in his mind, besides cleaning his body and mind, was remembering to strop his new razor before passing the blade over his chin again.'

'Wow, Larry, your family is right dysfunctional. Did they arrest him or what?'

'He wrote, "My virgin blade sliced the whore's throat easy, and with the minimum of effort on my part, I enjoyed it but lacked the courage to finish the job. I didn't relish spending more time mutilating the body as my father would, and I don't think I ever would, but with this, I have satisfied a hunger within me, and I departed the mayhem as a man. I showed her."

Later the same night, Jasper's parents visited him. Emily was upset, and learning what happened, made him swear to fight the urge. He must tell them, and they will smooth the way. She didn't want him to be Jack's son; she longed for him to be William's boy.

With her reproaches, his remorse was genuine, not for what he did but for upsetting his grandmother, and he promised not to do anything like it again. But she didn't say which urge he must fight, and he took it to mean no women.

His urge for blood lasted, pulling at him, the colour so vibrant, the odour earthy, but his oath pricked his conscience. He played back the scene of Phyllis in his head and the euphoria and power he experienced as the blade sliced her flesh and tempted him, taunting him to repeat the act. His promise irked him.

A few weeks later, after a beating about the head by his tutor for a minor infringement, he stole back to his room and grieved his lack of years. His thumb stroked his smarting cheek, where his stubble rasped against his soft touch. Taking out his razor, he played with it, being quite adept at shaving now. On impulse, he slashed his forearm. A sense of power surged through him, and he indulged in often, learning how to measure the depth of each cut.

Becoming accustomed to the pain, he gained a perverse yet exquisite sense of power in the execution of his self-harm. His scarred arms appeared masculine to him, and he continued until three weeks before his sixteenth birthday.

On this night, his tutor, along with two brutish men who called on his housekeeper, beat him within an inch of his life. They said they would kill him if he attempted to dismiss the tutor and housekeeper. Then they tried to force him to sign away his inheritance; not wishing their prosperity to end.

The unmerciful beating almost killed Jasper, and afraid of the consequences if he died, the two brutes vanished and were never seen again. The tutor revived him, and in doing so, in his desperation, he once again grasped a pen and shouted at him to sign a waiver to give them full autonomy.

Jasper cursed the woman in the blue gabardine dress and wide-brimmed hat, for abandoning him in a place akin to hell and swore revenge on them all. He cried out to his mother for the assured help, and Emily gave in. The time had arrived for her to ask his father William to confront them, which he did and has ever since.'

'Why what did he do?' asked Glenda.

Larry continues, 'Jasper needed an advocate to

plead his case for autonomy and so hired a barrister, informing him he had already dismissed the governess and tutor. With his bruises healed on his face, the man was none the wiser to what took place. Jasper argued that he had placed a vacancy advertisement for a private tutor. One who can teach him the sciences and be able to attend at his home five days a week.

The barrister made notes. Here is a young man who seems to have grasped his situation and is taking care of it. Jasper also said he would like the notary along with himself, to interview what are now a dozen applicants. The notary nodded his approval. Next, Jasper asked the firm to take control of his financial affairs until he reached twenty-one.

After signing, the law firm reiterates, that Jasper is a man of considerable wealth once he lodges the paperwork. He would revisit, bringing the deeds of the houses, and Jasper may choose where to deposit them.

Jasper informed him that he would retain the firm on the conclusion of the business, as they had represented his family through the ages. He also stated that he preferred them to manage any correspondence regarding his coming of age in their office.

Two days later, after receiving the deeds, they finalised the remaining legalities.

Before making his exit and in conversation with a clerk, Jasper overheard that the police had dragged the torso of a man from the Thames, so decomposed it is unrecognisable.

A ruckus began at the door, and a young clerk

rushed in gabbling, "The corpse, the one they pulled from the river. Well, they've found another, so one can but hazard a guess that we may be representing somebody soon." He grinned as he walked past Jasper, excited to be first with his news. Jasper was invisible to him, and he shivered, not from fear of discovery but as though someone had walked over his grave.

"Have they identified the corpse yet?" The clerk dealing with Jasper glanced at the messenger.

"No, except to say it's female. So, unless other parts wash in on the tide her identity may remain a mystery. If she was tart, then innumerable men may identify the part they found."

"Here, you, have some decorum, mate." The clerk shifted his eyes towards Jasper, standing and listening. "You'll be out on your ear if the master catches you talking like this."

"I'm just saying."

"Well, don't. She may be some skint creature fallen upon, murdered and tipped in like hundreds of others. They say t'is a giant graveyard is the river."

'Hey, Larry, what happened to the clothing? Couldn't they identify anybody by what they were wearing?' Glenda is engrossed in the tale of woe. Puzzled but pleased, Larry has never been able to relate the story, and this is a cathartic exercise for him, even so, he recognises the outcome will not change.

Chapter 12

SUICIDE AND MURDER
(Present Time)

'So, Glenda,' said Larry. 'Emily and William protected their descendants way back, and today they still do.' He took a moment and seemed to survey something above him. Glenda followed his eyes, but nothing struck her as odd. Is he seeking approval from heaven, she thought happily. He had placed his arm around her earlier, and it was something she found she longed for his attention. She allows him to rattle on, playing for time and trying to keep the mood light, racking her brains for something to say.

'What about the clothing and what happens next, I mean these are your ancestors, yes, is that correct; it's not a load of bull you're telling me?'

'Yes, of course, it's correct. How do you think I arrived on this fair planet? The stork is a myth, and as for the clothing, there is a simple explanation. Their things are up in the attic. Hidden behind a false wall. I have no idea how much because he used other places too. I'll show you later.'

'You sound so positive about all of this, Larry, but it's making my skin crawl.'

'When my wife and I moved in the plan was to renovate and I found the partition. I was searching in the roof one day, wanting somewhere to dump old things. I tripped over the cat and knocked a hat stand flying. A monster of a thing with hornlike arms. The ugly thing fell like a damn tree crashing down, missed me and hit the wall. You can guess my surprise when the horns went straight through.

Anyhow, I broke through the papered plywood partition. I admit finding a papered wall in the attic, which I assumed was servants' quarters at one time, struck me as funny, until I found old garments and other knick-knacks.'

'Other, what other stuff, and who would board an attic up in the first place?'

Glenda sounds genuinely interested, but inside she isn't grasping what's happening. She read more of the letters in the cardboard box than she admitted to Larry, but the more he said, the more it sounded like a fairytale.

Nonplussed, Larry is stuck for something to say. His top lip breaks out in beads of perspiration and his hand trembles a fraction as he wipes his sleeve across his mouth.

Removing his arm from Glenda, who wished she'd kept her mouth shut, she had been comfortable and enjoying the closeness. Taking a breath and with a gulp, Larry says, 'My father and I mean my birth father, erected a partition wall in the attic. I will try and enlighten you. Remember, this all started with you sticking your snout in about the house and from whom I inherited it. Yes, I was adopted, but not because I was unwanted; I am an orphan, but here's the rub: I learnt when I found the false wall something worse. My father murdered my mother.'

'Oh god, Larry. How terrible.'

'You needn't tell me.'

'I don't know what to say.'

'Don't say anything then.'

'How did you find out?'

'In the attic, if you remember me saying I found this chest.' He taps it with his foot. 'This contains Emily's scribbles along with Jasper's and Jake's. I also gathered facts about my parentage and found a letter written for me.

'All my life, I assumed I was unwanted, and they put me up for adoption. My adopted family gave me the same impression when they told me I was an orphan but never explained why or how I came into their care. So, I confess I assumed, and was wrong in thinking my parents didn't want me.' He stops to draw breath, and when he speaks again, his voice trembles, 'I found a suicide note.'

'Oh, Larry,' she made to take his hand. 'Why was it in this attic?'

He snatched his hand away. 'When I read through, I thought I was having a heart attack or would faint or some such stupid thing because he said what I had suspected all along. My family is not only ungodly but evil.'

'No, you can't say that; that's not right. Take you, for starters. A respected researcher only out to improve people's lives.'

Have you asked yourself, why, Glen? Because I can tell you, what I do is for selfish reasons and not noble ones?'

'What do you mean by that?'

'Later. Now regarding my parents.' He cupped her knee, and his warm hand reminded her she was cold.

'As I said, I found a note, well, more of a letter, in which he apologised to me. When I think I may never have come across if I'd ignored the will saying I mustn't sell this place, because my first reaction was to put it up for sale.'

Once more he pauses and stands, preoccupied, as if he's made his mind up about something. He ambles around the chaise, positioning himself behind Glenda, who stifles the urge to turn and face him. With his hands on both of her shoulders, he peers down on the top of her head.

There would be no benefit if she followed his gaze. It was unfathomable, and when he raises his hands, circling his fingers, it would do her no good at all to read his mind as he envisions them closing around her exposed neck, her nape inviting his touch.

Bracing himself, he flexes his fingers when her auburn hair catches a streak of light from the window, touching a memory of when they met as she raced past the cafe table and bumped into him.

He cups her head, tilts her chin back, kisses the glowing strands of hair, and begins to relax. For once, she understands, he doesn't want her to watch him as he talks.

'In it, he says he realised vileness runs in my family, and those are the words he scribed in his hand. He was not of strong character, and his wife, whom he treasured so much, was also a sensitive individual. I wish I had known them, Glenda. Honest, I do.' He gulps, 'He explained his life would be unbearable with the knowledge and his heart was so full of sorrow and love because they bore a son, me. He worried that the evil may flow through this innocent child, and the more he thought, the more he brooded deep inside if his heart was also black.

These ideas had never crossed his mind before and began to take over his life. He says he became more aware and weary of his lovely wife's daily mood changes as they drifted apart, all because of what he found in the attic. He couldn't explain to her, and over time she withdrew from him, as though afraid of him, something he couldn't tolerate.

He thought he was going mad because ghosts told him it was all true, ghosts who said they were his parents, William and Emily. But in his mind, only the insane listen to ghosts.

He denied them to himself, often shutting them out including his hapless wife. He beseeched them to leave him; he wouldn't accept who they claimed to be. He wrote he heard voices as a child but never submitted to them. How strange. He thought he was weak, and yet he never let them in.

I think he was stronger than any of us. His answer to the problem, though, was too harsh, for he took the life of his wife to save her more heartache, all this after boarding up the attic and leaving the note and then he took his own life, saying he would not harm his child. He prayed whoever brought me up would not learn of the vileness and therefore would not influence me in any way.' Larry finished his mouth was so dry, and he licked his cracked lips.

Glenda didn't move. Shocked and upset by his tale of woe and unable to provide help in any way. With no inkling, she searched her head for anything to say, which may offer hope or comfort, but how do you respond to a man who tells you his father murdered his mother and his whole family are evil murderers?

She thought she had better wait for him to be the first to say something. The time dragged heavily for what seemed minutes and an uncomfortable silence settled on them.

Larry, regretting telling her his deep secret, isn't sure what to do. He knows what Emily expects of him, but can he do it? He shrugs; time will tell.

'Righty-ho.' He claps his hands, rubbing them together, breaking the enforced lull. 'As for the other stuff, well, it's personal items, things like jewellery, some expensive and the rest just baubles. The pathetic showy display from the victims he disposed of. I did find a beautiful embroidered and beaded reticule, which I like to think belonged to Emily because a little drawstring purse suits my idea of her. I held it and sensed her so strong and real because it retained a trace of lemon verbena, a perfume I always associate with her.

Anyhow, the rest he displayed in order, like trophies or badges. Criminologists and police reports tell us psychopaths like to gather mementoes from their victims. The bag belonged to my grandfather's father and still held the tools of his....' Larry spits out, 'trade.'

'What, you are all psychos; how gross?' He can tell she's excited and desperate to ask about them as he studies her eager face.

'Thanks, Glenda; you don't even understand the meaning of the word psycho.'

'I do, murderous nutters.'

'Don't show your lack of intelligence like this, please. Not all psychopaths are murderers. One has a distinct absence of guilt, and therefore, in a way, they perceive no wrong in what they do, thinking it is for altruistic reasons.'

Glenda is about to cut him off with a sarcastic remark because she finds him so pompous, but he leaps in, 'As you understand, my work is...'

'Yes, the most important thing in your life; you don't let me forget...'

'Up there,' he glances upwards, 'in the attic, is what I can only think of as Jack the Ripper's bag and knives. There's one in particular, a long thin-bladed thing with a carved whalebone handle still caked in dried blood.' Larry's excitement grows as he speaks, absorbing Glenda in it.

'Think about it, Glen.' Using the diminutive form

of her name tends to remind her of old whispered endearments. Of late though, she thinks he doesn't care anymore; now she's longing to have him say it like he used to.

'Just think, it might be Jack's blood because, if you recall from the trial, Emily mutilated him and put the knife and the bag back behind the wainscoting because they never found it. I analysed the blood, taking a DNA sample to compare with mine.'

'Why?'

'Durr, to help with my research.'

'Are you joking? Your genetic investigations have something to do with this horrific story. This is getting creepier, Larry. What happened to the other two men and the woman?'

'What, you mean those who beat Jasper and the housekeeper?'

Attracted by what looks like a figure in the overmantel mirror, Larry turns, giving Glenda the notion he is acknowledging someone, before shaking his head and resuming a stern expression.

Glenda follows his gaze; the kaleidoscopic reflections from the stained glass window to the side of the room strike the gilded bezel as the sun struggles through the grimy pane and catches her in the eye. She squints as a flashing semblance of a lady dressed in old-fashioned attire and wearing a hat covered in spectacular feathers, seems to stare at her for a fleeting moment, and is gone. Glenda spins around. The room is empty except for the two of them.

Growing more uncomfortable and unsure what to think, Glenda is positive, he's enjoying regaling her with the horror story, but she still can't understand why he is so insistent on baring his soul now, here in this house. The thought that this is not only a house of secrets but one full of death strikes her like a hammer blow. She shudders.

'As for those you talk about who tormented him, that is the conundrum,' he says. 'Yes, I ought to tell you what happened to them. The trouble is, Glen, he doesn't say it in his diary. One can only surmise. Who can say if he killed them and got rid of the bodies himself? I don't know, but he suggests Emily and William were responsible. But think about it, Glenda.'

Larry's face suddenly changes. His eyes narrow, his forehead creases and his mouth leers. For a moment, his demeanour is inscrutable. He jerks his head back, tilting his nose in the air.

'Back in the late 18th and early 19th century, they pulled over five hundred corpses from the Thames, and over half of them remain unidentified. I like to think that the family added to this number by helping to rid the streets of filth.

The river's murky water served as a pathway to wash away the undesirable souls out to the channel and into the North Sea, where the hungry mouths of fish gnaw on the flesh. The fishermen trawl for these well-fed fattened fish and feed them back to us to make a living. You like fish don't you, Glen? Food for the soul. What goes around comes around. Ha-ha, one might say the Thames is the devil's river Styx, only without the ferryman.'

'Well, I did like fish, but I am rapidly changing my mind now,' she says as he gloats. Glenda is used to his sarcasm and anger, but she worries because this is a different unusual quirk she doesn't recognise.

'So, show me them. I'd love to see.' She tries to stand, but he clasps her wrist, not wanting her to move, at least not yet. She searches for something to say, anything to quell a growing sense of something sinister about the room. Charged with expectancy, the atmosphere sits heavy, but what she is expecting, she can't say. 'Tell me about this Arthur come, Jake, Larry, and you can show me the room, although I would rather go up now.'

Larry senses the excitement in her eyes, but can he also recognise fear? He doesn't want her to be afraid—not of him, not now. He recalls being in this situation before with his now–dead wife.

He shakes his head, trying to clear it. 'Oh yes, after Jasper came my grandfather, Arthur Jacob, but he was only ever called Jake.'

Poor Glenda. Saddened, Larry thought she would be different, but alas, no, and she has no clue what's in store. He must keep it from her for as long as he can. He smiles, a tenderness about his face, and she relaxes, happy to take his hand while blind to what his warped and damaged mind contains, the epilogue of her life. He continues with the story of Arthur.

Chapter 13

ARTHUR JACOB
(Jake)

Jasper hired a housekeeper at his ghostly mother's insistence. Unsure why she was persistent, he set out to do what she asked. He began offering interviews, and on meeting the third applicant, his instincts rushed to his loins.

The moment he saw this woman, the sense of pure joy was so overwhelming, that he almost forgot to find out if she was a suitable candidate. This was indeed love at first sight. "What is your name?" He asked across his mahogany desk.

"Ann Buttershaw, sir." She said, handing him her reference, written on embossed paper, declaring her excellent moral standing and contributions to the household of an elderly gentleman who had since passed away.

Under his breath, he thanked God, or whoever was watching over him, for sending her. In turn, she spoke of how she needed the position, having found herself in straits after her father died and left nothing but gambling debts. Her mother had died in childbirth.

They married in January 1915, and Ann fell pregnant on their honeymoon. With the war raging, Jasper made sure to write his will again at the insistence of his mother, Emily, and father, William, who still visited regularly.

This emerged as the only topic of discord in the Vincent household. Ann worried when Jasper spoke of the visitations, becoming anxious and afraid.

His love for her prompted him to stop mentioning them or their appearances; her happiness became his prime objective.'

'Larry, why are you called Emlison and not either Warren after William or even Vincent, after Emily?'

'Oh, well done. To be truthful, I didn't think you had it in you to notice.'

'Don't be so bloody rude never mind unkind, I don't deserve this.

Larry ignores her saying, 'Jake was the one who changed the name after he murdered a woman. Think about it, why not Emilson? We are Emily's sons. Anyhow, where was I?'

As the words left his mouth, his expression didn't alter. The word murder didn't affect him in any way, not like Glenda, who flinched but, for once, managed to keep quiet.

'Oh, yes, he, Jasper, I mean, left everything to his beloved wife including that Albury Street one and other properties. If anything happened to her, their child would inherit the lot, including a leather-strapped locked box containing letters and a diary from his mother. He wanted his child to treasure this, as one day he or she would need to learn about his or her background. He stipulated that it should only be opened if a need arose; what need I don't know otherwise, it must remain locked and passed down to the eldest of each generation.

Jasper didn't want his children to learn about the dark side of his grandparents or himself. They would acquaint themselves if necessary. Since his marriage, this fatalism was something he tried to bury, hoping he took after his mother rather than his father, not realising the bend in Emily's character.

He contemplated the best way to help in the war effort, and like hundreds of thousands who signed up before him, he recognised his duty—to serve his country and fight for the empire, his wife, and his unborn child. He enlisted in the Navy. Ann remained unhappy being on her own in the house and wanted to rent elsewhere and he encouraged her to do so.

It isn't known if his parents instructed him or that he didn't wish his wife to be left with them, I can't say but Jasper did stress that the Albury Street house must remain in the family and never be sold as stipulated in Emily's will.

'Ann took her husband's wishes to heart and moved out of the house to a small property in Stoke Newington, where she waited to bring her child into the world. He explained that on his discharge they would take their rightful place in the family home to make it a happy place to live.

Patting his wife's protruding stomach, making her blush, he told her, "With your help, Ann, and our children, of which I hope our quiver will be full, we can abolish all the sadness my parents left. Lay them to rest forever and bask in our lives together as a loving family, where no ghosts or bad memories can haunt us."

The sad news came through that Jasper's ship sank in the Dardanelles late in 1915, and Ann, who only days before had given birth to a baby boy, she named Arthur Jacob after her father, fell into decline.

With undue affection, and when she found the strength to hold him, she called him her little Jake, but she began to waste away no matter what they did for her.

Ann's health deteriorated, and her infant was about to become an orphan. His mother's lone siblings, two uncles, were already dead, fighting for their country, so it was the foundling home that awaited him. This was something Ann would not consider.

All the trusted nurses loved her and described her as a lovely and pleasant soul. One claimed to have a married sister who longed for a child, and she would care for the baby. Ann accepted, stating that she would claim him back on her recovery.

After meeting the woman and her husband, Ann considered them excellent foster parents for her son. Far better than any foundling home.

'Ann's strength rapidly deserted her, and before she succumbed to an infection, she gave them rights over her child, passing on the relevant documents. They took him to visit, and she held her baby in her arms as she fell asleep in death. People said the death of her Jasper was too much to bear.

They took little Arthur, known as Jake, from his mother's home to his foster parents, but not as they imagined, alone, he was kept an eye on by his sole relatives, neither of whom were living. His ghostly grandparents, William and Emily, were by his side when the foster parents adopted him.

The boy appreciated being one of the lucky ones as he matured. He was a quiet child who learnt of his beginning from his adoptive parents, who wanted him to believe they picked him, and that his biological mother chose them.

They were kind and took him as their own. They told him of his inheritance and why, at first, they tried to contest his grandmother Emily's will.

They didn't try to sell the Albury Street property for malice or self-gain, but because they thought the expense may be too much from his income to keep the house. They only wanted the best for him. Also, they believed he would not want to live in the old place alone because he would always have a loving home with them. Yet their friends laughed and reminded them that most parents held such foolish dreams.

Admittedly, at first, Jake was bewildered. but the couple helped to quell his anxiety, and he accepted their love. His problems began as the years progressed because he developed an inner craving for something unknown and struggled to figure out what it was.

His parents said of him, "Our Jake is a darling, and he's no trouble." While pleased when overhearing this, which he often did, with his habit of listening at doors, he still had an overpowering urge to do something different. Whether or not it was favourable he couldn't fathom, it was just something…

He matured into a lonely young man. He was unable to form lasting friendships. He forged strong attachments, and others found him suffocating and all-consuming.

His capricious ideas and some of his games made his playmates uneasy and they labelled him weird. He had an unhealthy occupation with death and talked about dissecting animals to examine their entrails. A couple of the boys didn't mind so much, but others kept out of his way when he spotted their pets.

His parents didn't see any of this, considering him a shy boy, and didn't push him to make friends. Their boy Jakey was far too sensitive for the rough boys.

He kept himself to himself with his quirky ways hidden from them and when he was ten, his family moved back to their Stoke Newington house. Back in 1916, with their new and precious bundle and fearing for their safety, his adopted parents had fled when the Zeppelins rained their deadly cargo on the homes of London.

They resided in the country not far from Brighton, where he was happy, so they stayed, but they longed for their old home, which, against the odds, and bombs was still standing.

In Stoke Newington, the place where his mother died, he grew into a strapping lad, and during the subsequent years when becoming aware, his weird feelings turned to lust. By fourteen they turned to licentiousness, and at that time came the first of many visits from Emily, his dead grandmother.

One night, full of adolescent lust, a woman's voice shocked him before an apparition appeared in his room saying, "Don't be fearful, Jake. I have watched over you since you were born, I won't hurt you. Please don't be afraid." Jake careered back, hitting the wall, petrified.

"No, I promise I am not here to harm you." Said the apparition.

Chewing on his bottom lip, he pressed against the wall, and when the corner of a shelf jabbed him, it didn't hurt. Not for the life of him, was he able to speak as he tried to become one with the wall. Frantic, his eyes calculated the distance between him, her, and the door.

"I'm your grandmother. Your father, Jasper, was my son. He died not long after your birth and he never met you, but I gave him my word; I would guard and support you. Your grandfather, William, is here too."

She glanced over her shoulder, but he couldn't see anyone, and all he could feel was the pounding of his heart.

"Oh, Grandfather William will come if you need him," said this apparition as calm as any old lady dressed in flamboyant costume standing in a teenage boy's bedroom. "I'm here to help you fight your dark thoughts and feelings."

Spittle dribbled down his chin. Is he losing his mind? Where did she spring from? Wherever it was she could bloody well go back. He didn't have any grandparents, and how did she slip into his room, worse still, his inner feelings are private. Please God, he thought, don't let her read my thoughts."

Finding his voice, he asked, "Who are you? Where did you come from?"

"We have met before, dear boy, and on many occasions. You may remember your fourth birthday. You couldn't sleep after you fell out with one of your closest friends, that night I came and sat with you until you drifted off to sleep."

Jake's breathing began to slow with the memory of the most awful day thirteen years ago leaving him forever hating that birthday.

His best friend called him a scary monster and didn't want to play with him anymore because he made him stand and witnessed him pulling the legs off a spider. It got worse when he held a live sparrow in a bucket of water to find out what would happen. The boy ran home crying, saying he wouldn't go to his party the next day.

The boy's mother had other plans and insisted. She dragged him there. She didn't listen to her son's pleas. She wasn't going to miss the chance of lunch with her friend for a four-year-old boy, who, by rights, should be with his nanny. "Damn the woman for being ill today of all days," she said, but it will not spoil her day out.

The child arrived and ignored him, pushing his proffered hand away. He avoided him for the rest of the day. It was the same night, an old lady dressed in funny clothes came into Jake's room, saying she was his grandmother.

She convinced him he was not scary, nor indeed a monster. He must, though, refrain from harming living creatures. Regardless of their size and place in the pyramid of life. "All," she said, "have a right to live."

In Jake's bedroom, Emily cut a strange portrait with her grey suit trimmed with yellow tassels, her hands covered with bright blue gloves placed on her lap, and she told a fascinating story, prompting him to ask if he was asleep and dreaming.

"No," she told him, "I'm here to help. I swore to your father and grandfather I would be here for you. You are struggling with strange feelings you may not understand. Don't be afraid, and don't dwell on them.'"

He fell asleep and forgot about her, but not before questioning why he knew nothing about having a grandmother.'

'How did you find all this out, Larr? It can't be all written down.'

'Shush, Glen, just listen.

Jake began to relax in Emily's company. On her third appearance, after questioning himself if he was halfway insane, he began to enjoy her visits. He found her company exhilarating and appealing to a quirk in his nature.

No matter how much she wanted, Emily could never keep the secret of his beginnings from him.

Her deep love for his grandfather, William still overwhelmed her, and told her grandson, Jake the story of William, a kind fellow, also known as Jack.

She had accepted his dark side and explained how they met and what happened. She told Jake that she knew he had a dark side and begged him to call on her if he was in trouble. She said she would help him with problems with the help of his grandfather. Together they would help and protect him.

Additionally, he would inherit from her, so he would never need worry about money—something he didn't do now as his parents; a wealthy couple had made provisions for him and were as extravagant with their money as they were with their love for him.

'The teenager learnt to live with his darker side and managed to keep it hidden, and his gratitude for his grandmother soared. Far more so than to the woman he called mother.

His life ran untroubled as he advanced into adulthood and Emily visited less. Although he felt lonely, he aimed to gain independence. What better way than to move into his house on Albury Street as soon as he was able? Like today, the completion of one's good intentions can be as far away as ever.

Over his many trips to the city, he grew to love the magnificent Georgian edifices while walking to Soho Square Gardens. He relished the tranquillity of the square, which reminded him of the time spent in the country near Brighton.

He strolled around, thinking of nothing more than walking in the warm sunshine and admiring the rococo plasterwork on the graceful structure of a building he hadn't noticed before. He scanned the frontage, where the plaster scrolls resembled those on Albury Street.

One day melancholy reflections of his unknown parents encroached on the apparitions of his ghostly grandparents, and his inner self began to deny their existence. His other identity shrugged in contempt at his thoughts. Aware of his excellent fortune with how life turned out for him and ready to stroll on, he stopped, for in the entrance of a building, framed in its beauty and complementing exceptional works of art on the cornices, stood a young man, and... Jake whispered, "beautiful."

For dizzying seconds, he stood transfixed as the man walked on, his strides compelled Jake to trail in his footsteps across the square. With each footstep away from Greek Street his thoughts conflicted, why on earth was he following a man he considered beautiful?

The young man stopped and turned to lean against a wall. His bearing was striking. A god-like Adonis in human form. He took out a cigarette and lit it. He inhaled and filled his lungs before allowing the smoke to drift. Puckishly, he popped his lips, which stirred excitement in the boy Jake, and gave him an inexplicable tightening in his loins.

Moderating his stride as he approached, Jake couldn't help gawping at this divine specimen of masculinity with dark hair parted down the middle, lengthier than fashion dictated. His smooth skin held no sign of acne or beard growth and with his perfectly fitting three-piece grey suit complemented by a pair of two-tone grey fashionable shoes, he was a vision.

This vision bewitched Jake, who walked by and couldn't resist glancing back over his shoulder. His heartbeat accelerated on seeing the man staring back. He almost choked on his breath. Why should a man cause such a reaction? He often tailed girls home while fantasizing about what they secreted under their androgynous clothing, but whatever, it didn't excite him, and yet the instant he walked past this man, his brow perspired, and his breath raced. Why should it be so?

He turned onto Carlisle Street, picked up his pace, and ran until exhausted. Stopping, he threw himself against rusty wrought iron railings, gasping for breath. He scanned his surroundings through bleary eyes, squeezing them tight and forcing his focus, but couldn't establish his bearings. Tears rained down his cheeks, but signs of a smile cut his face. Is he...? No, he spat. The thought disgusted him, but he has long battled with his inner life. He is different. Is this the answer?

He caught his breath and examined his feelings, each one he dissected and analysed with the brutal honesty of a seventeen-year-old young man.

He began to recall his boyhood experiments, launching an enormous explosion from which the blast hit him. He needed the closeness of a male friend, one who could understand his bloodlust and his desires and share them with him.

This revelation turned out rather radical. How does one take it in? Should his feelings revolt him? Should he find out more about them? His answer was NO, NO, NO, he must find a wife and settle down.

His adoptive mother wished him to marry. Often, she told him when he was ready, she would like him to think about settling down and bestowing her with grandchildren.

The Albury Street house grew more appealing as an escape from the pressure on him as a woeful loneliness began to overtake his mother's days since her husband passed away, the sad demise of a fine and upstanding man.

Jake retraced his steps to find his way home, making sure not to pass through the square. He lay awake throughout the night, arguing with the candid truth. He questioned his desires, fitful until a sense of peace out of resignation settled on him like a warm blanket. Peering in the corner, he spied Emily with a benign smile on her face. She nodded. He must find a woman to love.

Secure in his mind now, he avoided where the perfect young man leaned against the wall, smoking a cigarette as though caressing something of value. He didn't let it drag on his lip or hold it in his thumb and forefinger, he embraced it between his middle and pointer fingers, removing it from his soft, full lips, and exhaling a gentle curl of smoke before replacing it with reverence.

Convinced he would never set eyes on him again, but time unlocked his real desire, and he hoped he would.

Unable to explain this, he amused himself by pretending to prove his predilection is what he considers an ordinary man, but the truth lay deep within, gnawing away at him.

Jake revisited the square nine days later and was disappointed, the spot was vacant. His eyes swept the area, and he checked his timepiece. It was a similar time of day as before, another quick sweep, and to his regret and utter dismay, his frustration overwhelmed him.

He felt drawn each consecutive evening, and it soon developed into an obsession. The adolescent was still trying to convince himself of his normality. Cannot a man admire another if his demeanour is as startling as the one who stood on the corner, one foot against the wall, with a casual ease he wished he possessed?

On the third week of walking down, false in his conviction of hoping to find a beautiful young woman to escort, one petite and comely, with auburn hair and lips so sweet and full, he almost visualised her when he caught his breath, for wearing the same suit as before yet, different shoes stood the constant object of his images.

He swallowed, desperate to walk on, when a middle-aged man wearing a bowler and sporting a neat moustache approached and spoke to the adonis before he reached them. This left him to suffer the humiliation of witnessing them walk off together. His stomach churned. He gnawed at the knuckles of his right hand, devastated. How can he be so hurt? It's a man walking off with another.

He assuaged his pain. He considered the time taken building the courage to talk to him, and now he will have to wait again. What if his nerve deserts him? What next? Slapping his raw fist into his hand and gritting his teeth, he spun on his heels, embarrassed to retrace the way he came. What if they saw him? Oh, God, how awful!

He kept to an acceptable pace, not appearing to run when all he wanted to do was dash as far as possible from the scene, swearing he would never suffer this humiliation again.

Despite his protestations, he returned the next night, hoping to make the man's acquaintance. He had reasoned on his hair, attire, shoes, and even how he stood sporting his cigarette—anything but him. What drew him back to the same spot?

Building his courage to say something, befriend, and gain his secret with a longing to emulate him and his air of poise, which oozed and was apparent to all. Jake deliberated on these things as he walked. Who would make the first move? What would he say?

He stumbled, seeing him in the same spot as before. Nerves made him gauche and stupid as he turned to saunter past the object of his desire. His realisation disgusted him, and nausea threatened at the overbearing knowledge of the source of his lust. His lechery was overpowering, but most troubling was his craving for blood resurfaced.

Needing a release from these worrisome ideas, he planned to go out the same evening, ignoring his grandmother, who stressed he must fight his urges. Did she think he had this call to kill? Was this his inner being trying to stop him from going down a path, a route leading to death and destruction, one designated for him to follow?

Nobody could stop him. The door slammed on his heels. Hurrying to shrug on his coat, one arm caught in his sleeve, ensnaring his fingers in the silk lining. Swearing, he rammed his fist through, and when his hand emerged it was accompanied by a ripping noise, which fuelled Jake's internal fire.

'When he arrived at the Square, his heart missed a beat. He gulped and cleared his throat. The young man was stood in the same spot. Jake bit his lip but was unwavering; he would talk to him. He slowed his pace. "Err, hello, I trust you don't mind me speaking to you."

The man looked straight into Jake's brown eyes with his striking blue ones. A smile spread across his lips, which he opened to answer. His lips began to move, and time became immaterial as Jake imagined them pursing and leaning in for a kiss.

"Hello," said the man. His voice was strong and confident and almost melodious to Jake as he said,

"I've seen you before and wondered when you would speak. I've been waiting."

Assured of safer ground, Jake asked, "May I buy you a coffee? A Lyons coffee shop is not too far, on Tottenham Court Road."

The man smiled, and glanced down the road, giving him a heart-stopping moment before he said, "Why not? But let's go to the Strand on the embankment. They serve a wonderful pot, and we can chat while we walk. It's not much further. By the way, my name is Tony, what did you say your name is?"

"I didn't, but it's Arthur Jacob, although I have only ever been called Jake."

"Excellent. We can become better acquainted over coffee. There is a gorgeous little nippy who works on the ground floor, and she has such tiny feet."

Surprised and pleased at the mention of a walk together, Jake was less happy at the thought of a cute waitress in the coffee house.

"Yes, let's go," he said. "It will be a pleasant change, and we can spy out the being with the prettiest of feet. Do you have designs on her?" he asked.

"Not me," said Tony. "I thought perhaps you would like to meet her."

Not knowing what to say, and out of his depth, Jake worried, had he got it wrong? Was he about to make an utter fool of himself? His nerve plummeted.'

Chapter 14

Tony

'So, Larry, you are not only saying you once had a live-in lesbian lover; now you say you had a gay boy in the family.' With a tongue as swift as a slashing rapier, Glenda's cutting words belittle Larry, and he fails to disguise a squirm of embarrassment wriggling deep within.

He slaps the book closed. 'Oh, you are so not in the loop, darling. Now unless you want to stay here for the night, you better be quiet.'

He checks the diary. 'This is what Jake says about his new friend.

"Tony, twenty-three, was orphaned as a child but never settled into the workhouse way of life. He didn't listen to or conform to the strict discipline dished out, and he hated and fought against the mauling by the male members of the staff.

One little girl over the wall tugged at his heart when he peered into the girl's side through the fence dividing the sexes. One day, he told her he wanted to run away, and she pleaded with him to take her. He did so and he promised to always care for her. They spent weeks sleeping under hedges, stealing food from bins, and hiding in London's warren of underground tunnels until Tony learnt how to make a living. His feminine appearance attracted selective male attention, and he was adept at manipulating it and them, gaining money and gifts. He earned enough to rent a small room for the two runaways who planned to leave the dark and dismal streets of the city and England forever.

After ten years, he earned and saved enough to purchase the tickets for a new life in Australia, but now with Jake on the scene, a chance to earn a bit extra was on the horizon.

"Is this nippy important to you?" asked Jake.

"No, she's not my type. What about you?"

"I couldn't say, dear chap. I haven't clapped eyes on her yet, somehow I don't think she will be my type either." His glare bores into Tony.

"I didn't think so. Come on, let's go." They set off in tandem.

The coffee house was huge, and Tony was used to enjoying coffee and biscotti there. He led the way through the assortment of customers.

Jake spotted one or two surprised faces turning their way, which he put down to Tony's handsome way of carrying himself and not to the regularity of his visits, of which he knew nothing.

An attractive nippy swooped in with practised skill.'

The young waitress wore a starched cap with a large, red L embroidered in the centre, a black alpaca dress with a double row of pearl buttons sewn with red cotton, white detachable cuffs, and a collar finished off with a white square apron worn at the dropped-waist level. The public nicknamed these indefatigable, mostly women, who served speedily and efficiently, affectionately as nippy.

'Tony caught Jake's eye and peered down to the floor; Jake did the same. From below the knees, the waitress sported a short pair of legs finished with a petite pair of feet. Amused but not wishing to appear impolite, Jake controlled his laughter.

"Here again?" said the waitress.

"Hello again. Yes, this is my favourite coffee house," Tony winked, and she smiled.

"May we have a pot of coffee, please?" He eyed Jake, "Would you like something to eat?"

Jake shook his head, waiting for the nippy to leave them in peace, pretty feet or not. He wanted this new-found friend for himself. "No, coffee will be fine, thank you."

Adept, she strode off between the crowded tables to return quickly with their order. Once more out of his depth, he stared at his cup without seeing anything, but Tony, quite at ease, said, "Shall I play mother?" The boy nods.

"What age are you, Jake?"

"Well, I am almost eighteen. How about you?"

"That would be telling. How old do you think I am?"

The conversation between them ran smoothly, and by the end of the second pot, they felt relaxed in each other's company Tony paid the bill and left a generous tip for the nippy who thanked him and flashed a beautiful smile as they prepared to go.

"Have a good day, sirs," she said, with a cheeky lilting voice.

They strolled along the embankment. It was not a romantic or salubrious walk, but one suiting their mood and intentions. Inflamed with passion, a new experience for Jake, he longed to touch Tony's hand as they walked but rammed his fist hard into his pocket instead.

Taking a sly peek at him, Tony asked, "What do you do for your livelihood?"

"Ah well, I am as yet undecided," said Jake. "I can go to university. Science interests me, or to be more specific, the body. I have time to make up my mind. I don't need to worry about money if that's what you mean. I will receive two inheritances. Let me tell you, Tony, I will be a very wealthy man one day. So, I have choices ahead. I may indulge myself and live the life of a gentleman and enjoy the pleasures required by one."

"Yes, and why not?" Tony already experienced in life is sure he has uncovered an asset. His new friend is of the Nob class. He may take longer than usual, but he will be a profitable keeper once hooked. He hopes to have enough time before he leaves for the antipodes with pretty feet. This one will be worth spending a bob or two on coffee for now and at his expense. Afterwards, the world will be his oyster. He smacked his lips.

"Pardon," said Jake.

"Oh, nothing, I was thinking, can we convene again tomorrow? I have to go now." Tony peered at his watch, a grimace on his face. "I'm late and better rush. Same time tomorrow, same place," he said, reaching out to pat Jake's shoulder. The boy shivered.

"Yes, that's fine. See you tomorrow."'

'A classic case of grooming. Hey, Larry, only, I suppose they didn't call it grooming back then, did they?' said Glenda, grinning.

'Whatever.' Unconcerned by the interruption, Larry carries on.

'Elation lifted Jake's stride as he followed Tony, who glanced back while running for his appointment. When he turned the corner, he upped his pace and ran to the coffee house, where a man stood tapping his umbrella on the pavement. He was about to leave, when Tony called, "I am so sorry. I'm late, due to an accident down the road, and I got stuck helping."

The man in smart attire, a dark blue pinstriped suit and bowler hat, glanced up and down the way before he spoke. "Come, let's hurry. I don't have much time today so don't think you are getting the full money. I was about to leave."

Annoyed, he frowned and wiped his nose on a silk handkerchief.'

Glenda interrupts. 'I don't believe this, I mean a suited and booted gentleman and a well, what would you call him?'

'It's all here. It's his words, not mine, so shut your

gobby trap. There's a long way to go yet. You nagged me to bring you, and I said I would, once, and that's it. So, pin your ears back.'

Glenda squirms and stares at the floor, rubbing her arms for warmth.

Larry continues, 'Tony smiled at the man, the one he learnt gets him his way. "Aw, don't be a grump. I can make you happy, but let's make a move." He cast a furtive glance back, if Jake came around, he would be in deep trouble.

He didn't notice that just after he looked behind him, Jake walked around the corner and saw Tony scurrying off with the suited gentleman. He thought it a strange place to rendezvous but dismissed it in his newfound happiness. It would come back to haunt him later.

Jake arrived at the coffee shop the next day, ready to meet Tony. He spotted the seats where they sat before, happy because the table was unoccupied. Rushing over, he sat in the chair that Tony sat on and wriggled his bottom on the seat. The intense intimacy he experienced was unparalleled by anything he had ever sensed.

"Afternoon, sir. Are you alone today?" The same efficient nippy turned up at the table with a notepad ready to take his order.

"No, I'm meeting my friend, the man who was here yesterday."

"Man, oh, you mean, Tony? He's a regular, and he tips well. Would you like to order now or wait? Soon, we will be busy, though, and you may have to wait a minute or two. Oh, he's here now, Hello, sir. The usual?"

"Hello there, I'm starving; what about you?" said Tony, smiling at an anxious Jake.

'Jake, who ate a hearty breakfast and was not hungry, nodded his approval, and once again caught a wink pass between Tony and the waitress as she left to fill the order. Although unsure, he sensed they were acting out for his benefit, but why?

"I thought she wasn't your type," Jake said, his voice calm but his insides churned.

Tony's gaze was harsh, and he leered. "What's the matter, jealous or something?"

Jake was full of remorse; what had he done? "Err, no, it's just..."

Tony smiled and touched Jake's hand across the table. "It's all right, I'll tell you, she is a friend, but she is working, so please remember, we cannot go gaga over each other."

"Oh, sorry, but..." Jake gulps before mumbling,

"I was jealous, yes. Am I wrong to be?"

Conscious the room was beginning to fill with customers, Tony, with a slight movement of his head, afforded Jake a rapid flit of his eyes before he squeezed the younger man's hand, letting go straight away, saying, "No, for someone in love it is not wrong."

The nippy returns with their order.

"Nancy," said Tony, "I want to introduce you to

my friend, Jake."

"Oh, Tony I can't talk while I'm working." She set their order down. "You'll have me in strife. Hello, Jake, I'm sure we'll meet later." She flashed a toothy grin.

"Hello Nancy, it will be my pleasure, I'm sure." He spoke noncommittally.

Tony again took on the role of mother and poured, asking, "Where do you live, Jake?" As he placed his fingers on the coffee jug lid to pour the hot liquid, his long-tapered little finger pointed at Jake, inviting him to note his white, feminine hands. Was it a sensual thing?

"Stoke Newington?"

"Your place?"

"No, with my mother."

Tony grimaced. "Oh, I thought you were a man of means. Why are you still with your mother?"

Embarrassed, Jake mumbled. "I have properties, at my disposal, one I am considering moving into my house on Albury Street out Deptford way. My mother is still grieving the demise of my father, which is the only reason I am at home."

"A bit of a mama's boy, are we?"

Mortified Jake's dream seemed to slip away. Tony's acid tongue cut him deeply.

"Let me assure you, Tony, I am no mamma's boy. I am my own man." His bravado urged him on. "It's only recently I took possession of the house and will be moving in at the first opportunity."

Tony leaned back and lifted his cup to his lips. Flustered, Jake looked on. Was he imagining these flirtations? Every movement of this man appeared to send out hidden messages. Was this what he wanted? His life was lacking something, but what? Was this man the answer? Even while thinking, he answered himself with an emphatic no.

Tony asked, "Will you take me with you, Jake?"

Jake's entire body tingled. The question had a noticeable undertone.

"Yes, I'll take you. The condition is anyone's guess. I have avoided going up till now. When would you like to go?"

Tony glanced at his wristwatch, an Oris and the value was obvious to the younger man, and the fact that he was brazen in wearing a wristlet, surprised him. Most men prefer the traditional and manlier pocket variety. Convinced Tony was a definite bully trap with his facade of femininity and about to ask him how he made his living when Tony delighted him by saying, "What's wrong with now? I have a couple of hours free today."

Sucking in a deep breath, he couldn't believe his luck, but he had no keys to the house. He was bluffing, never thinking Tony would agree. He thought quickly; he could retrieve the keys from the family solicitor. Why not? He was anxious to take control and not to appear foolish when Tony asked,

"What's the matter; is now not convenient?"

Jake reckoned he was sniggering at him. He

dropped his head and rubbed his forehead, forestalling a threatening headache. "Actually, Tony, I have only seen the outside. The solicitor is in charge of the keys. If you want, and if you're patient, I can arrange a viewing in a day or two and get the option to view the inside too."

"No, let's go now. Where is this legal edifice and the holder of your keys?"

"Yes, let's. Come now, let's take a hackney,' said Jake.

"One moment, we must pay our bill, or they will be after our hides," Tony waved his arm with a flourish, and Nancy rushed over.

"Stop making a show; you'll earn me the sack. Here's your bill, sir." Even so, she tried to suppress a grin. The men took their leave, and Jake hailed a passing hackney.

"Deptford, my man." Said Tony reclining and taking in the aroma of Macassar oil and fresh cigar smoke mingling with the hint of leather soap on the upholstered squab.

"This cab is new," said Tony, impressed.

"Oh, this one is new, but we've used the Austin twelve-high lot for the past couple of years now," said the driver with a modicum of pride.

Twisting to face Jake, the driver says, "It's a fair trek to Deptford."

In no mood to engage in conversation, Jake said, "We are not trekking, are we? Now go, and at speed, I will direct you when we arrive on the high street."

It sounded more like a bark than an instruction. Tony sensed the panic in Jake's voice and patted his hand to reassure him which did not go unnoticed from the driver's seat, and unsettled Jake. Casting his eye on Tony, he indicated with a slight nod that care was in order.

They make their first stop at the family solicitor. One Emily first hired and whom Jasper, his father, retained. He asked the cabby to wait.

Jake introduced himself to the receptionist in the office, asking to whom he should speak regarding the Vincent estate, Emily's, and his father, Jasper.

The lady, a pretty, pleasant, rounded sort with an agreeable manner, picked up the phone and, after winding the handle, asked, "What name is it, sir?"

"Donaldson nee Vincent, Arthur Vincent. My adoptive parents told me all about my father and mother."

'The well-trained receptionist repeated his name in the mouthpiece and placed the earpiece back on the stand with a click, and a frail elderly gentleman stepped from behind one of the unnamed doors. His white moustache twitched as though he found something amusing as he invited the young men into his office.

"Well, I must say, you do bear a resemblance to the family, both of your father and grandparents. You say they informed you about your family and certain circumstances, and I say well done; it simplifies things. I need to verify one or two details with you before we can start your business."

After the receptionist served tea and cake and with all the business completed, Jake, on the understanding that he would produce any documentation of his adoption, and at his earliest convenience, accepted the keys.

During the small talk about the house, with the solicitor glancing at Tony more than once, Jake realised how remiss he had been in introducing him.

"I do apologise. This is Tony, my..." Tony jumped in. "Interior decorator."

They had one scare today and must be more vigilant, and this slight deception will cloak them in respectability. They made haste to the cab. "Driver, turn onto Albury Street down on the left," says Jake.

The driver swung onto the narrow street.

"Which one, sir?"

"At the end, on the left." He stopped outside the last terrace before an enormous green hedge. "Close enough," said Jake, alighting in front of Tony. He passed a folded five-pound note, which he placed in the driver's hand.

"Keep the change. He said," Convinced, he need not say more."'

'That, I take it, was loads of dosh back then.' says Glenda.

'Of course, but don't forget reputations needed upholding. Same-sex attraction was unlawful in those days, and they didn't want gossip.'

'And it should be today.' Another reminder of Larry's last live-in lover.

Refusing to accept or comment on her archaic rhetoric, Larry carries on.

'Jake walked along the front of the hedge with his friend to find the entrance. Tony halted on setting eyes on the abode; his first thoughts were encouraging—another jackpot. He couldn't believe his luck.

Contemplating his future and fortune, Tony rubbed his hands in glee, aware the handsome boy was his for the picking, with no ties except his mother. They wandered through each room in the house without comment until they came to the master bedroom, where, without warning, Tony leapt on the bed like a child and bounced up and down. "This is smashing fun; come and join me."

Jake surveys the surrounding room, thinking that this is where his parents lived and the probable place they conceived him. He visualises them together in a warm embrace, parents he would only meet in his head as apparitions, and he senses shame as tears pool in the corners of his eyes.

"Are you coming or what?" Tony's voice broke his sentimentality, yet the expression on Jake's face left him perplexed. What can he do to lift his mood and excite him? Stepping off the bed, he reaches for Jake's hand. The simple touch ignites a fire in the younger man. "Are you all right? You seem sad."

"No, I'm fine." He joined in Tony's mood and leapt on the bed, bouncing visions of his parents away.

Here he is with the man he loves. Tony rejoins him, "Hey you." Clasping both his hands as they embrace in unison, their smouldering eyes bore into each other until Tony breaks the mood with, "I hate your name."

"Don't spare my feelings. Come out and say what you mean." How can Jake be upset while holding Tony's hands? He is already halfway to paradise.

"Can I call you Jack?"

"It doesn't sound much different if you ask me."

"Ha, you're wrong. Jake is like a little boy, Jack is more manly, and I want the man, not the boy."

With a mere pause, he leaned in and kissed him. Caught off guard, Jake wobbled, afraid, and stared at the embodiment of his dreams. Waiting for a reaction, Tony understood the score.

"I prefer my name if you don't mind, and I can show you I am no little boy," he said, stepping forward and embracing Tony. Jake's mouth found his lips in a passionate kiss.

To his mother's chagrin, Jake told her he was moving into the house on Albury Street, at first dreading the apparition of Grandmother Emily following him. What if she starts appearing when it's inappropriate? Tony resisted all attempts to move in because if he did, this would cut off the supply of money and gifts from other clients, while always swearing to him that he would, and soon. Promising, he is the one for him. The lies slipped from his lips like melted butter off hot toast.

After begging him not to leave, his mother sensed he was going to, and although disappointed, as always when fighting the chains binding him, her adopted son's welfare and happiness came first.

She planned how to help by placing orders at the top London stores for all the accessories a young man of his stature may need: china, cutlery, glassware, linen, and a full complement of beverages to fill the cabinet for entertaining. All these goods his mother had delivered to the Albury Street address. Next, she tried to hire a valet and housekeeper, which he refused outright because people in the house would ruin any plans. "Once I'm established, Mother," he said, kissing her forehead.

Ignoring her pleas and arguments about trivial things, such as laundry, food, and other mundane matters he is clueless about. Jake was set on leaving, and his money would provide the necessary luxuries in life.

Not letting the maid help with the packing, his mother sobbed and folded his belongings. Stroking each item, reliving a memory in each one. She buried her face in one of his shirts willing herself to be strong and remember to include the box of letters and diaries his father and grandmother kept.

Tony called on his first night in the house, and they spent time exploring from top to bottom. Jake assumes a false wall was built up in the attics, as one room seems too small compared to the rooms below.'

'You told me about the false wall, Larry; is this

the one?' Although fascinated by Larry's story, Glenda is confused. He's amazed at her patience and, for once, doesn't find her annoying, as she lets him relate the story as he understands it.

'This is the house, isn't it?' She considers what he's said and imagines the building in its prime with two young men exploring, and before, with the boy Jasper, brought up here in torment and turned into a killer.

The word killer strikes a sense of horror in Glenda. 'Why are you exposing them and me to this now, Larry?' She rises from the chaise, rubbing her hands together. 'Are you saying something or someone, is haunting this house? You told me people said it is haunted, but you never rented the house to anyone, did you? You didn't book any agents either. You lied, Larry, but why?'

'Oh, hell, Glenda. How many times do I have to tell you? I told you right at the start, but no, you wittered on and on, and now you ask me, is it haunted? You wanted this. Now you can understand why I didn't want to tell you, because yes, I do believe the house is haunted.' He stands facing her, pulling at his hair like a chastised schoolboy. His shoulder twitches and a shadow crosses the room.

'Oh, come on, Larry, you're a scientist.'

The sun is still shining through the dirty pane, but Glenda shivers. The temperature drops and she feels something is present. She scans the room, but nothing has changed. It's imagination; it must be.

'No, you come on,' said Larry. 'You can't deny you experienced something downstairs.'

She spins around, looking in all directions, before stepping forward and offering her hand for him to take. 'No, you're pulling my leg. I don't believe in ghosts.' She says, attempting to laugh off the possibility.

'That's not what you said this morning.' Larry takes her hand. 'Let me finish. I can multitask. We can scout around if you want or stay here, but you need to concentrate.'

'Can't you tell me later?'

Puzzled and rolling his eyes to the top of his head, Larry says, 'No, I'll tell you everything while we're here. I can show you the clothes and other things too.'

'Those things–you mean the trophy things? I'm not sure I even want to be in the same house as them, never mind the same room.'

'Don't fret. No harm will come to you, not while I'm here.' He smiles. The old Larry is back. He kisses her cheek and pulls her down beside him.

'Shut your eyes, Glenda. You are safe. I'm hoping you learn to discern how events happened and why my work is important. Please, darling, close your eyes while I talk. Absorb my words and imagine the situation. Put yourself in their position and watch the story unfold.'

Gently, he eases her against his chest, placing a comforting arm around her. She relaxed; he called her darling. She peeks out of one eye to ensure they are still alone and chuckles at her fancies. Fancy being scared. Larry is here. She's safe. Glenda tries to concentrate and do as he bids.

'Where was I, oh yes, the false wall?

Jake thought so, but Tony had other matters on his mind dragging him off laughing with a carefree attitude while swigging from a Chateau de Laubade bottle before handing it to Jake.

One day, not long after, Jake begged Tony to stay and, for once, in a solemn mood, asked him to think about what they were doing and reminded him.

"Remember, the neighbours will hound us out of Deptford, and the law will throw away the key if they find out what we are doing."

"I don't give a toss."

Jake stroked Tony's cheek with his thumb as they lay naked on the rumpled bed, sweating with spent passion. Tony dressed with his usual care, and Jake noticed new studs on his waistcoat. Gold-rimmed with what looked like a diamond in the centre of each one.

"My, they are very handsome; where did you purchase them?" Jake gulped and pointed at the buttons. He recalled the last time Tony came round he wore a new cravat and pin.

Jake often gave him money, but these looked expensive, and since he usually bought these types of gifts for Tony, he wondered why he purchased them alone.

Tony's cheeks flushed, but he turned and grabbed Jake's hand. "Oh, gosh, don't tell me you forgot, you bought them ages ago. I forgot about them because you are so generous, and I only found them out the other day, but I'm so glad you noticed. Now give me a hug."

Jake seemed satisfied with the answer, although he was sure he would have remembered buying them.

The affair continued for months, and each day the boy grew more infatuated with Tony while becoming jealous of his frequent disappearances.

One day in May, an unexpected visitor knocked on the door, and everything changed. Jake was surprised to find Nancy, the nippy from the Lyons coffee shop, standing in the vestibule. He hesitated. What could she want?

"Hello, Jake, can I come in?"

"Oh gosh, sorry, yes, of course you can, Nancy," He opened the door to let her through, catching a waft of the perfume she was wearing. Tony's is so much more agreeable to him. A sudden horror hit him. His heart pounds. He asks, "Is Tony all right?"

"Yes, he's fine, but he's the reason I'm here, and I need your help if possible. Can you help me, Jake?"

"If I can. Come, sit down. Will you partake of a glass of sherry with me?"

"No, not for me; thank you. But you go ahead." He poured himself a glass. He didn't have time to say anything because, within seconds, Nancy burst into tears.

"Oh, my dear, what ails you?" He kneeled before her, and she sniffed. Jake reached into his pocket and produced a clean handkerchief before saying, "Here, wipe your eyes, Nancy. Tell me, why all this upset?"

"I'm so afraid, Jake. How do I tell him?"

"Tell him what?"

"I'm going to have a baby."

"Why should you be scared to tell him? I'm sure he will help."

"But will he marry me?"

Shocked, Jake stands, "Why should he?"

He doesn't want to witness her desperation or register the answer. What if she says the words he's suddenly dreading? He stared at the floor.

"He is the father, but I don't think to be one will suit his lifestyle."

Jake felt his knees wobble. No suitable response came to mind. He grabbed a chair to steady himself. This can't be right. Tony tells him that he loves him more than the entire world and everyone in it every time they meet. Why would he say it if it wasn't true? Those words made him feel unique, and she was jealous. It was obvious to him. She wanted to cause trouble. The blood drained from his face as he staggered to a seat. Nancy, shaken, reached out to him, but he slapped her hands away.

"What's the matter, Jake; what's wrong?"

Screwing his eyes, he saw nothing but the object of his hatred. How can she say these things? With clenched fingers, he stood. Before him stood the ruination of his future with his Tony, disappearing into oblivion. No; he won't accept it. Nancy stood back, startled by the rapid transformation of his face.

"Jake, what is it?"

"You are a liar," he said, gasping, breathing was difficult. He won't let this trollop, or whatever she was, take his Tony.

Here Jake says he was almost in a trance because he wrote.'

"Trancelike, I glanced at Grandmother Emily's apparition behind Nancy, her eyes downcast, and asked myself, was she trying to tell me something? Her doleful expression did something to me as she reached out to me, stepped through Nancy's body and faded to nothing. Yes, I believed she was showing me the answer. She was telling me not to let Nancy stand in my way.

"I howled like an animal, trapped in a snare, and I swear she pushed me, I want to believe that. I lurched forward, my fingers clasped around Nancy's small, dainty neck and I squeezed with all my might. The hyoid bone cracked under the pressure of my thumbs. I squeezed on until her eyes bulged out of her head. Her tongue lolled out and began to swell in her mouth, and her body urinated, an involuntary reaction that ran down her legs and pooled on the floor. Still, I clasped tighter, only stopping when a blow from behind from a horrified Tony knocked me to the ground."

'Good grief, Larry. It sounds like he enjoyed it.'

'Yes, anyhow, he landed on the floor next to the petite but lifeless body of the five-month-pregnant Nancy. A voice woke him. "MY GOD, what have you done?"

Tony dropped to his knees and eased Nancy's swollen head onto his lap, stroking her cheek. Jake gawped at the touching scene; he couldn't believe the tenderness played out before him. No, Tony can't love her. It's impossible. Tony loves him.

He asked him, "What does this mean, Tony? She says you were expecting a happy event." His voice rumbled around the room. Tony was aghast.

"No, Jake, she can't be. Not by me. I never did anything to her. She's lying." Was he trapped? Can he extricate himself from this mess? With his mind in turmoil, how can he convince Jake of the untruth and how Nancy had lied? It's true, he loved her, but he dared not show Jake.

He and Nancy were saving. They were going to leave this smog-ridden, shadowy world of grey. They had planned this move since they escaped from the workhouse system when he promised to care for her ten years before. Since then, he had employed every means available, and now she's gone. A couple more months, and they would have been ready to go. Why did she fall pregnant?

Jake asks, "Why would she come here and tell me such a tale?"

Tony stifled a cry. "I have no idea, but you didn't have to kill her. You are a fool. The whole situation would have led to me being able to move in if I had a wife and a child. Don't you understand you've made it impossible now?"

Full of regret, Jake cried, "You mean you would have married her even though the child is not yours? You would have gone through a ceremony to move in with me."

On safer ground, Tony begins to manipulate his lover, making him believe he cannot doubt his love, but what will they do with his Nancy? His needy little lover with petite and pretty feet.

Jake appraised his handy work; what has he done? One minute she was alive, the next she was gone. He examined his fingers, still taut and claw-like. Their impression around her cheating, lying neck. They would be around it now, but for Tony hitting him. Has he ruined things for them?

Jake seized Tony, crying. "Forgive me, please. I can tell now that she was a liar. I'm so sorry. I couldn't accept that you didn't love me when she said you were the father. You do love me, don't you, Tony? Please say you do."

Tony sighed and embraced him. "Of course I do. Don't worry." Jake detected unspilled tears forming in his lover's eyes and took for granted they were for him, and he was not grieving the loss of his love and his child.'

'Crikey, Larr, this gets worse. How many murders have taken place in this house? I don't want to live here. Let's go. It's scaring me.'

'You haven't heard the half of it yet, sweetheart. Again, may I remind you that it's your fault we're here.'

Glenda is unsettled, Larry places his arm around her shoulder, saying, 'Emotions were rife when Jake was down; Tony gave comfort, and so it went the other way around when Tony was feeling low.

I'll continue, and you'll understand what I mean. This is what was on Tony's mind. What happens if Tony loses his source of income now? Where would he be if Jake was convicted of the murder since he is his most affluent client? Tony enjoyed his work. He looked at it as his security, and the pay was excellent. The world was his to choose from.

'Visualise it, Glen, Tony is glancing at the body on the floor, thinking Australia is still an option. He can still make a living but now he will be without the worry of an old promise. Jake had done him a favour; only now came the problem of how to rid themselves of Nancy. Let me enlighten you. Shall I read it verbatim or tell you what it says?'

'I think you better tell me. I'm sure it's too graphic, I don't know how much I can stomach.'

'In Tony's arms, his hot breath on his neck aroused Jake and he kissed him on the lips. Tony led him by the hand into the bedroom. Nancy can wait. She can't tell anyone anything...

With a cigarette clasped between his fingers, waiting for the first curl of smoke to leave his lips, Tony asked, "What are we going to do, Jake?"

"Do?"

"With Nancy?" Tony lay satiated on the bed and turned. Jake said, "Oh God, what have I done?"

Raising himself on one elbow. "Will you leave me now? Will you tell the police?" More concerned about losing his soul mate than the murder of a young woman and unborn child.

"Of course I won't leave you, Jake, but we must do something about the body."

Jake rose from the rumpled bed and began to pull on his trousers. "Are you sure she's dead?" He glanced back at Tony smoking a cigarette in such a casual, untroubled manner.

"Yes, Jake, she is very dead."

"Come on, come with me. I don't want to go on my own." Tony got up already formulating a plan.

At the bottom of the stairs, Jake moved to one side, letting his lover pass. With a quick peek at her, Tony stepped over Nancy's prone body and whipped a heavy jacquard–woven cloth off the table. His lips move forming the word sorry as he dropped the cloth over her petite frame.

"Listen, Jake, it isn't that long since you moved in. Have you still got any tea chests or crates left from the move?"

"Yes, out the back."

"Bring one and we'll use it."

"What for?"

"You'll see. Let's get them first, while I think. She's giving me the creeps lying here."

They began to pick through old packing crates, growing desperate as Tony threw another one to the side. "These are no use; they are too small," he said, growing more anxious.

"Perhaps not. Come and give me a hand with this one." Jake realised Tony was thinking of packing the body into a crate. Come on, hurry."

Together they lugged a crate inside. Tony viewed the wooden box and then looked at Nancy. Petite as she was, he feared she wouldn't fit inside. Jake removed the tablecloth thrown over her body and grabbed her by the arms, telling Tony to help as he lifted her by the ankles, "Come on, help me upstairs with her, grab her legs."

"Upstairs why?"

"Just do it, Tony come on, or if you'd rather, you can witness me hang by the neck. You won't find me so pretty afterwards, so take your pick."

Negotiating the stairs proved more difficult than Jake thought. He tried to ignore Tony's whining when Nancy's head banged on a step. At the top, he guided them both into the bathroom.

"Put her in the bathtub," said Jake, heaving her under the armpits while Tony struggled with the reproach of having to hold her urine-soaked legs with her skirt flapping and holding his breath as the waft of ammonia assaulted his nostrils.

"Do I have to?" He said, exhausted.

"Yes, come on, get on with it," said Jake, taking charge. Tony closed his eyes; unwilling to witness Nancy's body callously dumped in the bathtub.

"If you want, leave this to me," said Jake. "You bring up the crate and the sharpest knife from the kitchen and try to find a saw of some description."

When he returns, Tony has qualms as he places the crate down and hands over the tools. "What are you going to do?" he asks. Thinking, his neck will be next in line for the noose if anything goes wrong.

"I'll make her fit in the crate, that's what," said Jake as he stripped to the waist. Tony sidled out.

With the knife clasped tight, he regarded for the last time the whole yet dead Nippy.

"Well, here we go." The knife ripped through the clothes as Jake stripped them from the corpse, taking little heed of her naked form. Setting about the task with relish, he removed Nancy's arms at the shoulder without trouble.

Starting at the joint, he pierced the skin with the knife, using it with skill as an extension of his hand. He sliced through muscle and ligaments to expose the white ball joint before snapping it back and cutting through the last tendon to remove the arm. All far simpler than he expected. His childhood delight in dead bodies flooded back, sweat formed on his brow, and a smirk touched his lips.

He thought the legs might be a problem, so he removed them near the pubis, thankful she wasn't tall because the work was arduous with a rusty blunt saw. Calling on more skill than he possessed to cleanly remove her head, his success involved hacking rather than cutting.

Instructing a sobbing Tony on the other side of the door, listening to the noise coming from the effort

Jake put into dismembering the body, "Go and find me some paper. Those packing cases have loads in, Tony, and bring another crate while you're at it."

Tony returns with the paper and cotton wool that packed their china. Jake set to clean the torso as much as possible and then arranged the pieces on the paper layered by cotton wool to soak up any leakage before wrapping the whole caboodle and tying it with the sash cord from the reception room curtains.

Both legs received the same treatment. Stuffed without ceremony into the smaller plywood crate, yet unaware of a single word written on one of the pieces of paper.

Jake worries more about the head and arms than anything, as they are the only form of identification, and he wonders what to do with them.

Eyeing her clothes, he lifted the remnants of the garment. He never liked it, and green did nothing for her colouring. It did nothing for her now with her puce face, or is it grey? Jake wondered as he studied rotating the head a little, hanging on to her hair. He shuddered and turned her away; she never was a beauty in his eyes.

Making sure not to gaze upon the face again, he rolls it in the dress with her arms. Bundling them and the rest of her clothes inside the tablecloth, he secures them, while churning over what to do next.

Opening the door, Tony bent double and leaned against the landing wall.

"Are you all right, Tony?"

Standing upright, startled by the voice, "Yes, I just..." He ogles at the doorway, Jake is naked from the waist up, trying to comfort him. "I do understand, Tony. Don't worry, but we had better clean and wash down the whole room, including the floor and walls. We can't leave even a speck of blood anywhere."

"What will we do then; I mean what do we do with the crates?" Tony couldn't mention any part of her anatomy or even her name.

"Leave it to me. I'll sort the crates, but I can think of one problem."

"One, you are joking, only one. We are right in it, Jake. The hangman's noose is calling for us." Tony panicked; his resolve disappeared.

"Stop it, stop it now," said Jake. "I told you, we will be fine, Tony, and yes, we do have a problem a mountain of one."

"Oh God, don't tell me, please," Jake whined.

Toy blanched, "I thought you were stronger than this, Tony. You always struck me as a confident individual. Don't give in now."

Tony sighed, "You're right, I'm sorry, I'll be fine. I promise. What is the problem apart from the bloody obvious?" He jerked his head towards the bathroom.

"The head and arms," said an emotionless Jake, making Tony retch.

"We can overcome this, Tony, but what do I do with them? They can identify her."

Tony closed his eyes and the sweat on his brow hinted at their dilemma. Jake's warm breath kissed his cheek, and he opened his eyes.

Jake tried to hug Tony, but he pushed him away, saying, "Will you put some clothes on, Jake?"

Reasoning Tony was in a state of shock, Jake washed and dressed. Tony slipped down the stairs and grabbed the sherry decanter; he filled a glass to the brim and swallowed it. He poured another. He continued one after the other.

By the time Jake joined him, Tony could barely stand. Jake cajoles, "I need your help to deliver these crates to the station."

"The station?"

"Yes, the bloody station. You know where the choo choo's are." Jake's tone dripped with sarcasm.

"Why, where are we going?" Tony's sherry-addled brain couldn't comprehend what he was suggesting.

"Nowhere, but the crates are... Brighton."

"Brighton?"

"Yes, Brighton. Be quiet and listen and pull yourself together."

"All right, Brighton, we'll picnic on the beach, Jake. A little party or a visit to the clubs while we're there, shall we?"

Tony slammed his glass down, spilling sherry across Jake's antique, drop-end brocade settee, saying, "Why the freaking hell Brighton; what's wrong with Buckingham Palace or Vauxhall Gardens?"

Sarcasm dripped from Tony's lips as he fell to his knees searching the cabinet for another bottle. Jake remained passive; his grandmother stood in the corner, nodding at him.

"Trust her to turn up." He wonders if she is his imagination appeasing his guilt, wanting approval from somewhere.

"I'll use a boy to deliver them to New Cross Station. We can address one to no one in particular, in Brighton," says Tony.

"Why Brighton?"

"Why not? Think about it, says Jake. It's so busy who would comment on an old crate or two, we can deliver one somewhere else or leave one in London, let's say, Kings Cross."

Tony sobered up enough to detect a flaw in Jake's plan. "What if they nab this so-called boy and what if he tells them where he picked the package up." He fingered the empty decanter before replacing it on the silver tray.

"No, Jake, you should leave this part for me to sort." He couldn't resist adding, "Life, like death, is full of irony. Nancy always wanted to travel."

Jake wants to hug him, but Tony steps back and says, "I am well acquainted with people who owe me, and big time. People who can deliver them without questions. One to Brighton, one to Kings Cross, yes, I can do that."

"What about the third package, Tony?"

"Third?"

"Yes, the identifying limbs. What shall we do with them?"

"Hang on," Tony turned away, seeming to search

for something. He faced Jake again, and asked "Did anyone see her arrive?"

"I doubt it. I'm not sure anyone knows we're here, and that's one of the reasons I don't want the hedges or trees cut. They make us private." Jake kissed Tony on the cheek arousing himself; death has this effect on him, but Tony spun away.

"No, listen, I saw something in the yard while searching for the crates–a manhole cover set in the flags. I didn't think anything of it before, but where does it lead to?"

"No idea," said Jake. "We have a cellar here. Is it a place for coal?"

"No, you don't have one. Your coal is kept in a shed," said Tony. "You make me fill the scuttle."

"Oh, yes, so what are you thinking?"

"Well, the city is full of tunnels. I found and slept in most of them when we first ran away."

"We?"

"Nancy and me."

"Of course, sorry."

"I doubt Deptford is any different, and with the old docks here, well, what if it is a tunnel?"

"What, you mean like a smuggler's used?" Jake is amused.

"I have no idea, but if so, we can put the third package down there."

"What if this is a cesspit?"

"Ideal," says Tony.

Jake ponders, "Why don't we put all the packages

down then?"

"No, we should stick to the plan for the crates. Let's make sure there are no markings that can identify them."

"Let's open this cover first, then we can decide what to do."

The slab was visible; why hadn't he seen it before? Jake wondered, and then again, he always sent Tony out here. Together, they pull on the rusty ring of the cover.

"Gosh, it must be years since anyone touched this," Tony grunted, dropping the ring in a huff as their joint efforts proved fruitless. Jake beckoned to heaven for help.

"I wonder if we can use anything from the shed?" Tony, now sober, sprinted over to examine the contents and returned moments later with a crowbar whispering, "Look what I found."

In unison, they examined the area. Was anybody watching? Reassured, no one was about, not even from, the stables behind the King's Head pub, their closest neighbour. Together they made short work of prizing the slab, gaining enough leverage to grasp it from underneath and lift it on its end.

"I'll fetch a candle." Jake dashed into the house while Tony peered down on well-worn, rough-hewn grey stone steps. Returning with a lit candle, Jake took his lover's hand and encouraged him down the steps behind him.

"Spooky," he said. "Come on, keep up with me...

and what is that repulsive stench?"

"I bet we'll end up in some cesspit," said Tony, disgusted, rubbing the palms of his hands down his expensive suit. The further they ventured along the tunnel; the sense of confinement grew when they both needed to bow their heads to accommodate the brick-lined ceiling.

"We'll be crawling soon, Jake. How far are we going?"

'Is the tunnel still here, Larr? You are still talking about this house and underneath it; if so, I'm off.' says Glenda.

'Not so fast, darling.' Once more, placing his arm across her shoulders, which was all she needed to stay. Larry knows the score. He must keep her calm. 'Not too long now; remember, this was all your idea.'

'How can I forget when you keep telling me?'

'Okay,' he shrugs. 'On with the story.'

"Mind your head and stop whining," said Jake, bending lower still and glaring at the barrelled roof. The candle highlighted slimy droplets of water clinging to the ceiling, shadowing their footsteps, and Tony dreaded his hair touching them, so he stopped.

"Oh, it changes here; come on," said Jake.

Intrigued, they entered a brick-vaulted dome-shaped chamber. Both can stand. "My back!" Tony thrusts his fist in, turning it to soothe the knotted muscles. In front of them is a tunnel stretching on, and on their right another bricked-up tunnel.

"Do you think we are under the road at the front of

the house, Tony?" Turning a full circle to adjust his bearings. "I think we are, Jake, and this tunnel may lead to the docks." He points to the passageway ahead.

The candle fluttered, and a wispy breeze flowed in like a spectre. They advance yards, bending their backs and walking, their knees at odd angles. Each step agonising until Tony groans, "Argh, do we have to, Jake, what about my shoes?"

"I'm surprised you can see them. Come on, I'll buy you a new pair," said Jake, persevering in ankle-deep water until he suddenly stopped and yelled as something wrapped around his foot.

"What is it? What's wrong?" cried Tony grabbing Jake's arm, almost unbalancing him.

"Watch it, Tony, you'll have us in."

"But there's something in the water," said Jake, spooked, wrapped around my foot."

Slowly, Jake lowered the candle with its flickering inadequate flame, uneasy yet trying to contain his fear and not appear a wuss.

"Whatever it is down here isn't moving," he said, reaching down to investigate. Gingerly his fingers reached in and touched something slimy. He retched and wanted to whip his hand away but swallowing hard he hauled the remnants of a stinking cloth from the water.

"Oh my, this looks like it was a cloak or coat of some description that's been here for years by the state, and stink, urgh, and rat-infested too."

"Oh, rats, I forgot about them." Tony peered into

the darkness, expecting them to swarm and surround them. "I hate rats; why aren't they here?"

"They must have something better than us to chew on, or they would be all over us by now." Jake chided his lover as they pressed on, until the water began to rise, forcing them to backtrack.

In the flickering reflection of the candlelight, Jake picked out the heel of a riding boot caught in the brickwork, noting that as the water level rose higher, the wet line above their heads became more noticeable on the return journey.

"It must be tidal. The tide line is quite high; I bet this flows to the creek," said Jake, but he is staring off to one side.

"What's wrong, Jake?"

"What?" Jake swung his gaze back at Tony.

"I said, what's wrong, Jake? What are you looking at?"

Jake believed he saw his grandmother Emily in his peripheral vision or was it another ghost? The essence of long-lost spirits watching them worried him, and what if this apparition wanted revenge?

"Nothing, Tony. No, nothing. Come on, let's go."

Tony wondered who owned the cloak and what else was floating around but they were almost back, and he wanted out. The faint light from the manhole filtered down ahead like a beam, beckoning them to the exit. "We can't leave Nancy here, Jake. Please say you won't; rats scare her."

They hurried to the entrance, sloshing stinking

water as they tried to run. Hanging on to each other, they reached the stone steps and gasped in lungs full of the fresher air as they climbed up to the welcoming dawn light. Jake glances back. Is Emily still behind them, or did he imagine her?

They stagger in silence into the house, divesting themselves of wet, foul-smelling clothes. One thought on both their minds when climbing the stairs almost naked, but it can wait. The crates needed moving first.

Tony hesitated at the bathroom door to examine the spotless walls, floor, and bath. He tried to block the image of Nancy in this bathtub cut into pieces.'

'Oh, no, Larry, please stop this. This is all about killers. What is it you are trying to tell me—are you related to these murderers or what? I'm lost; I don't think I can take it, and...' Apprehensive, she says, 'This story doesn't sound like it has a fairytale ending.'

'Family stories seldom do when you think about it, but I hope this one does. I'm working on it. This must be right, Glenda. This is what my life's work is all about; producing the right result.'

'I can see where you are coming from in one way, but why this house, and why the ghost stories? Is it true, or is this revenge?'

'Revenge for what, for making me come here. How shallow do you think I am, Glenda? If you don't take this seriously, I'm going.' Larry's temper rises, unlike the temperature in the chilly room.

'No, go on, tell me, but don't drag it out, and

please don't give me a load of bullshit. I'll try to take everything in, but if this is all true, it's an awful lot to digest. Go on, what happened to the happy killers?'

'Ah well, they got away with the lot, and then Jake changed the family name. As I said, he wanted her name to go on as a thank you for his wealth, which he meant to enjoy.'

'What happened then? I mean, you're here, so it's obvious he went on to have children, and I thought he was gay and didn't like women, so how come? I mean, considering what happened to poor Nancy.'

'True, but in a nutshell. Their relationship was illegal, and many gay people grasped at marriage to prove they were, shall we say, normal.' He signed quotation marks at the side of his head.

'No, not the quote fingers, Larry. They are so passé, no one does them anymore.'

'Damn you, woman, will you...?' he glared at her. 'The second point was the war. Jake and Tony would both have to join up, but before that, something befalls Tony, only weeks after posting Nancy on her travels, and at Jake's hands.

Nancy's remains surfaced on the 17th of June 1934, at Brighton Station, in a packing case. The extreme stench alerted somebody to the unclaimed baggage. The press reported the story everywhere because of a similar crime about seven years earlier, but this one, Nancy, was never solved. Her head was never found. Her legs did turn up at Kings Cross, packed in a plywood packing case and wrapped in cotton wool and paper.

The press took to it and gave her the name Pretty Feet, but none discovered her identity or the murderer. Only I and his son, my father, hold the secret of Jake being the murderer. We've all read the diary.'

'No, Larry, no. Are you sure? I mean, is this just...'

'What, Glen?'

'Gosh, this is too awful to think about, but you are saying that this Jake, what is he to you, is he your grandfather or what?'

Glenda stands and moves away from Larry, afraid. Something is wrong. She wants to leave.

'Can we go home yet, Larry?' She shivers. 'I'm so cold considering the sun's shining outside, and we've been here for hours. At least it seems like hours. I want to go home and warm up.'

'In a bit. Come on, let's go upstairs. You haven't seen the attic or the bathroom yet.'

'No, I don't want to. Let's do it another day.'

'I told you back home, Glenda, it's now or never because you won't be coming back.' Her mouth drops.

'Let me show you the bathroom, you'll love the tub. Quite an innovation at the time, although for a different reason than you may think. It saved Emily from that hateful place because her treatment was moved here and overlooked by Agnes and Dawson.'

'Is it the same bath? If so, I don't want to see it.'

Skipping up the stairs and tucking a letter into his back pocket with one hand while pulling her behind him with the other. Laughing, his voice is light. It makes her smile, and she skips on. Is the recent lull in their relationship changing and getting back to normal? Larry holds the door open for her to enter.

'Blimey, how huge is that tub; wow, I love it.' Forgetting the horror story, she runs her fingers over the roll–top, noting the green stain under the taps and the cracked enamel, which, with attention, would be magnificent. Larry sits on the roll top.

'Sit down, Glen. I'll tell you the rest.' Sitting on the floorboards, she rests against the wall and admires a worn patch of oilcloth under the bath, still bearing the remains of an azure diamond pattern. She pats the floor for him to sit beside her. He remains where he is.

'Tony and Jake kept up their pretence of being only friends and yet felt forced by convention at the time to escort young ladies out on occasion to avoid suspicion. Something Jake despised and believed Tony agreed.

Everyone dismissed or ignored the rumblings of war because of the awful reality that it may break out and develop into a second war so close to 'the war to end all wars' where Jake, as did his father and Tony, would have to fight for king and country was now significant. As it happened, Glen Tony never had the choice.

One night Jake followed him out of the house following an argument about the time Tony spent away from him. Tony left in a huff. Struggling with guilt about starting the row, Jake decided to chase after him and apologise. Not daring to cry out in the street because their reputations were at stake. He only wanted to catch him, but before reaching the end of Albury Street, he saw Tony meet up with a man. On its own, nothing was untoward, but to Jake, they were too close. They didn't touch or speak; they just settled into step, side by side in companionable silence.

Chapter 15

THE BODY IN THE TREE

'Jake's stomach knotted. It can't be. Tony wouldn't, but he still trailed after them, keeping them in sight until the high street where the stranger hailed a cab. Tony climbed in first, and Jake didn't miss the man climbing in after caressing Tony's buttocks, and Tony did nothing to stop him.

Jake was close enough to overhear him direct the cabby to the Caravan Club before the door closed on them, a fashionable venue that Jake was keen to join, but Tony said it was not their sort of place. So, why was he going there with a stranger?

Jake walked back along the street worried but surely nothing was going on. Tony would be able to explain when he got back of course he would, he always did.

Jake stopped walking and leaned against a wall, a pose he first saw Tony standing in and a feeling he hadn't experienced in a long time began to heat his blood. Why did Tony always have, what seemed a plausible excuse when he was away, what did he actually do?

When Jake gave it some thought, he had no idea where Tony's money came from apart from what he gave him. He began to remember his childhood, how he had no friends and how lonely he was. Had he jumped on Tony and accepted him because he was desperate and needy? Was there something sexual that cried out in him when he first saw Tony? All those desires from a child, his love of dissecting animals and his loneliness until his Grandmother Emily appeared to him, telling him not to worry, she was with him, and he must avoid these thoughts, but now they hurtled back.

He hadn't seen Grandmother Emily in a while to talk with. Oh, yes, sometimes he was aware of her like when she was there with Nancy, and he thought she was showing him what to do.

He thumped the wall tearing the skin on his knuckles and experienced a sense of fulfilment as he watched the beads of blood pool across the back of his hand, he enjoyed the colour and the feel between his fingers. "Well, grandmother where are you now?" He cried out.

A warm glow filled his body when he faced his home because standing next to his gateway was a lady dressed in a garish costume who beckoned to him and smiled though, this time, a man holding a thin-bladed knife stood behind her. Was this Grandfather William coming to help?

The rage bubbling in Jake exploded, instant and unstoppable. He knew of the club's reputation as the most unconventional spot in town and Caravan was a code word in the gay community.

Although he had had suspicions before while

watching Tony go out in the evening all dressed and saying he was off to a meeting, Jake was afraid to ask with whom and what he did at these meetings, but now the love filter cleared. Tony was a liar and a cheat.

Jake began to recall missed appointments and the extra shaving at strange hours on Tony's part. When asked why, he said, "Because you like it this way, Jake; you don't like beards."

Like a wrecking ball smashed into him, Jake came to terms with the awful fact that Tony wanted his wealth and not him. He also accepted the truth of Nancy's words; Tony was the father of her child.

The different presents Tony had explained away with a flourish, and the nights he didn't come around all began to make sense to Jake. "When the bastard returns, he won't need explanations or excuses, not again or ever." He spat the words out.

Nancy and her accusations came to his mind. "By God, Tony, I will teach you to spread your favours."

Jake's naivety vanished. The boy became a man, or was the devil reborn? What do you think, Glen?' Bemused, she couldn't say anything.

'Tony returned the next evening, all smiles and full of protestations of love for his rich lover, who did his best to conceal the rage bubbling under the surface. The hate built up through the long hours waiting for the man of his dreams to come home. Revenge would be sweet and something to savour.'

Larry waits for a reaction. Loving the harsh reality

of the diary's words and the control of his voice. The differing tones he uses for maximum effect begin to work on Glenda, like the hot and cold treatment Emily endured before a lassitude came upon her. Larry smiles. He doesn't have long to wait.

'I don't think I want to hear any more.' She says. 'This is all getting too much for me.' Larry, though, carries on as if she never opened her mouth.

'Jake takes Tony by the hand and leads him to this room. Larry tapped the edge of the bathtub. Tony, I suppose thought nothing was amiss as they enjoyed bathing together, but he didn't say anything.

Jake wrote, "I led a lamb to the slaughter; the only difference is Tony was no lamb. He is a wolf, preying on the rich and the lonely."

With Jake now understanding the source of Tony's acquisitions, his new watches, suits, and yes, Jake supplied most, but other gifts appeared too: gold snuff boxes and silver buttons, of which he did not know from where they came.

After those first few coffees in Lyon's coffee house, Tony had never once put his hand in his pocket. They took cabs, ate at the best restaurants, and had their clothes tailored by the best Savile Row tailors, all at Jake's expense.

'In here,' Larry gestured around the room, 'Jake locked the door and turned on the huge taps, while Tony began to remove his clothes.' Larry points at the taps, still enjoying Glenda's insecurity. He tries to keep a straight face as he talks. 'Tony is unaware of what is to come and climbs into the tub.

"Come on, Jake, come and join me."

Jake undressed but took his time and a strange expression masked his face prompting Tony to ask him, "What's wrong?"

"Nothing."

"Honest, you strike me as if we are going to have THE talk."

"No, Tony, no talk."

Tony stretched out naked in the hot water, wriggling his toe around the hot tap to curb the flow, ready to add cold. He gazed at his young lover with a smile on his face when without any warning, Jake took hold of Tony's ankles and dragged him under the water.

Tony's first reaction is to grasp the roll-top and pull himself up; this is a different game from what they play. Although shocked, he is not worried until Jake yanks his feet so hard that he cries out. His smile vanished, swept away by a gut feeling that something was dreadfully wrong.

Jake was well prepared and lashed his feet to the taps. Fighting to keep his head above the rising water, the sinews in Tony's neck strained to their limit with his frantic efforts to free his feet. His hands gripped the roll top, yelling at Jake to let him go. Instead, his lover smashes the butt of a knife on his fingers—a thin, long-bladed knife he hid under the claw-footed tub.

Tony yelled in pain, releasing his grip. Jake moved

to the head of the tub, brandishing the blade, swaying it from side to side, and circling the narrow steel, tormenting the half-submerged face of the man he once loved.

'You bought this on yourself, you bastard. I thought you loved me, but you are nothing but a lying thieving bastard and a whore. I loved you so much, Tony, how could you do it to me? Did I only mean money to you, you could have just asked, and me, being the idiot I am, would have given it to you. But to take Nancy and how many others, no, you took a step too far.'

In a last-gasp attempt to save himself, Tony thrusts his arms up and holds his last breath in his effort to grab Jake or the knife–anything to break free. This hell hole is not going to keep him. His goal is to go to the other side of the world, as far away as possible, and this is what he's worked for these past years. Jake keeps slapping his hands away.

Bucking his hips and knees in the constant struggle to emerge from the water, Tony's strength disappeared, desperate to free his feet while the bath filled inch by inch. He blew air from his nose, trying to gasp in breath as he fixed on Jake's angelic face, smiling down at him.

"You shouldn't have crossed me, Tony." Jake twitched and turned his head. "No, grandmother, I will deal with this.'"

By this time, severe doubts are unsettling Glenda. About what, she's not sure. Is it the murders or the enjoyment Larry seems to get while relating them? She's on edge.

'Almost finished.' Larry smiles at her. 'Tony begged forgiveness, coughing and spluttering for breath, his eyes pleading. His face was now under the water with his nose breaking the surface, one last breath to implore his lover.

Jake grabs a handful of Tony's hair, hauling his face out of the water. "It's too late, you son of a bitch. I saw you, you bastard. You whoring swine, you lied. Well, we are through now. Enough is enough.

We dismembered Nancy, yes. You may not have used the knife, but you are no innocent. You are right up to your neck in guilt, and now up to your neck in water. Ironic, hey. Well, Tony, I am going to do the same with you. You will join Nancy and the others in pieces, along with the sewer rats. You will be excellent company for the other rubbish. I wonder how long the rats will take to strip your bones of flesh and let you filter out into the ocean piece by nasty, lying piece? The only difference is that you will be alive while I set about my task."

Thrusting the blade into Tony's shoulder, blood gushed from the wound, spilling out like spilt ink from a bottle on blotting paper, colouring the water in a scarlet cloud reminiscent of a red sky at night, but not with any delight to follow. At least not for Tony, who screamed as Jake struck again, this time his other shoulder.

The blade was well-honed because he spent the

afternoon caressing it on a leather strap. Jake took his time. Delighting in the easy slide, the tugging, and the flesh puckering before yielding to the blade. He pressed the point hard into Tony's chest, enjoying the skin parting to reveal its layers before the last beats of Tony's heart pumped the bright, crimson blood into the gash.

It was almost too soon for Jake when the fighting stopped. Tony's face was under the surface, his mouth and eyes staring, crazed with fear. Nerves twitched in his body as the blade pierced the skin under his chin and glided down his chest with the minimum of effort.

Jake climbed into the bloodied water and straddled Tony, kissing his dead lips and cupping his cheeks in his hand.

"I was in love with you, Tony," he said, slicing the lips from his mouth.

The full tub prompted Jake to let the water out, but he left the tap running, trying to ensure no spatter. He stabbed the blade deeper into Tony's chest, where the tip scraped on his rib cage, before sinking into the once-firm belly.

The stench from the ruptured bowel rises. Jake laughed with an eerie demonic sound as he again grabbed him by the hair, lifted his head, and, with one swipe of his trusty blade, sliced the head almost clean off Tony's shoulders. He did not need to hack now.'

Larry appears lost in a world Glenda can't enter. His glazed eyes show no recognition. She shuffles to the doorway, his head turning, his eyes blank, and his voice monotone as he says,

'Jake ran away and joined the army; he had little choice, but he soon gained a reputation, and rumours began to infiltrate his section that he was a queer. To gainsay the speculation about him, he married in 1939, almost the first girl he met on leave in London, a naïve young thing to mould to his ways.

She never liked living on Albury Street and began spending more time with an old aunt when Jake was away in a house by the docks where she spent her childhood. She became pregnant and produced a son, my father, in 1940, but Jake never clapped eyes on him. You see, Glenda. I thought they abandoned me and left me unloved, but it turned out to be my father who was unloved.

Not able to settle in his enforced marriage, Jake spent no time with her, believing he made an awful mistake in bowing to society, and her confinement tied the chain of despair around his earnest desire to spend any Army leave in gay clubs in the seedier districts of London.

Aged twenty-four, Jake died in a bombing raid in September 1940. Only a week later, that psycho Hitler began to alter London's landscape forever, but not before Jake committed one more heinous murder.'

Larry, with an air of smugness, recalls the terrible drama. 'With his mates, they were on manoeuvres in Worcester, where they were all accustomed to heavy drinking sessions. All six lads were homesick, and they wanted home comforts.

Their passions increased with each pint of ale, and a lass was willing enough. Unable to take her near the barracks or the pub, they requisitioned a truck and set off in high spirits to a place of seclusion.

Of course, she wasn't Jake's type, but he must pretend to join in, he only wanted to act the part with no intention of doing it. Jake had had his fill of cloying women with his wife when they first married, and there was no way he would keep up the pretence away from home.

Apart from Jake, the rest staggered around drunk. When his turn came, he wrote, "She was well up for it."

Squaddies paid well if they thought they were due overseas. Regardless, he wasn't going to pay because he would not interfere with her. She, though, a typical woman, wanted money and demanded a considerable amount, or she would split on him and tell his mates he was a faggot.'

'What is it with you, Larry? All women are not the same.' Infuriated, she slaps at him.

'All right, present company accepted, now do you want to listen or what?'

'Yes, go on.'

'This fired Jake up when she began to shout. He must stop her cries. He was not going to spend his time in jail, not for a bloody, low-life street slut. The taffeta from the lining of her frock caught his eye, and he ripped a piece off and rammed it down her gullet. He even added how he enjoyed shutting her stupid mouth, but then her silence presented a new problem. How does he dispose of her?

His struggle left him out of breath, so when he beckoned to the other lads, shouting something was wrong, they would think he had had a first-rate time too.

Stumbling around, laughing and telling bawdy jokes, betting they could take her on again, the others returned to Jake when he called. He appeared worse for wear like them but was, in fact, stone-cold sober when he pointed the shaft of his torch in their direction.

Playing the torch beam, moving it up and down and making figures of eights, to act more drunk than he was. He highlighted their antics until he swung it like a spotlight on the girl lying close to his feet, pretending to call them for help as if something was wrong with her because she wouldn't move.

Jimmy Newman, the youngest, looked on asking, "What's up with her?" He was also the last to take his turn before Jake.

Garth Mulligan, believed all the girls fancied him, said, "She was all right when I took her, and she thanked me."

"You talk a load of bollocks and shite because she never said a word to me."

Neither man foresaw the significance or the dire events that would befall them if they were found as they began a battle of words about their manliness until Eric Burrage stopped them.

"Shut your stupid faces, the pair of you. She's dead!" He dropped to his hunkers. His bloodshot eyes stared, but he appeared to have grasped the gravity of their situation better than the others.

Jake waved his hand, shaking his head in mock disgust. He needed to convince them that this was their fault. "You killed her. When I got here, I thought she'd had enough, but no, I'm telling the lot of you. I found her like this. When I tried, she didn't move. Are you listening to me? She was already dead."

Jock Washington stuck his two-penneth in with, "Aye, dead tired because I gave it to her good and proper."

Five pairs of bleary eyes stared at Jake; feet shuffled, and hands thrust into pockets. Jock fumbled with a packet of cigarettes, dropping them; his fingers shaking, yet no one said a word. A vixen howled over yonder, like a woman screaming in fear.

"Concentrate," said Jake; he'd shifted the blame. They won't remember who did what in the morning. He reinforced the deed: "You killed her, Jimmy, but we are all in this together and better do something or the noose will be greeting the lot of us."

Larry pauses, waiting for Glenda, who remains speechless, to respond, so he continues.

Fred McGoogan was the quietest of the bunch and hailed from a poor and disadvantaged family. He wanted acceptance from his new comrades but now wished he were anywhere but there, and he threw up.

Eric, the driver who got the vehicle to take them to

the woods, began to run, saying he wasn't taking the blame, and that he had better get the lorry back unnoticed. Jock soon brought the coward to his knees with a rugby tackle, yelling, "We're all in this together, laddie."

Jimmy, a dependable sort, ran around like a headless chicken, but in his panic, he came across an old hollow tree, not twenty yards from where they were, and suggested they dump her inside the rotting trunk.

The eastern sky was already beginning to glow with the looming dawn. They needed to move her fast before she stiffened up. And that's what they did. Between them, they lifted her body and dumped her in the hollow tree. Ironic, really.' Larry sniggers. 'They wouldn't have had to go on the run because their orders were for imminent overseas postings.

Jake decided to use his 48-hour pass to visit his wife. Whether to tell her the truth or have a sly peek at my father is anybody's guess, but it never happened.'

'I bet Emily knew,' Glenda finds the story more interesting now because of its relevance to Larry and his Emily.

'Shush, he was only around the corner from where his wife lived, hurrying as the air raid sirens began blaring when the street took an almighty hit, and he perished in the blast or falling debris.

My grandmother died only months later from her injuries, and while it was a direct hit that claimed my aunt outright, only my father survived, found in his cot. A fallen beam straddled over his crib where he lay, it supported part of the roof. The rescue team followed his cries, discovering him unhurt but covered in dust.

Once again, as I told you, Emily and William found their descendant was adopted as an orphan, He was a sensitive soul who inherited everything, as his father had left a will.

No matter how hard Jake spent, he hadn't even made a dent in his capital. This included property and of course, they would have gone to his wife had she lived but came to my father instead.

I could say he was the only normal one in the family until he discovered the curse when he moved here into this house. Why did he open the chest and read the letters? Who can say because he left it locked for such a long time? I was already born when he succumbed. She never told me.'

Chapter 16

REVELATIONS

'Well, it doesn't say much for Emily. One son dies in the first war, then a grandson in the second. I thought you said she looked after them, yet they were all... hang on, Larry, what does, "she never told me mean?" Who never told you what?'

It strikes Glenda that Larry may be making a fool of her. He often accuses her of being slow on the uptake and unintelligent but, she had reasoned out before saying anything, that if Jake died in a blast, how did he write this in the diary or anywhere else for that matter?

Larry tries to ignore the question, 'She saved my father, so, in theory, she guaranteed the family line continuing through me. I never divulged about the tests to you, did I, Glen?'

'Which ones?' She snuggles closer to him, and with her fear diminishing, curiosity grows.

'Don't be funny, the DNA ones. Glenda, this is important, or why bother?

'I assume this has to do with your research.' In a sotto voice, she mumbles, 'Isn't everything?'

Silence pervades. The floorboards groan under the bathtub as she shifts her weight next to Larry.

'Bloody typical.'

'Why do you say that?' She lifts her head and fixes his gaze.

'Give me a minute, and I'll try to clarify.' His eyes move and fix on the corner of the room, so much so, Glenda is unsure whether he is talking to her. She shudders.

'If William and Emily understood what I do, this would never have happened.'

'Wh...?'

'No, I'll explain. Genetics is the way forward and one day, we will be able to remove faulty genes. Now and with more screening, we could stop flawed ones from coming together.'

'Damaged people or genes?'

Larry hugs her close to keep her interest. They have never talked about his work before, and he likes it.

'Much of a muchness in a way, I am beginning to think people should be forced to take genetic tests before they inflict their genetic biology on another body. This is complex for a layperson such as you, Glenda. Think of a kind of reverse of natural selection. The genes progress in strength, and the strongest grow ever stronger. I think this gene in the family in my research will grow too, and yet, what if I, with my work, can put an end to it?

'Let's say it's a living organism that won't die out. It's alive and appears to hunt for like-minded people. After they meet and combine, the results can be devastating. Now concentrate. Say, I am the one to end it, and the only way I can is to prevent it from procreating.'

'You mean people with faulty family genetics? You want to stop them having children. But, Larry, you can't engineer children or take away the rights of parents. That can't be right.'

He keeps his composure and continues his efforts to make her understand and it is an effort in his mind. 'Yes, put like that; in a way, you're right. Glenda, you must understand how vital my work is to help put an end to the monsters of the 21st century. If I can highlight these recessive genes alter them, eliminate them, or at least ensure they can't be passed on, my work may aid humanity.

'I'm sure screening will be the norm soon, and this will help eliminate any chance of, how can I put this... half of a gene meeting its counterpart, and the result is a full-blown disease or a malady that causes death and blights families for centuries.

'These days it's inconceivable to think of another William and Emily, like Bonny and Clyde, Brady and Hindley. Was theirs a genetic flaw? My research is about people and the lives of the families at stake.

'If the gene is damaged or evil, what about their offspring? If it were possible to stop them from procreating, the horror they inflict on the world would not happen. It's still a theory, this gene, but if proven accurate and we can remove or alter it, think how much better mankind would be. Take Hitler, was he the product of two evil genes coming together, or did he choose his vile path?'

'Yes, I get it, Larry—but you are so passionate as if it's personal. This is the bit I can't come to grips with.'

'Well, Jack the Ripper came back, not in person, but he passed his genes onto his son and with the help of his beloved Emily, who, I admit, did at first try to stop the mayhem. Alas, bless her; she was never strong in the head, but her love for William and those to follow down the line, overcame her. She failed to stop her family's murderous reign, so, typical of Emily, she changed tack. I suppose back in the day, she would need the cold bath treatment to keep her placid, but now she keeps control by trying to eliminate the problems for her family and calls on William when she wants him. Despite all her efforts, Jasper followed on a murderous track, Emily, though, is never one to falter in her love, even after something triggers him to kill Phyllis. This is a part of my research; what the triggers are, and all I pray for is the time to complete it.'

'Are you telling me you're ill?'

'No, nothing like that. You're barking up the wrong tree.' Larry shrugs her fears away.

'Another one, Jake, my grandfather, was never apprehended for his murders, and again, what was the trigger point?'

'But you said they wrote down the trigger points that started them, and I'm not sure if I wouldn't have knocked off a couple after what they went through.'

Glenda reaches for the paper Larry tucked in his pocket.

'No,' he said. 'You won't find the answers in that one. I learnt about this through the inheritance left to us all.'

'You said it was all here, Larry, and you haven't explained about Jake yet, or how he managed to write his events down.'

Taken off his guard, Larry rekindles his feelings for Glenda from when they first met, the respect she showed him, and how she would always bow to his knowledge and give him his due. Where did it all go wrong? Oh, yes, she brought his grandmother back like an avenging angel.

Emily always seems to hover in the background; her shadowy figure appears between her bouts of chaos, but Larry accepts her as a quirk and in his head, he has put her to one side. Glenda's nagging brought the phantom back, but rather than remain in the shadows, she now talks to him with that insistent voice in his ear. She tells him what to do and how.

She's like an annoying fly; okay on the window, but when it buzzes around your head you want to swat it. The voices, led by Emily, had stopped him from doing his work, which to him is paramount to saving the world.

To think he can do all this—no more wars, no Pol Pots, or dictators needing Godlike worship such as Kim Jong Un. Inferior little beings who think they are omnipotent. The real truth is that they should hold on high, such as himself, those who can manipulate and cure humankind of evil.

He should be revered, and no, not worshipped. His thoughts bring calming utterances back. He shakes his head to clear it because if the trials work, success will be his. All this distraction is misusing any time. Yes, Glenda is wasting his time.

'Larry, you're miles away. Is everything okay?' Her words break into his thoughts like an exploding bomb bringing him back to reality.

'Emily may have understood more than I give her credit for in her demands for her letters to be handed to the eldest child of each generation. She came and told each one of us about our past. Why did each generation only bear one child, a son? Why, Glen? What if the gene controlled them, limiting them until it came across another half?' He shakes his head in despair.

'I'm not following you.' Glenda stifles a yawn.

'Okay, Glen, there are conditions one can only inherit in an autosomal recessive pattern. Simplified, autosomal means genes. We all acquire twenty-three pairs of genes, twenty-two pairs of autosomes, and one pair of sex genes, the x and y, at conception. What if one of these autosomals is a killer gene?'

'TMI, Larry, sorry.'

'What?'

'You are not with it, are you, Larr? It means Too Much Information.' He ignores her.

'This means the condition can only be passed on

to a child if both parents receive a copy of the faulty gene, or, in other words, both are carriers of the disease.

'If the child only inherits one copy of the flawed gene, they are carriers but won't suffer themselves from the condition. If a mother and a father carry the faulty gene, there's a one in four probability that each child they have will inherit the condition and a one in two probability they will be carriers.

'So, if Emily and William both carried this defective or rogue gene, they may have bred a family of killers. It goes beyond all this, though; in my eyes, what if this killer gene searches out partners?'

'Oh, come on, that's Si-Fi gone wrong.'

'No, think about it. It's possible. They say people fall in love at first sight, accepting that fate made them for each other. What happens? Who is to say it's not the genes forcing them together?

According to the evolution theory, the strongest survive. What if it's all down to these genes? As for your question about Jake, Emily told me the stories. Yes, the accounts are in her diaries, but picking out the relevant pieces needs somebody to go through them with a fine-tooth comb.

'I understand why they never took heed of them dismissing them as the rambling of the mad. Emily explained it to me, and I went through and found all the details of my family. The whole squalid affair.'

Dumbstruck by what he's saying, Glenda thinks he's nuts, or at least halfway. No, but then again, who talks about their sodding grandmother's talking to them and can claim they are not insane? She wants to edge away, but his grip is firm with his arm across her shoulder.

'My father, a gentleman, I believe from what I discovered but also afflicted in the same way. The difference is that he read the letters too soon, just after my birth. His last scribbles said he couldn't bear the thought of one day being a murderer and admitted that, after reading them, new and strange ideas plagued him. Ghosts haunted and spoke to him; so much so, he told his wife, my mother, who became hysterical. My father decided to have none of it, unable to live waiting for his world to crash down on them. So, Glenda, Emily is here with her motherly instincts outweighing her sense of duty, and it's up to me, the last of the line.'

Glenda shivers. What is he on about?

'What you mean here—here in this house, or this room, and it's up to you to do what? Are you saying you want a child now?'

'Oh God, Glenda, put your brain into gear. A child is the last thing I want. Don't you still understand?

'Over the years, I wondered what was wrong with me. I'm not stupid, as you well know, but they used to visit me. I pretended to ignore them, but when I told my wife, another mistake in my naivety. I told her about the house like I'm telling you, or to tell the truth, you are dragging it from me. This curse is not new to me. I have known about it for years, Glenda, but like most people, like an ostrich, I hid my head in the sand right up to my arse, and I married. Why did I? Anyhow, she was a right pain. She didn't believe a word, nag, nag, nag and she wanted a hoard of kids even after I told her they would never be on the agenda. I think she was the one who sent me mad.'

He surveys her, 'Well, all but mad.'

Glenda shifts about to speak.

'No, don't say anything. When I couldn't stand it anymore, I was almost ready to do her in, but Grandmother Emily came to me and assured me she would sort things out, saying she wanted to keep me well. She and William visited and took care of the problem, and now they are here again to help me solve this, my new predicament.'

'What is this new dilemma?' Sweat breaks out on Glenda's baffled forehead. Things don't sound too wholesome.

'My wife died, Glenda. You made me smile when you asked if Jenny was under the patio, because no, she isn't. As I told you, she is off somewhere but she was alive when I last saw her, unlike my wife.'

She thinks better of asking where his wife is. Intimidated now and fearful, can she leap up and run? Will he stop her? Is he still out to frighten her? Larry continues:

'Don't you want to find out where she is, Glenda?'

'Stop it, Larry. Stop it, enough; you've gone too far. If you want rid of me, say so. I'll be off and never bother you again.'

'I wanted to show you; I did give you a clue, Glen. As I said, it tickled me about the patio. Okay, it has no patio, but tunnels are under the house, leading to the docks, the creek, or both. I never followed them all the way, but I plan to one day soon.

'Emily showed Jake how to use them to hide any evidence. It worked. My beloved spouse is in them. I do have plans to concrete the yard. It's getting a bit dicey don't you think? Emily says one or two disiecta membra, including Jasper's tutor and the woman who set herself up as a housekeeper, grace the tunnels too.'

'What?' Stunned, Glenda says, 'I didn't do Latin, which I am assuming that is.'

'No, you didn't, and it's one of my proudest achievements until I complete my research. It's quite a charming language. The literal meaning is scattered remains, far nicer than body parts spread about, don't you think so, Glen?'

'You can be so weird, Larry, and you're scary.'

'Ha, here's a quote you will love from Seneca. It's a pity you won't have time to learn it, and it applies well, Timendi causa est nescire. Ignorance is the cause of fear, which fits you to a T, Glenda.

'Poor. Pretty feet. Well, part of her is down the tunnel. I went in once, but it scared the bejeebers out of me. They blamed me for their incarceration as if everything was my fault. I haven't searched further because what does it matter in the grand scheme of things? But you, Glenda, you will have the honour of being the last.' Larry squints through his screwed, slit eyes.

'I hope–well, it's not hope. You are to be the last one, Glenda, because she assured me, and I, with no heirs, am the last in line. With the help of Emily, I can end this curse.'

A blast of sulphurous air spews from the plug hole, bringing the stench of death and sewage into the room so thick, they seal their lips in a grimace.

Unnerved to the extent of panic, Glenda spins around. The Bombay cat is tiptoeing on its claws, looking fearsome with its short hair standing on end, resembling a toilet brush. She remembers they closed the door, so when did it come in?

Why is she worried? Larry promised she'd be safe, but from what?

A quick revision of events brings her to a scary conclusion. Larry is unsafe to be with; how can he save her? She needs to escape.

A crushing sensation of severe doom closes in, forcing breath from her lungs and. a woman's voice screams out: "NO, Larry. You will not stop it. You cannot and never will."

'I'm sorry, Grandmother; I must, and you have to help me. You said you would.' He shies away as a blast of polar air separates him from Glenda, who clasps her throat. Her eyes brim with tears and fear. She stumbles to her feet sure her end is near. She is going to die. Larry is pitching his delusional grandmother's wrath against what he believes is his normality, and his remaining tiny grasp on reality catches Glenda, slumping to the floor, she notes the decorative oilcloth without admiration now.

He reassures her. 'It's all right, love. I've scared you. Don't worry, it's a panic attack. Breathe in deep. You'll be fine. I'm sorry I took it too far.'

Annoyed, he glared into the corner and seething says in muted tones, 'Stop it and leave it to me. You agreed to let me do it my way.'

'I agreed, what, Larry?' Whispers a frightened Glenda believing he is talking to her.

The last thing he wants to do is frighten her.

'Aw, love, come on now. Don't take on so.' He lifts her to his side and places her on the edge of the bath, slinging his arm over her shoulders. He gives her a little hug.

'What's going on, Larry? I can't stand any more of this. I swear, I'm sorry. I know I'm such a fool, but I want out. Something is dead wrong here, and why is that damn cat following me around?' She struggles to make a joke.

'It's Emily, Glen. She's here, I told you, she's in the corner.'

'I can't fathom any of this. You don't mean THE Emily?' Glenda stares around the bathroom; a shadow looms, resembling a person but disappears when the sun emerges from behind a cloud giving a little respite to the gloominess of the green-tiled room, which was once fashionable but is revolting now.

'She is not here, Larry. Honestly, I think you need help. Come on, let's go.'

'Help, yes. You're right. Yes, thank you. That's why grandmother is here; to help me.' His voice deepens. 'You wouldn't stop,'

She checks the room; if he's not talking to her so, who else?

He stands. His stature fills the room as he squares up to her while she steadies her balance on the roll-top edge. 'You had to pry, didn't you, Glen? Well, this is the last time you'll butt in where you don't belong. I tried not to, but you made me remember and answer their call. Your chance to escape was downstairs if you had just asked about the DNA test. I wanted you to run, but Emily said no. I told her you would never say anything or let on about family secrets. But you couldn't keep quiet even if your life depended on it. Oops, silly me, your life does. Remember, I am Jack's descendant.'

Neither a grin nor a smile sullies his thin, straight lips. 'William was a myth. The coaching accident altered his character, but he returned to finish his mission. It's in the genes, Glenda, and that's why I'm passionate. This is why my research is so vital.'

'What is it you're telling me, Larry? Please get to it?'

'I will die childless. You will just die. I can do nothing to stop it now. There can be no more Jacks or Emilys running around causing havoc, death and destruction, and you know too much with your snooping. You'll want to hear this bit, Glenda; this is where you come in.' His laughter echoes around the bathroom, his eyes wild and staring.

'No, it's not true. You are not well, Larry. Let me help. You have your work, and you're trying to scare me, and you've succeeded. But enough is enough. I'm sorry, sorry for everything. Please, let's go home.'

Menace and evil filter into the room Glenda covers her mouth, screws her face and stares in disbelief at the man she loves, the aroma of lemon verbena suffocating her. His features are soft and feminine one minute, harsh and cruel the next, with eyes burning into her soul, weighing heavy and crushing her spirit. His hands reach out, grasping her wrist; she raises her arms to protect herself from a rain of blows she believes is coming and screams, 'I'm begging you, Larry. Listen to me, please. I'm pregnant!'

Shocked and shaking his head, 'No, don't say anything. It won't save you. You have sealed your fate. I told you I cannot have a child. I am the last in the line. Only I can break the curse.'

Letting go of her wrist, impotent for a moment on what to say, his lips work yet emit no sound until he spins around, 'Grandmother,' he cries, ripping at his hair.

Glenda eyes the door he's blocking, can she pass him? A thin-bladed knife turns on the shelf, catching Larry's eye. Its white bone handle gleams in the semi-darkness.

'I understand, Grandmother. Leave this to you,' he says like a small boy being told off.

Taking her chance, Glenda dashes to the door,

yanking, screaming, kicking, and pulling. It remains stubborn and fixed as his demonic laugh chills her soul, more so because he does not attempt to stop her. A bruise appears on her wrist from his substantial grip, belying his sedentary work.

'Come now, Glenda; have some dignity, please. I've told you; you won't leave here. Do you think a bit of kicking and screaming will save you?'

'What about the baby, Larry?'

'What about it? You are not pregnant, at least not by me. I made sure of no children on my part after Jennifer. I think that's why she left. She got all broody and moody, but I wouldn't give in. I had the snip, and blow me, she ran off with a sodding woman. There's no pleasing some folk.' He snorts, amused at his comment.

'If you are pregnant, the father is somebody else, which means you have been playing around and would have to go regardless. Remember Jake's revenge on Tony? He wouldn't put up with it, and I won't either. So, all in all, Glenda, darling, I will say BYE, BYE.'

Wide-eyed and sick to her heart, Glenda drops her gaze, beaten, with no more strength to fight, and succumbing to his superior will. 'I won't struggle now. I can't. Do what you believe you must. I can't take anymore. I can't fix this monster in you, can I?'

'That's not fair, Glen. No, I am not a monster. I'm the one trying to put order back into the family. It's me who wants to bring this all to an end. Don't call me that.'

For a moment, hope returns; the scientist is back. Has she hit a nerve? Can she awaken from this nightmare?

'You told me your family are monsters, Larry. You told me you are different; what about your research? You are the same. Please, Larry, think about it if you kill me.' She gulps, 'You are like them. Don't let her do this to you, please.'

Her eyes sweep the room for something to use as a weapon. A microsecond of peace breaks out, nothing, not a sound. Seconds tick by. Is she getting through to him?

A strained metallic grinding noise cuts the silence and fills the bathroom with the squeal of rusty metal. The huge twisting handle on the tap over the clawfoot tub shudders open, spitting and gurgling blood-coloured water and filling the bath.

Larry grabs her wrist, pulling her forward. 'Mad, am I? I'll show you mad. I told you I needed to work. Well, now look what you've gone and done.'

Glenda wriggles in his grasp, trying to loosen his painful grip. 'I'm sorry, Larry. I didn't mean to upset you and yes, I made mistakes. I can change. Let me go. What the hell is happening in the bath? Come on, let me go. For God's sake, let's go home.'

She struggles, once more pleading to the side of him she thought she knew, but his face is a façade. A veil, devoid of emotion, and in one awful moment of clarity, Glenda registers that Larry has slipped over the last barrier to insanity.

To think she is living with a madman—has she pushed him too far? Is this her fault? He glances around the room; a smile flickers, curving his lips. He asks of fresh air, 'Are you sure?'

Glenda still won't accept the presence of Emily, and she tries to keep him talking. 'Sure, of what, Larry? I don't understand. Let me go, please. Let's go home?'

'Be quiet. I'm not talking to you. I'm done trying because you don't listen. You pretend to, but you don't. Now—well, it's too late. We are home, or at least you are.'

He stares at the bath. Glenda is about to speak when a woman's voice interrupts her. "Yes, you can leave her here. You know what to do; don't worry, Larry, I hate the baths too, but they work."

Glenda's face is a portrait of fear and a frozen image of terror, as the man she has lived with for years, an eminent academic, addresses a pussycat.

'This will be the final one, please! I'll do as you say, but I can't do this anymore. It must stop. I left last time because of my wife. I wanted to stay. It's my mistake, and I understand you want to protect me, but no more, please. I won't slip up again. No more women. I want to come back here, back to my home.'

Glenda stutters, desperate to say something. As cool as she can, her mouth is dry as she forces her words, 'Who are you talking to?' She stares at the cat and back at Larry. 'Cats can't talk, so where the hell did the voice come from?'

The black cat sits and lifts its back leg long and straight in a ballet-style movement. It begins to clean itself, spreading its toes and licking between each one, looking satisfied and smug.

Muddled, Glenda's brain isn't functioning. Why is he talking to the damn cat? A terrible thought bludgeons her, is she the one who is insane, but he quickly disabuses her of the idea by saying, 'Oh, it's my grandmama, Emily. Sorry, we have no time for introductions.'

'What are you on about, Emily? It's a bloody cat. Look at it, Larry; it's a cat, not somebody's frigging granny.' He turns his glazed, unseeing eyes her way, and she whispers in a moment of pure fear. 'It's you, Larry. You are insane!'

His grip slackens. She wriggles her wrist free and grabs the doorknob. The door still won't budge. It may as well be a brick wall for all the impression her banging and kicking make.

Larry sits quietly as she cries for help, shifting his buttocks on the bath rim. Glenda hammers her fists on the door scraping off skin trying to get out. Spots of blood appear. He swirls his fingers back and forth in the rising bloodstained water still bucketing from the rusty taps, delighting in the touch. He likes the colour.

'You wouldn't leave things be. You kept on digging, didn't you, Glenda?' She stares at him; he won't hurt her. She's sure, isn't she? Her heart leaps, she lets go of the knob and takes a tentative step towards him.

An impression of calmness emanates from him, producing a smile. Reaching out, hoping she can still sway him by convincing him he's right and she's wrong. He loves being right; it's his job. He's a scientist, and they all want to be the ones who understand everything or at least search out the truth. What's the truth about this situation, though?

Different scenarios race through her head: is she ill, dead, or dreaming? The events before this don't indicate being a dream. About to touch him, he speaks again.

'It's true. What they say is true. You are all the same. You go on until you win, like my wife did. I can finally understand why William, my great-great-grandfather, disliked all women, all apart from Emily, who was a wonderful, kind-hearted person.'

'Come on, Larry, please. Who are they? I may deserve you having a go at me, but don't you think this is taking things too far?' Her heart leaps as he smiles. At the same time, she still hopes this is all a sick joke but is soon disillusioned. The colour of the bathroom walls changes and crimson-coloured rivulets run down the wall.

'I'm sorry, it's too late. You made her choose you, Glen.'

Staring at the man she loved her mind can't grasp what is happening or how the room is turning red. A knife spins on the floor, and the cat sits grooming itself in the corner.

'I don't fucking care. Let me out of here!' she retches. The stench of the blood-filled bath stings her nostrils. Fear is causing physical pain.

Larry glances around, his gaze settling where Glenda can see the cat, but he can see Emily.

'What do you say, shall we get on with this Grandmother, or what? If you let me go now, I can leave her to you.'

Glenda's hand clasps his arm. Her fingernails dig into his skin with the strength of talons drawing blood. 'No, tell me everything, Larry, please, please tell me. If I must die, I should know why...?'

His attention swings back to her. 'Don't speak like that, Glenda. This is a necessity.' The Bombay purrs and curls around Larry's ankle.

A blood-curdling scream fills the house; Larry leaves the bathroom without looking back and the door slams behind him. He races down the stairs and outside, he glances at the window where the walls inside run red. It's over; at last, he's free.

He waits until the walls change to a delightful, albeit dated, pink and grey rose–patterned wallpaper before he achieves the confidence to turn away.

He climbs into his car, nods at the house on Albury Street saying, 'I'm coming back to you soon,' and drives back home to his research and normality.

Larry feels relaxed and vindicated for the first time in a long while. He won't need the medication anymore and will never need it again. At last, he conquered his episodes. His grandmother promised him, that the voices would leave him alone now.

Slapping and running his fingers over his leg in rhythm to Debussy's Ondine, reminding him of the sparkling waters of a country stream he visited as a boy, which used to refresh his worn spirits.

The louder the music blasts through his stereo, the more intense the memory. Happy, bouncing his head in the 3/8 time, he glances down at blood spots on his trousers, annoyed, he had tried so hard not to get blood splashes on them. His pet hate is sloppy work.

'Damn,' he mutters, 'These are my favourite trousers.'

Chapter 17

JACK

Larry smashes his forehead into the living room wall, leaving a growing lump and a fleeting blurring of his vision. Busy packing, Albury Street awaits him, and his plans are going awry.

This morning, he received a notification telling him, his funds were being withdrawn because his genetic trials didn't meet expectations or provide enough evidence to warrant the vast amount of money required to achieve his goal. They promised a review in three years.

'Damn and blast them.' Larry smashes his fist against the wall, and twitches as a voice in his ear warns, 'Calm down.' His inner self cautions him. 'You must learn to relax.'

Larry doesn't want the voices back or his great-grandparents. He doesn't need them now. He won by severing the line. Emily swore that after Glenda's demise, the family's reputation would not be under any more threat, and they would leave him in peace. He assumed her role to be complete. She helped him all she could in his work to conceal their lineage and shroud their real beginnings, those of the murderer and the mad, and she promised to leave. So, why would he need to warn himself to chill?

His inner voice repeats, 'Come now, relax, Larry. You don't need or want them back.' He assures himself that the need is gone, so why would the voices still talk to him? They should have stopped. Why won't they leave him in peace? They are at fault, delaying him with his tests by insisting he do away with Glenda.

It's strange to admit there is a gap in his life now she's gone, and he's resigned to a life alone, but he has to learn to bear this existence. He dare not consider a repeat of all he's been through in these last years.

His house on Albury Street is being refurbished and he hopes the work will help to expunge Emily and William.

'Sorry, Grandmother,' he says, with his tongue in cheek and continues, 'Get on with your packing, Larry, old boy.'

He rubs his knuckles and continues talking aloud, recalling that he's always most at ease in his own company when a knock at the door interrupts him. 'Who the hell is that?' He surveys his lounge with the packing cases and boxes neatly stacked around the walls. |He doesn't like untidiness.

Well, one thing's for sure they won't be invited in with the place looking like this, whoever they are,' he grumbles aloud, edging his way between the cases and furniture, wondering if he ought to buy new and leave the old suite behind, because she chose it not him. The doorbell rings.

'Okay, I'm coming,' he calls, fixing his mind on changing everything for a fresh start.

Flicking the Yale lock, he yanks the door open to face a young police officer, who quickly steps back. With his helmet tucked under one arm, he appears nervous.

'Er, hello, yes, what can I do for you? Is there a problem?' Larry eyes the young man.

'Are you Larry Emilson?'

Visions of Glenda leap into Larry's head. He catches his breath. How the heck did they find out? Emily is so thorough and has never slipped up before. He glances over the young man's head, peering each way up and down the road, wondering how many curtains are twitching, and how many officers are waiting to pounce All seems clear, he inches away from the door, thrusting his hands into his pockets and winces as his raw knuckles catch on the material.

'Yes, how can I help?'

'May I come in?' The officer sounds humble and apologetic. Larry thinks he looks more like a boy than a man of the law, but what the devil is he doing on his doorstep?

The young man stutters and gulps. 'My name is Jack, sir, and I believe you are or were acquainted with my mother.'

'What? Are you sure, sorry, I mean, who is your mother, because I am acquainted with a lot of people if you mean Glenda, I never knew she had a son.'

How did this come about, why didn't she say

anything? To be honest, this is the first I've heard about a child.'

His heart races, missing a beat. The last thing he needs is somebody on the hunt for her after all this time, a dark horse she was. He had only ever known three women in the biblical sense, and two of those are dead.

'Err, no, you are mistaken. I'm sorry, I haven't done this very well,' says the young officer. 'May I step inside?'

'I'm in a bit of a mess. I'm moving and beginning to wish I used a firm.'

'Please, I won't keep you?'

'Is this police business?'

'No, it's personal. I'm sorry about the attire, but when I plucked up the courage to call, I found my uniform gives me the confidence I lacked.' The constable strokes the buttons on his jacket with pride.

'It suits you,' says Larry beginning to relax but still puzzled.'

'Okay, so what do you want?' He pulls the door open, allowing Jack to enter.

'Watch your step. I don't want you to blame me if you break your neck tripping over my stuff; never mind where there's blame, there's a claim.'

'Is that what happened to your head?'

Larry's hand whipped to his forehead and feels a lump the size of an egg. He grins. 'Yes, but I can't claim for my stupidity, I tripped over a box,' he lied.

'Yes, like the stupid human rights bill, another is

where the criminal is endowed with more of those than the victims they murdered,' said the officer.

Is this a cunning plan to trap him? Larry's thoughts grapple with the word murdered. His immediate reaction is to call on Emily, but what if she is behind all this?

The young man puts him at ease 'No, sir, I'm happy to say, nothing like that.'

A weight shifts from Larry's shoulders, leaving him mystified. If not police business, what does this boy want with him?

Stepping over the threshold, Jack follows him into the front room. Larry feels the temperature drop. His eyes flick to the thermostat, the green light is on, and nothing has changed.

'Well, spit it out, lad, I'm busy.'

'Okay, here goes.' He fidgets with his helmet. My mother's name is Jenny.'

'My God, so she did have a baby, well, I never, but wasn't she, I mean, isn't she gay?'

'Yes, I do have the ubiquitous two mums if you want. Not so queer these days, though.'

'How is she? You do know your mother walked out on me don't you, she left me devastated, well unhappy, but I did love her.'

'Mum told me she regretted leaving you, but she had her reasons.'

'Yes, she fell for a woman.'

'Err, yes, but she said you didn't want children and would not give her a child. She reckons she almost grovelled, but you were adamant.'

'Yes, true enough, and I never regretted my decision, but it seems she got what she wanted, and I'm happy for her. I am. Can I ask, although it's none of my business, and tell me to mind my own, if you want, but are you from a donor or adopted? I mean, if you have two mothers and, if, you don't object to me asking, what about a dad?'

'Well, we come to the crux of the matter, Larry. May I call you by your first name?'

Although Larry stiffens, imperceptible to the man watching, the blood drains from his head, replaced by an icy trickle, leaving his scalp tingling.

What is this lad saying? At that exact moment, a wave of a familiar fragrance wafts between them, triggering a pleasant memory from his childhood. As the scent permeates the room, Jack smiles. 'You like lemon verbena? It's my favourite perfume.'

Larry feels nauseous, the aroma can only mean one thing. His eyes hunt around the room and his heart seems to stop mid-beat. In the corner, by the packing cases, stands Emily with a broad smile plastered on her face. Wearing a ridiculous fruit and feathered concoction on her head, her blue gloves clash with her favourite grey dress piped with yellow tassels.

'May I, sir, call you Larry?'

'Why not? It's my name.'

'Thank you, Larry.'

'Come on, Lad, what's the point of your visit?' Uncomfortable, Larry wonders why Emily is back.

Didn't he lay her to rest? This old apartment is dear to him, but he longs to move back to Albury Street now because she won't be hovering anymore with her guidance. He eliminated the need for her presence.

He worked diligently for or with her over the years, sensing the need to protect the family name and not reveal the secret of their antecedents.

Now is his time. He can concentrate on his work and finance the project for a while. In time, if left alone, his progress will be enough to justify the return of his funds. Emily is gone, so she can't delay him anymore. Warning himself to relax, he doesn't want to nurse his mind now he's back in control. He twitches. Jack waits.

'Mine is too.'

'What?'

'My middle name is Larry'

'Ha, she didn't forget me then.' Larry shrugged, finding it amusing.

'She never forgot you. She is one of the reasons I'm here, I have a son now.'

'Congratulations, you don't look old enough, but I'm not sure what this has to do with me.'

'Yes, they say I look too young but remember the adage regarding policemen looking younger than you and your peers. It's a sign of ageing.

The older man throws him a black glare.

'Sorry, I didn't mean to be rude,' says Jack flustered, taking in the upheaval in the room. His eyes scan the packing cases and cardboard boxes stacked in a pile; they waver for a second. Larry is convinced he smiled, but at what...?

He tries to remain level-headed, but something sinister is happening, and he senses a familiarity of sorts, but not amiable. He's almost shouting in his head, telling himself to calm down, but he thinks one thing: that this young man flaunting his manhood must go. Why is he here telling a stranger he has a child? Of what interest is it to him?

Jack stares at the floor. A smile plays around his well-formed lips, and Larry decides the boy is a trifle effeminate looking, with his long, shapely fingers and delicate cheekbones.

'Let's get to it, shall we?' says Jack standing to attention and brushing the front of his jacket with one hand. 'My mother, Jenny, thought you ought to understand that I am why she left. You didn't want a child, but here I am, and I have a son, your grandson.'

Larry's world explodes as the word, 'Noooo,' escapes his lips. 'This can't be true. They are gone. I am the last of the line. For years, I put in every ounce of effort to succeed in this, and now it's at an end. She promised me and I believed her. My God, what has she done?'

He glares, wishing to hurl the fires of hell from his eyes and blow Emily out of his house and out of his life. Send her back to where Purgatory spewed her from.

Larry had done everything in his power, at his grandmother's insistence, including the slaying of what may be innocent lives, and all to bring his family line to an end. He resisted to the point of madness, and now when he's convinced his hateful task is over, his sweet-grey-haired old granny, whom he did love and respected, that daughter of Satan, turns up, with another two in tow.

That's why she smiled. She had lied and deceived him. In her twisted way, she had enjoyed keeping his son from him until it was too late.

Losing self-control, all Larry can focus on is his partner and what he put her through in the name of humanity. His legs give way as he sinks to the floor.

On his knees, he rants aloud. 'It can't be. I have been so careful checking the family line, fighting my urges, and suffering the indignity of surgery to eliminate any risk of passing on these evil genes, and now this. You throw two more into the pot. You misled me and ruined my campaign. Why, granny? I didn't realise the extent of your capabilities, but you must have worked bloody damned hard to keep me away from the truth, and now I have it, you want the line to continue.'

Jack is horrified at the response and throws his helmet on a chair. He drops to his hunkers beside his newfound father but hesitates before placing his arms around him, embarrassed as this impressive-looking man breaks into uncontrollable sobs.

'I'm sorry my visit is causing you so much distress, but I needed to find you. In one way, I have searched all my life for you, at one point becoming obsessed. Ha, I thought I would go mad.'

Larry shakes free from Jack's arms and peers through inflamed eyes and sniffs, wiping his face dry with a handkerchief dragged from his pocket. They face each other on their knees. What do they say now?

Larry raises his voice. 'Mad, why do you say mad?' Spittle foams in the corners of his mouth.

'Well, not crazy but I suffer from hallucinations, which scared me. However, since I always wanted to be a policeman, I couldn't disclose them. Can you picture turning up in court to testify about a convicted felon, for them to mention, that I hallucinated?'

'What kind?'

'What do you mean?'

'What type of illusions?' Larry ignores his grandmother beckoning in the corner.

'They sound silly.'

'Please. Tell me what they are?'

'Oh gosh, well, I'm embarrassed.' Jack twitches and rubs his nose, and for the first time, a resemblance to Emily is obvious to Larry—the laughter of a female charges the atmosphere like an unexploded bomb sitting on the floor.

'WHAT FUCKING SORT?' Larry struggles to his feet. Jack faces him, and as one, they turn towards the place where Emily acknowledges them smiling and, for the first time, extends her arms to encompass both of her grandsons.

Larry cries, 'Oh no, you promised.'

Emily's smile is not one of welcome but of the

victor belittling the defeated.

The End

ABOUT THE AUTHOR

First of all, I would like to thank you for buying my book and I hope you enjoyed it. Could I ask you please to spend a moment or two in giving me a review? I would appreciate any feedback, but please be kind in your wording. It took years to learn how to write and publish a story I felt confident with. I am still learning.

Thank you.

Printed in Great Britain
by Amazon